THE ECHO OF BONES

MICHAEL BRADY BOOK 3

MARK RICHARDS

AUTHOR'S NOTE

The Echo of Bones is set in Whitby, on the North East coast of England. As I'm British and the book's set in the UK, I've used British English. The dialogue is realistic for the characters, which means they occasionally swear.

This is a novel. I've taken some slight liberties with the number of police officers there would be in Whitby. Other than that I have tried to stay faithful to the town and the surrounding countryside.

As it's a work of fiction names, characters, organisations, some places, events and incidents are either products of the author's imagination or used fictionally. All the characters in this book are fictitious. Any resemblance to actual persons, living or dead, is purely coincidental.

www.markrichards.co.uk

THE NORTH YORK MOORS: JANUARY 2016

"How many times have we disturbed Lilla's slumber now?"

"Three for me. What's this, your fourth?"

"Yeah, four. First time in winter though."

"All downhill now. More or less."

"Apart from that last set of steps. I tell you, Andy, either those hills in the first ten miles are getting steeper or I'm getting older. Speaking of which, I'll catch you up..."

"We'd have finished by now if you weren't incontinent."

"Wait 'til you turn fifty. You'll be diving behind every second bush you pass. Give me two minutes."

Paul Jarvis walked away from the main path. Not a bush in sight. But the middle of the North York Moors. Ten o'clock on a winter morning. Frost on the ground. A watery sun.

Who needs a bush? We haven't seen a living soul since we crossed the Pickering road.

He unzipped his walking trousers.

Not bad. The Lyke Wake Walk in mid-winter. Thirty-five miles gone, five to go. And another one crossed off the bucket list...

"Paul!"

"What?" He didn't bother looking round.

"Paul!"

Shouting. More insistent. This time he did look. And saw the group of ramblers coming up the path.

Where the hell did they come from?

He zipped his trousers up and stumbled clumsily over the heather.

Ten more yards will have to do. Can't wait any longer. Christ, it's no fun getting older. Not that there's anything to see on a freezing cold morning.

This little patch will have to do. Looks like the heather's been burned away and not grown back. Odd...

Paul Jarvis unzipped his trousers a second time. Picked out what looked like a tiny, white piece of wood.

Sighed with relief.

How many years has it been out in the sun to be bleached that colour?

Took aim.

The piece of wood bounced as the stream hit it. Bounced, turned over, caught the pale winter sun.

What the –

He bent down. Picked up what he'd thought was a piece of wood.

Ignored the urine dripping onto his fingers.

Felt the scene burn indelibly into his memory.

"Andy!"

"What's wrong? However bloody cold your fingers are I'm not zipping your trousers up."

He turned round, still holding what he'd picked up. His fingers still wet. "Andy," he said. "Come over here."

Andy Boulding walked reluctantly over the heather. "You've not put your foot in a bog have you? I had enough bogs yesterday to last me a lifetime."

"No, I haven't." Paul Jarvis held out what he now desperately needed to be a sliver of wood. "This," he said.

"What is it? Let me get my reading glasses out of the backpack."

"No. Don't bother. Blow your whistle. Get that group of ramblers back here."

Andy Boulding shook his head. "What the hell are you talking about, Paul? We're no more than five miles from the finish. The girls will be waiting for us. What's the matter?"

Paul Jarvis sighed. Shook his head. Saw a class of children in front of him.

Knew that he would never walk this path again. Sucked in a great lungful of air. Looked at his brother-in-law, the man he'd walked with for ten years.

What was I thinking two minutes ago? The Lyke Wake Walk in mid-winter. Another one crossed off the bucket list...

"This," he said again. "It's a bone, Andy. I've spent the thick end of thirty years teaching biology – and I'm telling you it's a human bone. A finger bone. Ring the girls. Tell them we'll be a long time. A bloody long time. It's a finger bone. And it's from a child."

.   .   .

"Go through it again for me," Detective Constable Dan Keillor said. "Let me make sure I've got it straight."

Paul Jarvis took a deep breath. A man coming to terms with what he'd found. Who knew that teaching human biology to 12 year olds who only wanted to embarrass him with sex questions would be very different now.

"We were doing the Lyke Wake Walk. We'd just passed the Lilla Cross." He gestured towards the top of the hill.

"That's about forty miles isn't it? Forty miles across the Moors in winter?"

Jarvis nodded. "Forty miles. And you have to do it in twenty-four hours. Mid-life crisis, I suppose. I was fifty on Christmas Day. Some men buy a motorbike, some start chasing young girls. I bought a new pair of walking boots."

Dan Keillor smiled. "Physical challenge?"

"And then some. Prove to myself I'm still young."

"Except he's not," Andy Boulding said. "Needed to find a bush every two miles."

"That's how you found the bone?"

Jarvis nodded. "Yeah. I had to walk an extra ten yards. A group of ramblers turned up. Not that they'd have seen anything. So bloody cold."

"So..."

"I saw something white – I thought it was a piece of wood. Took aim. Like you do. And – Christ, I'm embarrassed. I hit it. It moved. I realised what it was."

"You picked it up?"

Jarvis nodded. "Yeah. I bent down. Picked it up. Couldn't believe what I was looking at. Still can't..."

"You were certain?"

He nodded again. "I've taught Biology for nearly thirty years. Yes, I was certain."

"What did you do then?"

"Called Andy over. Showed him what I'd found. Told him to blow his whistle. Get the ramblers back to help us look."

"But you didn't?"

Andy shook his head. "No. I told him not to. Said we had to phone the police. If it was a crime scene... Lots of people... All they could do was contaminate it."

Dan Keillor raised his eyebrows. "Not many people would have done that. Thank you."

"I watch a lot of detective programmes. You know, *Prime Suspect* and such like. People are always contaminating crime scenes."

"So the ramblers carried on rambling. At least until they saw the patrol car. What did you do? Apart from call 999."

"We had a look round. And phoned our wives. Said we'd be delayed."

"That's when you found the other bones?"

Andy Boulding was an unhealthy shade of grey. Paul Jarvis looked like he was going to throw up. "The ulna and the radius," he said. "Year nine. That's when they learn it. They can remember 'radius.' 'Ulna' is the one they forget. The bones in your arm."

Dan Keillor looked out across the North York Moors. It was going to be dark soon. They'd need to secure the scene. Leave someone on duty overnight? That wasn't his decision.

"What were you planning to do?" he said.

"What do you think? We'd have walked forty miles. Eat sandwiches, drink tea. Fall asleep in the car. Get home. Long, hot soak in the bath. Sleep for two days."

"I'm sorry. You'll have to stay over. My boss will need to speak to you."

"We know that. But we've been walking since first light. We're freezing. And starving. We're not going to have to wait around for him are we? Where *is* your boss?"

"Where is he?" Dan Keillor smiled, tight-lipped. "Where else would a Detective Chief Inspector be on a freezing cold afternoon in January? He's in church."

1

Michael Brady reached across his niece and took his sister's hand. Felt the tissue clasped between her fingers. Squeezed. Smiled at her as she turned towards him. Saw her blink away the tears.

Then he stood up, adjusted his black tie and walked to the front of St Mary's Church.

"Full of life," he said.

It's packed. Absolutely packed. Just like the church was for Grace...

"Nine times out of ten it's a cliché. 'He was full of life' we say, meaning someone told an occasional joke. But with Bill it was true. You only had to spend a minute in his company – whether he was talking about his police work, golf, football or the family he loved so very much – to know he truly was, 'full of life.'

I remember the first time I met him. Kate – a bag of nerves I now realise – brought him round to the house. 'Well,' Dad said when he'd gone. 'He's a bundle of energy. And he'll get on. You can tell that.'"

I remember what Mum said as well. 'Too bloody full of himself is that one. He won't make her happy. Not for one minute...'

Brady carried on with the eulogy. Looked up at the congregation.

Kate in the front row, wiping away the tears, trying to smile at one of his jokes. Maddie and Lucy next to her, their poems haltingly read out, more tears flowing. His daughter Ash next to Lucy. Bill's brother and sister and their families on the opposite side of the church.

And then the great and good. The pecking order of the pews neatly defined. The Chief Constable behind Bill's brother, with Detective Superintendent Alan Kershaw, Brady's boss, sitting next to him.

For now. Maybe not my boss for much longer...

And Frankie Thomson.

Black jacket, black trousers, hair tied back. But not wiping away a tear.

She was sitting directly behind Kershaw.

A fine view of the back of his neck. That must be hard for her. At least she's got her sister for moral support.

Less than a year since we came to Whitby. Less than a year since I was facing her in Kara's kitchen after Patrick's murder.

'Your boss has arrested the wrong person.'

'He's still my boss.'

And she let me walk out with Patrick's backpack...

And then the extended family. Friends. Old police officers who'd known Bill, suddenly vowing not to waste a day of their retirement. The three golfers who'd needed to find a fourth at eight o'clock on Sunday mornings.

"Let me finish where I started," Michael Brady said, "Bill was full of life. Full of energy. Full of love. For the police force he served for nearly thirty years. For his friends, his passions. For Whitby. 'The best place in the world to live.' But above all, for Kate. For Maddie and for Lucy. There is nothing I can say to them – "

Don't cry, Kate. I'm nearly finished...

" – That will ever make up for their loss. But look around you. Take comfort from everyone you see here today. Take comfort from knowing that we will always remember him. Bill Calvert. Full of energy. Full of life. Above all, full of love."

The vicar took over. The funeral service ended.

Inevitably, it was *My Way...*

BRADY WATCHED his sister touch her fingers to her lips. Hold them there. And then touch them to the coffin. Whisper something. Turn and take her daughters' hands. He put his arm round Ash, followed them slowly out of the church.

Just the crematorium to go. A lot less people, thank God.

"A good speech, Michael." Brady turned and saw Kershaw. Silver haired, silver tongued, and – if the rumours were right – about to leave Whitby and climb another rung on the ladder. "I admire you," he said. "A fine exercise in hypocrisy."

"Ash, sweetheart, just go and see if Lucy's alright, will you? Thanks... Maybe not, sir," Brady said. "I had a lot of time for Bill at the end."

"You're saying William Henry Calvert was improved by the prospect of meeting his Maker?"

I'm saying Bill bore his final days with bravery and humour. That there was no self-pity. No 'why me?' That he was determined to say 'Happy New Year' to his wife and daughters. And that he made it. Only just, but he made it...

"Will you excuse me, sir?" Brady said instead. "Bill's sister is over there. I haven't spoken to her yet. Family duty..."

Brady walked a few paces through the church graveyard. Smiled to himself as he looked at the headstones.

*Half of them illegible. Worn away by the wind and the salt. The other half as clear as the day they were erected. There must have been an 18*th *Century stonemason selling cheap headstones. Knowing that he and his customers would be long gone before anyone found out...*

He smiled at Bill's sister. Made a determined effort to remember what her children were called. Completely failed. Opened his mouth to speak. Was interrupted by his phone.

Do you answer your phone at a funeral? I'm a copper. Bill was a copper. He looked down at his phone. *And it's Dan Keillor. So that's that...*

"What's up, Dan?"

"I'm sorry to trouble you, boss. I know it's the funeral and all that. It's just that..."

"What's happened?"

"There's been some remains found on the Moors. Human remains. I'm up there now."

"Give me a minute, Dan. I'm surrounded by people."

Michael Brady walked to the edge of the churchyard. Made sure he couldn't be overheard. Looked out over Whitby. At the town where he'd been born. At the hill where he'd scattered his wife's ashes. At the twin arms of the piers stretching out into the North Sea.

Looked up, across the harbour. The fishing boats. Looked past them. Found the house he'd bought.

Wondered for the thousandth time why he'd bought a house where he could see the end of the pier. Where he'd be reminded of Jimmy Gorse every day...

Because it's the right house. Especially for Ash. Because – good or bad – you can't run away from your memories.

"Sorry, Dan. We were just coming out of the church. Tell me the story."

"Two walkers, boss. Doing the Lyke Wake Walk – "

"In January?"

"They look like they know what they're doing, boss. Said they wanted a challenge. One of them stops. Call of nature. Sees what he thinks is a small piece of wood. Realises it isn't."

"And what is it?"

"It's a finger bone, boss. A finger bone from a child."

"How did he know?"

"He's a teacher. Biology."

Brady was 26. Back in Greater Manchester Police. His boss, his mentor, Jim Fitzpatrick, telling him about his first murder.

'Just outside Bolton. One of those clear, crisp autumn mornings. A hint of the first frost. A clearing in a wood. A shallow grave. She was sixteen years old.'

He'd gone home and told Grace.

'What am I going to do? When people are calling me 'boss?' Supposing she's the same age as one of our children? The same colour hair? In the same class?

He could still hear her reply.

'You'll deal with it. And I'll be here with you. I'll always be here.'

Daisy Stoner, Grace. You remember. And I didn't deal with it very well...

"Have you taken statements?"

"I'm still up on the Moors with them. Thought it was better to ask questions up here. So they could show me everything."

"Have you got the photographer?"

"Yeah. He's complaining about the cold and the fading light."

"Photographers are always complaining about the light, Dan. Is he there? I need him to do something for me."

"Do you want him, boss?"

"No, you're fine. Ask him to photograph the bones will you? On his mobile. Then send me the photos. I know this guy teaches Biology but I need to get it confirmed."

Brady looked at his watch.

Not much more than an hour until sunset.

"Then secure the area, Dan. And make it big. Up to the path. And then fifty or sixty yards in each direction. And a tent over the grave. Let's try and minimise any more weather damage. And that'll do for tonight. It'll be dark soon. I'll send the cavalry first thing in the morning.

And I'll come up with Geoff Oldroyd. What are you doing with the two guys?"

He heard Dan Keillor laugh. "They're both cold and hungry. I've told them you'll need to talk to them. They live over near Leeds. I think one of the wives has found a B&B."

"Good work. Have you looked around yourself?"

"Briefly, boss. I thought I should leave it to the experts. But it looks like a shallow grave."

"Have you looked at the piece of bone?"

"Yeah. It's definitely bone. I'm not sure how he could have thought it was anything else. Then again, I've never walked forty miles across the Moors."

"Have you got them there?"

"One of them. Do you want a word?"

"Very briefly. And thanks, Dan. Do what you need to do and get yourself home. It's bloody freezing here on the cliff so God knows what it's like on the Moors."

Brady heard Dan Keillor say, 'my boss wants a word.' Then a nervous "Hello?"

"This is Detective Chief Inspector Michael Brady."

'Ask the question they're not expecting.' The most valuable lesson he'd learned from Jim Fitzpatrick. *'Ask the obvious question and they have the lie ready and waiting.'*

And it wouldn't be the first time a killer had 'found' his victim...

"How cold are you?"

"Sorry? What?"

"How cold are you?" Brady said again.

The man on the other end of the phone laughed.

"Very. And thanks for asking, Mr Brady. This is Andy Boulding. What can I do for you?"

"Nothing," Brady said. "I wanted to say 'thank you.' I'll need to speak to you in the morning and I just wanted to say thanks for staying in Whitby."

"No problem. I think the wife's looking forward to it now she's got used to the idea."

"Was it you that found the remains, Mr Boulding?"

"No. My brother-in-law, Paul Jarvis. He's just walked up the hill to try and warm up a bit."

"OK, thank you again. I'll see you in the morning. Enjoy your night out in Whitby."

On a Monday night in January? After they've walked forty miles? They'll fall asleep halfway through their fish and chips...

THE PICTURES TOOK LESS than five minutes to arrive. Brady excused himself from a conversation with Kate's next door neighbour. Walked to the edge of the church-yard a second time. Dialled her number.

Two years since I last saw her? Maybe more.

"Good morning. Or afternoon. Or evening if you're lucky enough to live in Melbourne. This is Julia Grey. I can't take your call right now but leave a message and I'll get back to you."

"It's Michael Brady. Long time, no speak. Hope you're well, Julia. I'm just going to send you some pictures. We've found some bones on the Moors. I don't think there's much doubt, but I'd be grateful if you could confirm it. And we need to recover them. Hopefully you're not busy. And feel like a morning in Whitby..."

Brady looked up. Saw Ash waving frantically at him from across the churchyard. She pointed at the funeral car. Time for the crematorium.

I can't sit in the funeral car with Kate and send pictures of bones...

He mouthed 'one minute' at his daughter and hurriedly opened *Photos* on his phone. Copied the first one. Remembered Ash rolling her eyes when she'd shown him how to do it. Copied the other two. Sent them to Professor Julia Grey at Sheffield University. Knew what one of the country's leading forensic anthropologists would say.

Hoped she didn't ring him while he was in the crematorium.

JULIA DIDN'T. She waited for the reception.

"Julia, thank you for getting back to me. Give me a minute to find somewhere quiet."

He walked out of the hotel lounge and stood in the corridor. Looked out of the window over the manicured gardens.

"It sounds like you're at a party, Mike."

My favourite accent. Bolton. Julia and that presenter on Gardeners' World...

"Sadly not, Julia. I'm at a funeral. Well, the reception."

"Nobody close? Ah, sorry Mike. This is the first time I've spoken to you since... Since we heard about Grace. I was... well, 'devastated' isn't an adequate word. Neil too. All our love."

"Thank you, Julia."

"And you're back in Whitby?"

"Yeah, I..."

I don't want to explain it on the phone.

"You and Neil should come over to Whitby. I've bought a house overlooking the harbour. Come for the weekend when it's finished. How is Neil?"

"He's good. He's cut down to three days a week. But that wasn't what you were asking..."

Brady laughed. "No, I wasn't."

"Yes is the answer. He's reached the age where he's being stalked by ads for incontinence pants but twice a week he exchanges his stethoscope for a lead guitar. And as he constantly tells me, he's ten years younger than Eric Clapton. And I have to tell you, Mike, I'm all in favour of it. My hair's grey, I need about four different pairs of glasses but I'm married to a man who can still use the word 'gig' with a straight face. And as I tell him, I'm five years younger than Suzi Quatro."

"You should *definitely* come over. I've missed your humour."

"But in the short term you need an answer on those photos."

"Please, Julia. The guy that found them teaches Biology. He says a finger bone and the two arm bones."

"Sadly, he's right. Looking at your photos, Mike, I'd say a teenager. Well, 'teenager' covers a multitude of sins. Still a child to six inches taller than his father. A young teenager. And looking at the colour I'd say the bones have been there for some time. You're not looking for someone who disappeared last week."

"When can you get over?"

"Immediately? I can't. I'm needed on the other side of the Pennines. Like I need to drive over Snake Pass in January. But it's every homeowner's worst nightmare. Your dream house – or it will be your dream house when you've done the alterations – "

"And the builders find a body?"

"Two bodies. Mother and child. I'm going to be there for two days at least."

"Understood. I don't really want to leave the bones out there that long, Julia. It's the North York Moors, it's a bloody big open space and it's the middle of winter."

"And you can keep people out but you can't keep predators out?"

"Right. And I can keep the snow off but I can't control the temperature."

"Geoff Oldroyd moved to Whitby didn't he?"

"Yes. Ten years ago. Or thereabouts. Same time as our SOCO. Guy called Henry Squire. He's good. Very thorough."

"I've worked with Geoff. And I'll happily trust your judgement on Henry. You recover the bones, Mike. Just make sure there's a big search area. And I'll be over as soon as I can. I'll call you."

2

"I could have been a solicitor," Brady said. "Did I ever tell you that? Nice warm office, someone bringing me a coffee. Or I could be out here freezing to death. Tough decision."

"You're going soft in your old age," Geoff Oldroyd replied. "Crisp, sunny, winter morning on the Moors? As good as North Yorkshire has to offer. But you're missing the most important point, Mike."

"What's that?"

"Solicitors don't have to wear fancy dress. I reckon me and Henry have reached the age where a pale blue plastic romper suit doesn't do a lot for us."

Nine o'clock on Tuesday morning. Brady had been due to have a one-to-one with Dan Keillor. His six monthly performance review. It would have to wait. Looking at a patch of bare earth on the Moors, knowing what they were going to find, Dan Keillor's performance review might have to wait a long time.

"Point taken, Geoff," he said. "I'm going to leave you to it."

"Squeamish?"

"A child's skeleton on the Moors? I talked to Julia yesterday – "

"Julia Grey?"

"Yeah. I know our guy's a Biology teacher but procedure's procedure. So she says yes, they're human bones. And they've been here for some time. 'You're not looking for someone who disappeared last week' were her exact words."

"She's not coming over?"

"She is, but she's not sure when. So it's up to us – well, you and Henry – to remove everything as carefully as we can. So yes, I'll leave you to it. And I need to think."

Brady watched Geoff Oldroyd step carefully over the heather into the small clearing.

Not even a clearing. Just a gap in the heather. Barely bigger than my desk. Nothing growing...

Brady could only just make out the edges of the grave. And only because he knew what he was looking for.

How long has she been out here? And why am I saying 'she?' Because a body on the Moors is going to be a girl. Because I have a daughter. Because of Daisy Stoner...

"Jake!" Brady called to PC Jake Cartwright.

"Yes, boss?"

"How long have you been on sentry duty?"

"First light, boss. As soon as it was light enough to walk across the Moors."

"You had anything to eat?"

Cartwright shook his head. "We're in the wrong business," Brady said. "If we were out here filming *Harry Potter* there'd be a fully equipped catering truck. As we're coppers – " Brady pulled a £20 note out of his pocket. "Is the car handy?"

"Five hundred yards, boss. On the perimeter road. By Fylingdales."

"There's a garage just back towards Whitby. Let's hope it has a coffee machine. Buy us all one. Any change you've got spend it on Mars Bars and biscuits. And bring me some sugar. It's too bloody cold to give up this morning."

"Suppose they haven't got a coffee machine, boss?"

"Arrest them, Jake. Endangering the life of a police officer. Half a dozen police officers. Then keep driving 'til you find one."

Brady walked towards the Lilla Cross. Went five yards past it and read the plaque.

The Lilla Cross. Erected about 620AD over the reputed grave of Lilla, an officer of the court of Edwin, King of Northumbria, who died saving the life of the King. Believed to be the oldest Christian memorial in the North of England.

Walked up onto the burial mound. Stood by the cross. Stared out across the Moors.

You've got a cracking view, Lilla. The Moors, the path sloping gently downhill. The heather when it's in bloom. The sea in the distance. Richard III got a car park in Leicester...

Brady looked down the path towards the Pickering road.

That was the way they came. Gently uphill. They reach here. Do they see the cross as the start of the home straight? All downhill to Ravenscar? One of them needs a final pee? Stumbles to the exact spot?

He saw someone digging. A shadowy figure.

Night. It had to be at night. So it has to be murder. There's nothing else it can be. No-one commits suicide by climbing into a shallow grave. And it's a child.

How did she get here? Was she alive? 'Let's go for a walk on the Moors, sweetheart.' Or did he carry her body up here?

The protective screens round the grave were fluttering in the breeze. Geoff Oldroyd and Henry Squire still on their hands and knees.

When did this happen? It had to be in the winter. If he was digging he'd have needed wetter, softer ground. And no people. But why here? Why bring the body all the way out here?

Brady couldn't help it. Impatience got the better of him. He walked down. As close to the grave as he dared. Spoke to the two middle-aged men in blue romper suits.

"How are you doing, Geoff? And it's sorted, Henry," he added. "I've sent Jake for some coffee."

Henry Squire, scene-of-crimes officer, twisted round and looked up at him. "Bacon and egg sandwich too much to hope for then, Mike?"

"North Yorkshire Police, Henry. You cocked-up. You should have joined the Met. Worked in London. Michelin star restaurant on every street corner."

"He's right, Henry," Geoff said. "'Where's the body, guv?' 'Just round the corner from Gordon Ramsay's place...'"

It was a coping mechanism. Brady had seen it – done it himself – any number of times. The more the crime affected them, the blacker the humour.

And if this is a child in a shallow grave it's going to be very black...

Geoff Oldroyd finally, painfully, straightened up. Put his hands on his hips. Stretched, tried to ease his lower back. Walked over to Brady.

"Christ, I'll pay for that in the morning."

"What have we got?" Brady said.

Geoff sighed. "Not much. The predators have done their work." He gave Brady an anguished look. "But a child, Mike." he said. "And if you want my best guess – "

"You know I do."

"Then twelve. Thirteen. Somewhere in that area."

Brady nodded. "That's what Julia said. 'A young teenager.' Girl or boy, Geoff?"

"Girl. Definitely. The pelvis is still there. So I'm sure."

Brady nodded.

A girl. It had been inevitable.

"What did you find? No, hang on. Tell me in a minute."

Jake Cartwright was back. He passed Brady and Geoff a coffee. Handed Brady a sachet of sugar.

"Thanks, Jake. Good work. Drink your coffee and then get yourself off. Go and find some breakfast. Get warmed up."

"Thanks, boss."

"Sorry, Geoff," Brady said. "I didn't want to discuss it in front of Jake. I want to keep this quiet for now. Whoever we've found was reported missing at some point."

"There was a story wasn't there? Twenty years ago? Twenty-five? A girl went missing in Whitby?"

Brady shook his head. "Not twenty-five years ago. I was still here. I'd have remembered something like that. Twenty? I don't know. I was travelling. Or falling in love. Whitby didn't register. When did Henry come here?"

"Ten years ago. About a month after me."

"It doesn't matter," Brady said. "It'll be in the records. I'll find it. But whoever she is she'll have parents. We need to find out who she is before we've got a queue of grieving relatives banging on the door. That sounds harsh. Sorry. Murdered children... It gets to me."

Geoff Oldroyd pulled his coat round him.

Protecting himself from the cold? Or from what he's found?

"You're not alone, Mike. I've got someone on the table in front of me. Sixty-five, seventy maybe. I'm thinking, 'fair enough, mate. Not quite your full whack, but close enough.' When it's a child..." He shook his head. "Stays with me for days. The wife doesn't even have to ask."

"So what've we got, Geoff?"

"Bones. Bones that have been out here for ten years. Maybe longer. Very definitely not someone who disappeared last week. And not all the bones either."

"Why not?"

"Like I said, predators. Scavengers. You've seen it, I've seen it. A sheep dies out on the Moors, they strip it to the bones in a few weeks. And they carry the bones off. So down there – " He nodded towards the grave. "We've got all the big bones. Skull, pelvis, thigh bones. The ones that are too heavy to carry away. Some of the others... We're never going to find them."

"So we'll have to make do with what we've got?"

Geoff nodded. "Get them back as soon as we can. But

I'm going to need some help, Mike. This is a job for a real expert. So the sooner Julia can come over the better."

"I don't suppose there's anything…"

"To say what she died of?" Geoff shook his head. "Nothing at all. The skull's intact. That's about all I can say right now. It's a jigsaw, Mike. It's a jigsaw where we need to find the pieces. And accept that two-thirds of them will be missing."

"Nothing else?"

"No. No fragments of clothing. No jewellery. No ligatures, ropes, cable-ties. Nothing."

"Nothing at all?"

"Not that I can see."

"So you're done?"

Geoff nodded. "More or less. I'll stay here with Henry. See what else we can find. Bag it. Label it. Bring back everything we can. Are you going to organise the search?"

"Organise the search, tell the lads to make sure the site is secure and try and keep a lid on it. Which is going to be bloody difficult. If not impossible."

"And talk to the two guys that found her?"

"Next job. They've stayed one night. I can't ask them to stay another. Whitby in January…"

Geoff looked at him. "It's a hell of a longshot you know, Mike."

Brady nodded. Looked back at the grave. "Finding the body? I thought that." He swept his arm out. "What are we looking at? From here to the sea? Three miles, four miles? How big are the Moors? Five hundred square miles?

"About that. And our guy stops to relieve himself in exactly the right place?"

"It's a bloody strange way to confess."

"So what are you saying? He suddenly feels the need to confess after ten or fifteen years? A lot easier to walk into the nearest nick."

Brady laughed. "Especially in January. But never say never. I'll see what he has to say for himself. And thanks – you and Henry. I appreciate what you've done."

Brady turned and walked up the moorland path. Back past the Lilla Cross, leaving the man who died saving the life of King Edwin to gaze across the Moors for eternity.

You could have had company, Lilla. Someone to share eternity with.

But now she's been found. So my job is simple. Find out who she was. And who put her here...

Brady sat in his car. Turned the engine on. Mentally added heated seats to the checklist for his next car. Dialled the number.

She's been in Whitby almost all her life. If a girl had gone missing she'll know about it.

"Frankie Thomson."

She sounds stressed. Under pressure...

"Morning. It's Brady."

"I know. My phone told me. What can I do for you, boss?"

"I thought you were calling me Mike while you were on sabbatical?"

"Sorry. I'm not thinking straight. I've got to go round

to Mum's. There's a problem with her medication. More than a problem."

So she hasn't got five minutes...

"OK, you go and sort that out."

"What did you want, Mike?"

"No, it doesn't matter. Go and look after your mum. I'll deal with it. Find it in the files at the station. It's not a problem..."

3

Brady knocked on the door of the B&B. Showed his ID to the middle-aged woman who opened it.

"You'll be the new copper, then?"

Brady nodded. Was shown into a tired, out-of-season residents' lounge. Waited five minutes. The door opened: two men with weather beaten faces walked stiffly into the room.

"That looks painful," Brady said.

One of them smiled. "Rigor mortis. Nothing terminal."

...And then realised what he'd said. "Ah, not very tactful. Sorry. Andy Boulding." He stuck his hand out. "And, by a process of elimination, Paul Jarvis."

The door opened again. The landlady with a pot of tea.

"Shall I bring you some biscuits to go with your tea?"

"That'd be lovely," Paul Jarvis said. "We've still got a few calories to catch up from yesterday..."

"I appreciate this," Brady said. "Thank you for staying over. I accept that Whitby in January – especially when it starts raining – might not be to everyone's taste."

"You're fine. It's either stay over or come back isn't it? And our wives walked up to St Mary's before breakfast. Saw the Dracula graveyard."

Where I was standing when Dan Keillor phoned me...

"I know you've told this story once," Brady said. "But... what you found up there. I can't say too much for obvious reasons. But you look like intelligent guys. Apart from walking across the Moors in winter, obviously..."

They laughed. Brady warmed to them. Felt some sympathy.

You've found a body, gentlemen. Welcome to three o'clock in the morning. And the chances are, you'll have to cope with the demons on your own...

"You can guess what I'm going to ask," Brady said.

"You'd like to hear the story again?"

"Yes, I would. Rather than play Chinese whispers with Dan Keillor."

Paul Jarvis poured himself some tea. Looked questioningly at Brady and Andy Boulding. Both of them nodded.

"So I turned fifty," Jarvis said. "Fifty on Christmas Day. Crap day to have a birthday but what can you do? No-one asked me. And I wanted to do something to celebrate. And something to challenge myself. So the Lyke Wake Walk in winter seemed a decent option."

"It's forty miles isn't it?" Brady said.

"Forty miles across the highest, widest part of the

Moors. Osmotherly to Ravenscar. Supposedly the route they took with the monks' bodies. And you've twenty-four hours to do it."

"I can't believe you camped?"

Paul Jarvis shook his head. "Stayed at the Lion at Blakey Ridge. The last bit up to it is easy. You can do it with a head torch."

"So you're walking in the dark?"

"We're experienced walkers," Andy said. "We've done it before. And... This may sound silly. Have you ever been in the middle of the Moors at night, Mr Brady? Pitch black? No light pollution? Bloody hell, it's beautiful. I'm not a religious man, but I defy you to stand in the middle of the Moors and look at the stars and tell me there isn't a God."

No I haven't. But I'd like to...

"And then you set off at first light the next morning?"

Which will be easy enough to check...

They both nodded. "They left us something out for breakfast. And yeah, we're off again. About an hour before sunrise."

"So eventually you cross the Pickering road – and then you walk up past Fylingdales?"

Jarvis nodded. "Up there – blimey it was cold – and we get to the Lilla Cross. If you're doing the Walk it's a big moment. Well, it is for me. You know you're nearly finished."

"And you can see the winning post," Andy added. "The mast at Ravenscar."

"So you're what – an hour away?" Brady said.

"No, longer than that. Closer to two."

"Were you going to do it in your twenty-four hours?"

"Yeah," Andy Boulding said. "With an hour or so to spare. I was starting to worry about it not being tough enough. Thinking what he'd dream up for his next birthday..."

"And then you found the bones." Brady made it a statement.

Paul Jarvis nodded to himself. "I did. Yes. I had to answer a call."

"Why there?" Brady said. "Why did you choose that particular spot?"

Jarvis laughed. "I didn't. You know that poem, Mr Brady? *Desiderata?* 'Gracefully surrendering the things of youth?' Well I seem to have surrendered my bladder. Especially on a cold morning. So I just stood in a clump of heather. Then Andy shouted. Said there were some ramblers coming. So I went a bit further. Five, ten yards. And there was this patch without any heather. So I stood in that."

"And..."

"It's... Well, it's embarrassing. Do you need it in graphic detail?"

"Yes," Brady said. "I'm sorry, I do."

Because I want to 'see' what happened. Because if I can start to see what happened yesterday maybe I can see what happened ten years ago. Or however long it was...

"I started peeing," Paul Jarvis said. "I saw what I thought was a tiny piece of wood. Like I said to your Constable, I'm embarrassed. Ashamed. I aimed at it."

"And now you're feeling guilty?"

"Yes. I'm a teacher. I teach children. I don't..."

He didn't finish the sentence. He didn't need to.

Yep, three o'clock in the morning. And when you're face to face with a new class in September you'll think, 'It could have been one of these kids...' Welcome to my world, Mr Jarvis.

THE DOOR OPENED. The landlady was back. "Would you like your tea freshening up?"

No-one did. She reluctantly retreated.

"So you realise what you've aimed at?" Brady said.

"Not immediately. I just know it isn't a piece of wood. Honestly, I don't know. You have this feeling when you're walking. Especially early mornings. 'I'm the only one out here. Supposing I find a body?' Same as dog-walkers I suppose. But once I bent down and picked it up..."

"You knew what you were holding?"

Paul Jarvis nodded. "Yes, I did."

"And then..."

"Then we looked around. I told your Constable. Dan was it? We found two other bones."

"Then we stopped," Andy said. "Because..."

"Because you're normal guys and you're starting to feel sick. Don't apologise," Brady said. "You did what anyone would do."

"Do you know anything yet?" Paul Jarvis asked. "Any idea who it was?"

Brady shook his head. "No, not as yet."

And if I did I couldn't tell you.

"I've got some basic details from DC Keillor," Brady

said. "Let me fill in some background. You live in Wetherby, Mr Jarvis?"

He nodded. "Live in Wetherby, teach in Leeds. New term starts in a couple of days. I was supposed to be in today."

"You're married. And children?"

"One. One lad, fourteen."

"He doesn't walk with you?"

"Fourteen? You clearly don't have a teenage son, Mr Brady. His bedroom's a cave. Lit only by his computer..."

Brady laughed. "I've got a daughter. So make that 'lit only by her mobile phone...' What about you, Mr Boulding?"

"Spofforth. It's a village near Harrogate. About three miles from Paul's place. And yes, three of the expensive buggers to answer your next question. And I'm an engineer. And I married his sister. So I'm stuck with him."

Again, all easy enough to check...

Brady stood up. Held his hand out. "Thank you. You may think you haven't told me any more than you told DC Keillor. But it's been helpful. Thank you. We've got your phone numbers?"

The men nodded. "Your DC made a note of them."

"Thank you. There may well be an inquest. You'll need to come back for that. Not for a while though."

Brady handed them both a business card. "If you think of anything else. However trivial – anything that comes back to you. Don't hesitate. Call me. And I hope the rigor mortis wears off."

·   ·   ·

BRADY STOOD on the pavement outside the B&B. Felt the wind coming off the sea.

Someone's got to find the body. There's always someone who finds a body. 'It's a hell of a longshot, Mike.' Finding any body is a hell of a longshot, Geoff. But you're right. As longshots go this is right up there...

4

Ten minutes to walk back to the office. Brady turned the collar of his coat up and walked down Church Street.

Crossed the swing bridge. Changed his mind about going straight back to the office. Stood by the side of the harbour.

I love that. Love that I can see the house from half of Whitby. Let's see what Chris has to say on Friday. And maybe Ash and I can finally eat together tonight. Spag Bol. I'll need some mince...

He walked out of the butcher's and into the wind. Decided that Whitby in your forties was infinitely colder than Whitby in your teens. Remembered that he needed to see Kate.

Tomorrow night. It'll be the same. The same as it was with Grace. The arrangements. The funeral. And then everyone's gone. Suddenly you're on your own. Now what do I do? Get on with it, pal. You're not the first person whose lost his wife. Learn to cope. Come to terms with it. Do the paperwork...

He turned left and walked up the steps.

I need to start Dan on missing persons. How far do we need to go back? Ten years? Twenty? Before Geoff Oldroyd arrived.

There was something going on outside the police station. Jake Cartwright talking to a middle-aged woman. Judging by the body language not an amicable conversation.

What is she? Forty-five? Fifty?

Brady was close enough now. Close enough to hear the conversation.

"I need to see him."

"There's nothing he can tell you. Please, madam, for your own sake, go home. We'll be in touch – "

"Everything alright, PC Cartwright?" Brady said.

The woman turned to stare at him. Light brown hair pulled straight back. A face that said, 'Life has not been kind to me.' A denim shirt open at the neck. Coat unfastened. Red, puffy eyes.

Like she's been crying all night...

"You're him aren't you?" she said. "You're him. Brady. The one in charge."

Jake Cartwright stepped across to restrain her. Brady held his hand up. "It's alright, Jake. Yes," he said. "I'm Michael Brady. What can I do for you, Mrs..."

"Ruby Simpson. I'm not married. And you can show me where those walkers found my Alice."

Alice? Is that her name?

How does she know?

Does the whole of Whitby know?

And how the hell do I deal with it if she's right?

. . .

BRADY PASSED Ruby Simpson a cup of tea. Told her, no, she couldn't smoke in the interview room. Suspected it might not be the first time she'd seen the inside of Whitby police station.

"I want to see it," she said again. "The place. The place where they found her."

He'd had to take her inside. Couldn't have a discussion on the street. Just as clearly couldn't send her home.

Brady had sat her in the interview room. Told her he'd make her a cup of tea. Left her with Jake Cartwright for five minutes. Desperately tried to find out what she was talking about. Found it after two minutes' searching the records. Didn't have time to read the full report. Read enough to hold a conversation.

And worked out who'd told her.

Brady took a deep breath. "I've looked in the records, Miss Simpson. I know – "

"Ruby. I'm not a schoolteacher. Everyone calls me Ruby."

"I've looked in the records, Ruby. I know what happened to your daughter. I simply cannot tell you how sorry I am. But right now that's all I can tell you."

Ruby Simpson stared at him. "She's been found. On the Moors. Some walkers found her on the Moors. I want to see her. If you don't let me see her I'll go up there. My brother will take me."

The landlady at the B&B. She heard them talking. Paul or Andy. Or their wives. And she's broadcast the news round Whitby.

Brady spread his hands. "Ruby, I can only repeat what I said. I've read – very briefly – about your daughter. Her disappearance. I am truly, truly sorry. But that's all I can say. The best thing you can do – the *only* sensible thing you can do – is to let us get on with our job."

She looked across the table at him. An equal mix of loathing and contempt. "You're all the same you coppers. Twenty years on and it's the same shit. 'Leave us to do our job.' 'We'll be in touch.' 'No, we're not looking for anyone else.' 'Your daughter's body? No idea where it is, love. He won't tell us.' 'But you're a pretty little thing, Ruby. Young enough to have another one.'"

Slowly, carefully, Ruby Simpson rolled the saliva round her mouth. Spat into her cup of tea. "Pigs is fucking right."

Brady held his hand up to stop Jake Cartwright for a second time. "I don't need this, Ruby. Clearly, I wasn't here when your daughter disappeared. I've been on the Moors all morning. And then speaking to – "

"Speaking to the two blokes that found her."

"Yes. But you know I can't comment on that. And I haven't had time to read all the reports. So I can't say any more. And spitting into your tea won't make me change my mind."

How must she be feeling? If it is her daughter? How would I feel if... I can't even put it into words.

"Jake, give me five minutes will you?"

Cartwright looked at him quizzically.

"Five minutes, Jake," Brady repeated.

"You want me to wait outside, boss?"

"No, you're fine."

Cartwright walked across to the door. Gave Brady another 'are you sure, boss?' glance. Brady nodded.

"Just the two of us then, Ruby. And like I said, spitting in your tea won't make me change my mind. But I... I'm sorry. I was going to say I understand how you feel. Obviously I don't have a clue."

She carried on staring at Brady. "No-one can. No-one. People say to me – " Ruby shook her head. "Fuck. What does it matter what people say? Just answer me this."

"If I can."

"Why did you give up? Why did you stop looking for her? You police – you can spend fucking millions looking for that McCann girl. Me? 'Cos I'm a single mother on a council estate. 'Cos I don't look good in a press conference. *My* daughter. You don't give a tuppeny fuck."

I've no idea what happened. Has she got a point? Probably...

Brady sighed. "Do you want me to tell you the truth, Ruby? Or do you want me to lie to you?"

Ruby Simpson laughed. Her front teeth were stained from smoking. "The truth. If you coppers know what the truth is."

"The truth is this. When your daughter disappeared – twenty years ago – I'd just left university. I only flicked through the file. I don't know the exact date – "

"October the twelfth. Twenty years this year. She would have been thirty this year. I'd have been 'Nana' by now. Bairns to collect from school. Babysitting. October the twelfth. A month after the other girl."

Brady stared blankly. Had no idea what she was talking about. "Other girl?"

Ruby shook her head. Laughed to herself. "And there's me wondering why you lot never found her. Two girls. Becky Kennedy. And then a month later, my Alice. Two girls. No bodies. No news. Nothing. For twenty long years."

Brady fought to regain some control. "So... if there were two girls. And I'm sorry. Like I said, I was on the Moors all morning. And at a funeral yesterday."

"Bill Calvert."

"Yes, Bill Calvert. He was married to – "

"Your sister."

Dear God, is nothing private in this town?

"So if two girls went missing, Ruby, how do you know Alice has been found?"

"Because I'm her mother. How else would I know? And that's my question. Why did you give up? Fair enough, you've got the bloke that did it. But why did you stop looking for her?"

I should have videoed this. Put it on the training course. How to lose control of an interview...

"Ruby, I asked you two minutes ago if you wanted me to tell you the truth. So the truth is this. When your daughter disappeared I'd just joined Greater Manchester Police. I'm from Whitby – as you clearly know – but I was away."

And I'd just started seeing Grace. So I wasn't paying any attention to Whitby...

"I didn't know what was happening at home. But I'm back now."

"Why?"

"Why what?"

"Why did you come back? I've heard stories. People talk. But..."

But you want me to say it. You think if I'm honest with you about that there's a chance I'll be honest about your daughter. Fair enough.

"My wife died," Brady said. "I have a teenage daughter – "

"Ashley."

No, nothing is private in this town...

"Yes, Ash. That's right."

Ruby nodded. "Same year as our Karen's lass."

Right. Obviously...

"So I'm back," Brady said. "And as soon as you've gone I'll read the files. *All* the files, And I'll sort it out."

"Every copper I've ever spoken to has said he'll sort it out."

Brady looked at her. Held her eyes. "Every copper you've ever spoken to wasn't me, Ruby. You need to trust me."

Less hostile now...

"Maybe. You seem different to the others. I'll not go on the Moors. Not for now. I've waited twenty years. Two more days won't make any difference."

"Thank you," Brady said. "Trust me. Let me do my job."

She nodded. "Like I said. Maybe. Maybe you are different. We'll soon see."

"And Ruby. Do something for me will you?"

"What's that?"

"Don't tell anyone. If it *is* your daughter, we don't want a circus. You said you'd wait for two more days. Do that. Keep quiet for two more days. And..."

"What else?"

"Ask your cousin – is that Karen? Ask her to do the same will you?"

Ruby looked at him innocently. "My cousin? What are you talking about?"

Brady smiled at her. "She looks like you. But not enough like you to be your sister. And she called me 'the new copper.' You've already told me there are no secrets in Whitby. She's the landlady at the B&B."

Ruby nodded at him. Weighed him up. "Someone told me you were a sharp bugger. Said you'd never have sorted that business at Grosmont if you weren't. Maybe they were right. Maybe Alice will get justice after all." She stood up. Walked to the door of the interview room. Reached for the handle. Stopped. Turned and looked at him.

Suddenly vulnerable. Stripped back to the bone. A mother who's lost her child.

"Find her for me, Mr Brady. I know she's dead. I know I'll never see her again. But find her. Give me a place to go on her birthday. Christmas Day. Somewhere I can take her teddy bear. Lay flowers. Find Alice for me, Mr Brady. Please."

5

Brady heard the front door open. "Hi, sweetheart? Everything alright?"

"We won, if that's what you mean."

Ash stood in the kitchen doorway, school uniform on her top half, then tracksuit bottoms and trainers. "That smells good. What is it?"

"Spag Bol. I thought it was a while since we ate together."

"Oh..." His daughter had the good manners to look embarrassed. "I said I'd go round to Bean's. Fiona said seeing as we had to be at school early in the morning..."

"In the morning? Have I forgotten something?"

"Stratford, Dad. The English trip. *Macbeth*. You paid for it, remember? Anyway, we have to be at school by seven. So we can spend half an hour sitting in a freezing bus while Mrs Clarke counts everyone eight times and then realises Jamie Watkins has slept in. Like he does on every school trip."

"So you don't want to eat?"

Ash shook her head. "I'm going to get a shower. Then can you give me a lift to Bean's when I've sorted my stuff out? It smells good though. Why don't you freeze it? Or eat half yourself and give mine to Archie?"

"I'm not going to give my best Bolognese sauce to the dog. Well, not before it's been on my plate. You sure you've got to go?"

"Sorry, Dad. I promised..."

Brady knew he was beaten. "I'll freeze it," he said. "Archie can have yesterday's leftovers."

AN HOUR later he'd put the Bolognese in the freezer, delivered his daughter to her best friend's and walked his dog along a cold, windswept beach.

Now what? Another lonely sandwich?

She didn't have five minutes this morning. Maybe she's got five minutes now...

Frankie answered on the third ring.

"Boss. Sorry. Mike. How are you? And I'm sorry about this morning."

"No problem. You know that. Did you get it all sorted out?"

"Sort of. It's round two tomorrow. Round two of about twenty, I think. What can I do for you?"

"I wanted to pick your brains for five minutes. I – "

Sod it. Just ask her.

"Have you eaten, Frankie?"

"I have two slices of toast in the toaster as we speak. And some pate which is winking suggestively at its sell-by date. Tuesday night is gourmet night..."

"OK. Give the toast to the birds. Throw the pate away. I've some Bolognese that I was going to eat with Ash but she's eating at Bean's. If you put some pasta on I'll be round in ten minutes."

"Pasta? That is *so* seventies. Don't you know everyone in Whitby eats quinoa now?" Frankie paused. "Tagliatelle or spaghetti?"

"You choose. And I'll get some garlic bread on the way."

GARLIC BREAD

...And a bottle of Shiraz.

It was only the second time he'd been to her flat. "Hi," he said as she opened the door.

I'm nervous. Why am I nervous?

"Hi yourself. You brought wine. And garlic bread."

"And Bolognese sauce that's been in the freezer for half an hour and thawing out in my car for ten minutes."

"So not properly frozen and not properly thawed? A gastroenterologist's wet dream. I'll put it in a pan. What happened to Ash?"

"She stood me up. Went to Bean's. They're off to Stratford early tomorrow morning. The Scottish play. Or a mini-break for the teachers. What's that quote? 'For this relief much thanks.'"

She took everything from him and went into the kitchen. Blue jeans, maroon sweatshirt, dark brown hair pinned up as always.

Is that a faint hint of perfume? Alien? Was that it?

She stopped and turned back to him.

"That quote? 'For this relief much thanks?' The one from *Macbeth*?"

"Yes?"

"It's from *Hamlet*."

Brady walked over to the lounge window. "You need to move fifty yards to the left," he said. "Then I could wave to you across the harbour. When I finally move in."

"How's it going?" she shouted from the kitchen.

"Good, I think. I've got the plans. And I'm seeing the builder on Friday."

"So what do the plans say?"

"They say I've spent too much time watching *Grand Designs*. I'm going to turn the house upside down. Have the lounge on the first floor with a balcony. So I can sit and have a beer and look out over the harbour. Watch the lights when I'm worrying at three in the morning. Eat out there in the summer."

"Two words," Frankie said.

"What's that?"

"Triple glazing. You're looking right out to sea. And the wind travels in a straight line. Siberia – frozen tundra – North Sea – Michael Brady's lounge.

Brady smiled ruefully. "So another five grand? I've already thrown the budget out of the window. The triple-glazed window..."

SHE'D GRATED SOME PARMESAN. Sprinkled basil leaves over the top. "You're not going to be offended are you?" she said. "I added some garlic to it. And a pinch of chilli flakes."

"*More* garlic? Suppose I was in front of the promotion board in the morning?"

"Then you'd have to walk into the room chewing parsley. I like garlic. And it's the price you pay for talking shop over dinner."

"How do you know I want to talk shop? I brought a bottle of wine."

"...And very nice it is too. But every man and his dog knows about the bones." She paused to break off a piece of garlic bread. "You could have got all the details off the file."

"I could. I fully intended to. Except that Kershaw ambushed me. Wasted most of my afternoon with some more 'management initiative' bollocks."

"Rumour has it he's leaving."

Brady shook his head. "I don't know. He's certainly distracted by something. But the rumour's been knocking around for two months at least. So far there's plenty of smoke and absolutely no fire. But he's got a new best suit if that tells you anything."

"No. It tells me I'd rather not talk about him. Decomposing bodies if we must. Maggots crawling through eyeballs. Not Kershaw." She reached for another piece of garlic bread. Twisted some pasta round her fork.

"How much do you know?" Brady said.

"Leaving aside the speculation, the basic facts seem to be that an incontinent walker found some bones on the Moors yesterday."

Brady nodded. "A bone from a child's finger. And the two bones from the forearm. And like you said, I could have read the files. I'll go in early tomorrow and do that. But I wanted the anecdotal, not the analytical..."

And someone to eat pasta with.

"From someone who was in Whitby at the time," he added.

"I was fourteen," Frankie said. "No, fifteen."

"So twenty years ago?"

Frankie nodded. "Two girls went missing."

"Together?"

"No, separately. Maybe a month apart. September and October, I think. Alice Simpson – "

"I've met her mother."

"Ruby? Everyone knows Ruby."

"She made a fool of me this afternoon. Turned up at the station demanding to go up on the Moors. Knew far more about the case than I did."

"So you need to know everything?"

Brady nodded. "More than everything. You know I don't like being second-best."

"So Alice," Frankie said. "And a girl called Rebecca – Becky – Kennedy."

"No connection between the two?"

"Apparently not. Different schools, very different families. Nothing in common. No gymnastics, no swimming club, nothing. Except they both disappear and neither of them – neither of the bodies – has ever been found."

"And no-one arrested?"

"In Whitby? Yes, Alice's step-father was arrested."

Ruby didn't tell me that...

"Maybe step-father is overstating it. The man who

was living with Ruby at the time. Questioned and released. And eat something before it goes cold."

Brady did as he was told. Drank some of the wine. "Which one disappeared first?"

"Becky. And then a month later, Alice."

"What was the feeling in the town?"

"I remember two things. The first one's simple. We were teenagers. We were terrified. We didn't dare go out for about three weeks. But it was that teenage girl mixture of terror and excitement. The Whitby Ripper? Maybe Dracula was real? I sat next to Melanie Johnson. She had a clove of garlic in her pencil case. Every time she opened it..."

Brady couldn't stop himself laughing. "I'll suggest that to Ash. She already thinks I'm going senile. That should convince her. Did you know them?"

Frankie shook her head. "Like I said, I was fifteen. Alice was at the same school – maybe she'd just started when she disappeared – but I didn't know her. Becky was at Fyling Hall. Someone said she boarded through the week. I don't know. You'd need to check."

"I'll need to find their friends..."

Frankie nodded. "You'd guess most of Alice's will still be in Whitby. Becky? Anywhere but Whitby."

Brady broke off another piece of garlic bread. Mopped up what was left of the pasta sauce. "I concede," he said.

"Concede what?"

"More garlic. The chilli flakes. It's better. More... I hate to use the word. It's total surrender. But I admit it. More taste."

"And sugar," Frankie said. "It brings out the flavour of the tomatoes."

"Did you hear anything?" Brady said, steering the conversation back onto safer ground. "Gossip? Rumours?"

"Like I said, we were teenage girls. So gossip and rumours were what we did. Serial killers. Dracula had returned. Werewolves... You know Alice disappeared on the day of the eclipse?"

"The eclipse?"

Frankie nodded. "There was a partial eclipse that day. We were outside at the farm. Mum made us look at it through a piece of glass."

Brady reached out for some more garlic bread. Stopped. Worried that he might be eating it all.

"How often is there an eclipse? Once every ten years? One day in three thousand? Four thousand?"

"Like I say, the rumour mill was in overdrive."

"But nothing more down to earth? No-one local that people were suspicious about?"

"No. Just the guy who was living with Ruby. But no-one took it seriously."

"What about the town? What was the reaction?"

"What you'd expect. Fear. Anger. Criticism of the police for not doing enough. And for taking sides."

"Taking sides? How?"

"Every news conference – all the statements – seemed to be about Becky Kennedy."

'Cos I don't look good in a press conference. My daughter. You don't give a fuck.'

"They'd only been here for two or three years. Both

her parents were university lecturers. The mother at
Teesside Poly. Or had it become a university by then? I
don't know. The father was at Leeds. A Maths professor."

"So they ignored Alice Simpson?"

"Not ignored her. But there was a feeling – especially
in some parts of the town – that she was second best."

Like I felt this afternoon...

"That they were looking for Becky's killer. She was
higher profile. A better story. And they seemed to be
hoping that whoever had killed her had done the decent
thing – and killed Alice as well."

"They? Who was in charge of the investigation?"

"Day to day? Macdonald."

"Niall Macdonald? He was still Chief Constable?"

"Who else? A year or so before he retired. Every time
you turned the TV on there he was. And a DI called
Roberts? Robertson? Something like that."

"I've never heard of him."

"You wouldn't. He died. Ten years ago? Retired on
Friday afternoon, died on Sunday morning. Heart attack
on the thirteenth hole. Unlucky for some. There was
someone else as well," Frankie said.

"Who's that?"

"An ambitious young detective called Bill Calvert."

"Bill?"

Brady did the maths. *He'd be thirty. Thirty-one maybe.
That's about right.*

"He never mentioned it," Brady said.

Frankie shrugged. "Why would he?"

"But then suddenly it was 'case closed?' They found
the guy?"

"Macdonald's two favourite words. There was a guy arrested in Middlesbrough. He'd stabbed a girl. A sex attack. Dumped her body on some waste ground. Turned out he was in Whitby on the day Becky disappeared. Said he'd come for a fishing trip. But the forecast was bad and it was cancelled."

"So he didn't go fishing, hung around in Whitby all day but no-one came forward to say they'd seen him?"

"A point Macdonald made very forcibly. The official line was simple. There wasn't enough evidence to charge him, but they weren't looking for anyone else. The good people of Whitby could stop worrying."

"What was his name?"

"Norman Blake. And he ticked all the right boxes. Single guy, always been a loner. Neighbours described him as odd. Healthy stash of pornography. One girl said he'd exposed himself to her. The dead girl's mother said he'd been stalking her. Or maybe stalking her older sister. I can't remember..."

'Four boxes: four ticks. That's enough for me. Sometimes we get an open goal. So let's kick the ball in the net. Stan, take Mike and go and arrest him.'

My first murder case. I can hear Jim Fitzpatrick saying it. We walked out of the office, climbed into Stan's car and went to arrest Gary Cooke. Stan had a heart attack. I woke up in hospital. Cooke had ticked four boxes. But not the right four boxes...

"So Blake is still in jail?"

"As far as I know," Frankie said. "And no-one else disappeared. So maybe Macdonald was right."

"And they stopped looking for the bodies?"

Frankie shrugged. "Manpower and resources. The old story. Macdonald was pinning his hopes on Blake telling him where he'd buried the bodies. But he didn't."

"So he's kept quiet for twenty years?"

Frankie nodded. Took advantage of Brady's pre-occupation to finish the garlic bread.

"And now our incontinent walker has found one of them."

"It looks like it. And I tell you, Mike, you'll wish he hadn't."

"Why do you say that?"

"Because Whitby's learned to live with the truth. No, that's wrong. It found a story it could *accept* as the truth. That's what Macdonald did. Blake was arrested and Macdonald said they weren't looking for anyone else. All the reporters went home. He'd given the town what it wanted. Someone to blame."

"You mean someone other than the police to blame?"

"Right. Somewhere for the town to focus its anger. A target for the Kennedys and Ruby Simpson. Somewhere to direct their grief."

"So that's why I won't be popular?"

"Not if you re-open the wounds."

"I might have to."

Frankie nodded. Stood up and took his bowl. Stacked it on top of hers.

"You might have to. But you won't make friends."

She walked into the kitchen. Said, "finish the wine" as she came back. "I'm at the GPs at nine in the morning. Like I said, the medication wars, round two."

"How's she doing? I should have asked earlier. I'm sorry."

"What was it I said before? What were bad days are now good days. And the bad days are worse. We made a real fuss of her at Christmas. I don't think... you know what I was going to say. I don't want to put it into words."

Brady reached across the table. Tentatively put his hand on hers. "Are you alright?"

Frankie looked back at him. Nodded. "I'm good. I'm OK. Louise and I cope between us. And it was the right thing to do."

"The sabbatical?"

"Yes. Not just Mum. Everything. I needed a break." She freed her hand, picked the wine bottle up. "You want this?"

"Thank you, no. One I'm driving, two I want a clear head for the files tomorrow."

He paused. Looked across the table at Frankie. Knew there was no point asking her to come back to work. "I should tell the builder to crack on with the balcony," he said. "I can see a lot of three-o'clock-in-the-mornings with this one."

"Ruby Simpson?"

"Not just Ruby. Let's say it *is* one of the girls. I'll have to go to one family and tell them their daughter's been found. I'll have to go to the other family and say, 'She's still out there somewhere.' I'll have to find the killer. Stop the whole thing becoming a circus – "

"Like it was last time."

" – And do it all without pissing off Kershaw."

It was Frankie's turn to laugh. "Do it, Mike. Treat yourself. Every job has its compensations..."

Brady smiled at her. "You might be right. A leaving present..."

Frankie looked at him. "Just now. You said 'find the killer.' You don't think it was Blake?"

"Right now, I don't know. But what's your first thought? There's a hell of a difference between dumping a body on waste ground and burying one on the Moors. Where would *you* bury a body, Frankie?"

Two months. Not much more than two months. I hadn't realised how much I'd missed talking to her...

"Personally I don't bury bodies at all. Although the receptionist at the GP surgery is fast becoming a possibility. But I know what you're saying. I'd bury it somewhere I knew."

"Right. You're not going to murder someone and then drive to the Brecon Beacons on the off-chance you can find somewhere to dig a grave. Have you been up on the Moors – "

Brady stopped. Looked at her. "Enough. Not tonight. I don't want to go inside the killer's head tonight. My first murder case as an SIO was a child. An eight year old girl. It stays with you. And I need to go. You've got to be up early, I've got to be up early."

"And Archie..."

"Right. And Archie."

Brady stood up. Walked over to the sofa and picked his coat up.

Why do I feel nervous again?

"I enjoyed tonight," Frankie said. "Thank you."

Brady laughed. "No, thank *you*. All I did was make Bolognese sauce and get rejected by my daughter."

"We should do this properly, Mike. Mum goes into the nursing home next week. We've got a week's respite care. I'll cook. Come round for dinner." She paused. "If you'd like to."

"Yes. I would. But supposing I'm in the middle of the Moors?"

"Then you'll have to leave your wellingtons in the hall." Frankie shook her head in mock exasperation. "Seriously, Detective Chief Inspector. How hard can it be? Identify the body. Break the news to the families. Keep Kershaw under control. Keep a lid on the press. And solve a twenty year old murder."

"Two murders..."

"Right. Two murders. But you've got a week. Come on, Brady, call yourself a copper?"

6

Starbucks. Costa. Caffé Nero. All the independents. If an alien landed in London he'd think the sole purpose of the human race was to drink coffee. If he landed in a police station he'd think the sole purpose was to avoid it...

Brady took another sip, accepted that he'd put far too much faith in the new machine, and pulled the file towards him.

He'd decided to do it in geographical order. Start with the murder in Middlesbrough: travel south for Becky and Alice.

Is that what the killer did? Start in Middlesbrough? Drive across the Moors for his second and third victims? Let's see...

He opened the file. Still in a Cleveland Police folder.

They must have copied it for us.

Sandra Donoghue. Murdered by Norman Blake.

What did he get?

Brady checked a note on the file.

Life, with a recommendation of twenty years.

It had all hinged on the report. The report and the

confession. There was no forensic evidence, no witnesses. So the SIO – DCI Fraser Hogg. Brady trawled through his memory, didn't find anything – had reached for the latest shiny new toy.

A report from a forensic psychologist. A profiler. Brady skimmed through his qualifications – a psychology lecturer at Newcastle University. An academic. But he'd spent a month with the FBI. In 1996 that was more than enough to tick the 'expert' box. More than enough for a desperate copper to have you on speed dial.

Wade through twenty-five pages – or the expert's 'executive summary?'

Brady turned to the last two pages.

The Murder of Sandra Donoghue. A Psychological Profile of the Killer

Sandra Donoghue was murdered on Thursday August 22nd. Her partially-clothed body was found on waste ground behind Westmoreland Road Industrial Estate. There was no evidence of sexual assault. Cause of death was multiple stab wounds leading to loss of blood.

The victim was reported missing at 21:05 on the night of August 22nd. Time of death was put at 9pm to 10pm. The body was not discovered until 10:30 the next morning, when two staff from Coyne Tyres and Exhausts went for a 'kickabout' in their break.

It rained heavily in the night of August $22^{nd}/23^{rd}$ and no DNA – apart from the victim's – was recovered from the scene.

My key findings for the police officers investigating the case, based on the above summary and my own expertise and extensive research are as follows:

1. The stab wounds appeared to be random. The pathologist was unable to say which particular stab wound was the fatal one. However, she was able to say that the wounds had been inflicted with some force.

2. I would suggest that this was an attack from someone who had been rebuffed sexually, with the random nature of the blows and their severity suggesting anger. The killer is unlikely to be married or in a stable relationship and is unlikely to be 'successful' with the opposite sex.

3. He may well have had a recent experience where he was rejected by a member of the opposite sex.

4. The victim was only partially clothed. The blouse she was wearing was not recovered. Her bra had been pulled to one side: her jeans had been unzipped and tugged down in a sexually suggestive way. I am strongly of the opinion that the killer masturbated after the murder, but that all traces of semen were washed away by the subsequent rain.

5. Linking this to points [2] and [3] above you are almost certainly looking for someone with a collection of pornography or whose computer evidences frequent visits to such sites.

6. The obvious conclusion to draw is that as the body was found near an industrial estate the likely killer is someone who knows the estate. In fact the waste ground is not easy to find

from the industrial estate, but is used as a short cut between the nearby housing estate and the town.

7. In my opinion you are far more likely to find the killer on the housing estate than on the industrial estate. I would suggest that he was following Miss Donoghue, made sexual advances to her and was re-buffed, with tragic consequences.

8. The pathologist has said that the stab wounds, were inflicted – in her opinion – by a chisel. In my view this does *not necessarily* mean that the killer is a tradesman. A chisel is an everyday object that will be in most houses. This was a disorganised, spur-of-the-moment attack. Sunset on August 22nd was at 20:17. There may well have been some light when the attack took place. The killer does not, in my view, have the organisational skills necessary to work as, say, a joiner.

9. As noted above Miss Donoghue's blouse was missing. As evidenced by the 'Rotherham Shoe Rapist,' taking of clothing as a 'trophy' is well known. The killer may have discarded the blouse – however, when you search his home you will certainly find other 'collections.'

10. In summary, you are looking for someone who lives alone – or perhaps with his mother: who has an unhealthy interest in pornography; who 'collects' things: who is unsuccessful with the opposite sex, who lives locally and – based

on the severity of the attack – is likely to lose
his temper if he does not get his own way.

Timothy Farrell BSc PhD AFBPS
Consulting Psychologist
September 7th, 1996.

BRADY READ the report a second time. Decided he'd taken
a wrong turn in life. That anyone who'd read *Teach Your-self Psychology* could have written it. And attached a suit-ably large invoice.

*Stop being cynical. It's twenty years ago. Profiling was the
new kid on the block. Or on the waste ground behind the tyre
and exhaust place...*

*But Fraser Hogg had run with it. What had Frankie said?
'Norman Blake. Single guy, always been a loner. Neighbours
described him as odd. Healthy stash of pornography. One girl
said he'd exposed himself to her. The dead girl's mother said
he'd been stalking her.'*

Brady nodded to himself.

*Hogg had found someone who ticked the boxes and not
looked any further. Closed the file and taken the team down
the pub to celebrate.*

If only it was that easy...

THERE WAS a newspaper clipping attached to the file.
Someone had scrawled *Yes! Result!* across it. A grainy
picture of a nervous looking young man in his twenties.

Nervous and frightened, even in what looks like a holiday photo.

NORMAN BLAKE GETS LIFE FOR MURDER OF SANDRA DONOGHUE

Norman Blake was today found guilty of the murder of 13 year old Middlesbrough girl Sandra Donoghue. Blake (22) of Osborn Flats, was told by Judge John Quick that he had 'committed a despicable act, cutting short a life that was full of promise and bringing unimaginable pain to her family.'

Detective Chief Superintendent Fraser Hogg praised the 'thoroughness and attention to detail' of his officers. "We have no doubt at all," he said. "That had Blake not been apprehended he would have continued to prey on other vulnerable young women, perhaps with equally tragic consequences."

Reading a prepared statement on behalf of the family, solicitor Jessica Young thanked the police for their efforts, and those people who had given evidence against Blake. "Sandra's parents, her brother and sister will never get over their sense of loss. A light has gone out in their lives and it can never be rekindled. Sandra had already represented her county in gymnastics competitions and was widely expected to represent Great Britain in the future. Now we will never know what might have been."

There was a brief footnote. 'Having been taken ill during the trial Blake's mother was not in court to see her son sentenced. The accused cut a sorry figure as he was led away, still protesting his innocence, to begin a richly-deserved life sentence.'

.   .   .

BRADY CLOSED THE FILE. Reached for the one on Rebecca Kennedy. There was nothing he couldn't have guessed.

She'd been with friends in Whitby. Last seen getting on the bus. The driver remembered stopping. About a mile for her to walk home. He'd told her to walk quickly because it looked like rain. Had anyone else got off the bus? Yes, a man he hadn't seen before. Any description? Medium height. In his twenties. But he wasn't really paying attention. The ticket machine wasn't working properly. So no, he didn't see which direction the man went in. Rebecca? He'd dropped her off before. Straight down the lane. About a mile to walk home...

Except she never arrived. Reported missing by her mother late that night. They'd phoned all her friends. Of course she didn't stay out late. And if she missed the bus – she'd done it once – she phoned them.

They appealed for the man to come forward. He never did.

They started searching the next day. Nothing. No trace. Not a piece of jewellery. No clothing, no signal from her phone. Nothing.

And they were still searching when Alice went missing a month later...

Brady sighed. His coffee had gone cold.

Maybe twenty seconds in the microwave will improve it...

It didn't.

IT WAS the same story with Alice. Saturday October 12th. She hadn't come home. Ruby didn't report her missing until the next morning. There was a note on the file.

The mother – Ruby Simpson, who is known to the police – thought that her daughter had stayed with friends and "forgotten to phone." She had done this before. The mother said that she was not worried and that "Alice could take care of herself, could Alice."

Ruby Simpson appears to be living with Dennis Henry McBride, who has convictions for theft and breaking and entering. When officers visited the house on October 13th McBride refused to answer questions.

Brady read the rest of the file. Niall Macdonald had focused all his efforts on finding Becky. The search for Alice had been half-hearted at best.

Maybe I should be charitable. Find the first girl's killer and then you find the second girl's killer. But finding Alice's body? He may as well have stuck a pin in the map. The town centre? The steps leading up from the harbour? McBride had been hauled in and then released a day later. The police didn't have a clue...

Alice had vanished, exactly as Becky had vanished. The annual cold case review had been little more than a box-ticking exercise.

Two girls, a month apart. And now one of them has been found.

Brady looked at Alice's file again.

October the twelfth...

He went online and checked.

No, not a full moon. So Frankie's pal with garlic in her pencil case didn't need to worry...

7

Michael Brady locked his car. Turned and walked slowly to his sister's front door.

Less than a year. Less than a year since I came for Bill's birthday party. Less than a year since Kate told me to open the door and I saw Patrick. Now he's dead. My best friend. My sister's husband. Both of them. How is that possible?

"How are you doing?"

Kate smiled at him.

Her brave smile. I've seen it a lot lately...

"I'm doing alright, Mike. Come in. Let me make you a cup of tea. Do you want something to eat? And – " She shook her head, an 'I can't believe it' expression. "I'm making a list. 'Things I need to do after my husband's death.'"

"What's at the top?"

"A billionaire with a six-pack. Move to a Greek island. Learn the saxophone. Or was that the other list? Bill's clothes. Then paperwork. More paperwork. Police pension. Death-in-service."

"Let me know what you want me to do. With the clothes. If you can't face it... I'll come one Saturday morning. Take them all to the hospice shop for you."

She reached up and kissed him on the cheek. "Thanks, Mike. I know. I just... I don't know. It's part of saying goodbye, isn't it? I sort of feel I owe it to him. We were never closer than..."

The sentence trailed away. Brady held his arms out. Hugged her until the tears stopped.

"Me too," he said. "Enjoy is the wrong word but... I did. I enjoyed sitting with him."

"Smuggling whisky in," Kate chided.

"I did. Guilty as charged. He was so determined to make it to New Year. It was the least I could do. I put some on my finger. Touched it to his lips. 'One last time,' he said. Even found the strength to wink at me."

"Not the best way for you to see in the New Year..."

"I don't know. Ash was at Bean's. Her mother was having a party. I stayed for a drink but Bill seemed... More important. I didn't want him to be on his own. And I knew you'd been there all day. So I sat on his bed and we talked into the night..."

I talked. Football. Police work. Golf – what little I know... Sometimes Bill answered. Sometimes he rambled. Drifted back in time. Like Dad did before the end.

"Those were his last words," Kate said. "Did I tell you? 'Happy New Year.' I'd left the girls asleep. They were exhausted. So just me and him. And one of the nurses. He opened his eyes. Looked at me, said 'Happy New Year.' And he was gone."

Brady hugged her again. This time the tears took longer to stop.

Kate pushed herself away. Blinked back the last of her tears. "His clothes, sorting it all out. It stops me feeling guilty," she said. "Slightly..."

"You did everything you could, Kate. No wife could have done more."

She shook her head. "You don't need to butter me up, Mike. That night you came to his party... I'd made my mind up. As soon as Lucy went to university I was leaving him. Before it was too late. And then the bugger gets cancer. And suddenly I find... Well, you know what I found. And here I am making two piles. Charity shop and recycling."

"And paperwork."

"Right. And paperwork. Did you say you used to do it at three in the morning?"

I did. Sitting at my desk doing paperwork. Sleeping on the sofa because I couldn't face being in the bed without her. The funeral's over. Everyone's gone home. And you're on your own. Except I had Ash. And we sat on the sofa and hugged each other. Sat on the floor and hugged Archie. And then one morning her hormones start and she doesn't want to hug me.

And I missed it more than she did...

"How are the girls coping?" Brady said.

"Surprisingly well. Maddie's focusing on work. She got an offer, did I tell you?"

"Her first choice? That's brilliant."

" – And Lucy's... She's just a teenage girl. I think she's got a boyfriend. Not that she'll tell me. How's Ash?"

Brady smiled. "Growing up. My little girl has almost disappeared. I miss her. But what can I do?"

"Looking forward to the new house?"

Brady laughed. "Her or me? Ash is looking forward to it. More than looking forward to it. I'm envious. A top-floor penthouse overlooking the harbour. What more does a girl need?" He paused. "Me? It's complicated."

"How?"

And if I can't tell my sister who can I tell?

"It's... I'm enjoying it, Kate."

"And you're feeling guilty?"

Brady nodded. "Exactly that. Because it's a new house and I should be doing it with Grace. Or part of me thinks I should be doing it with Grace. And the other part of me is thinking I always wanted exposed brickwork and I'm going to have a balcony overlooking the harbour. And I'm looking at the plans and suddenly I think, 'I'm enjoying this.' And then a small voice says I shouldn't be enjoying it."

"But Grace would want you to be happy."

"Yes, of course. And if it had been the other way round I'd have wanted her to be happy. And I know all the logical stuff. But there you are. I'm lying in bed thinking, 'I'm seeing the builder this week' and this bloody voice starts whispering in my ear. Why don't you come round on Sunday? Bring the girls. Family Sunday lunch? I'll buy a joint."

Kate smiled. "I'd like that. If our daughters aren't too busy. But..."

"But what?"

"But you have a life to lead, Mike. Remember that. I

know you feel responsible for us now. So of course we'll come for dinner. As soon as we can. And you'll probably have to take his clothes to the charity shop for me. And I know you'll do anything else I ask you to do. But..." She smiled at him. "You don't need to worry about me all the time. I'm not the first woman to lose her husband. And you're not the first man to lose his wife. So stop feeling guilty about the house. You can grieve. But you can't grieve for ever."

Michael Brady stood outside the front door. Breathed in the clean, crisp winter air. Tasted the slight tang of salt blowing off the sea. Turned round and looked up at his new house. Felt the same mix of excitement and guilt he'd told Kate about. But knew he'd made the right choice. Knew he'd found somewhere he could call home.

See the end of the pier every morning? Reminded of Jimmy Gorse every day? A few months and I won't even notice it...

A white van came round the corner. A blue house roof painted on the side. *Chris Kenton Builders* written underneath it.

...And stepping out of it, Chris Kenton himself. Older, rounder, greyer – but unmistakeably the boy Brady had known at school.

He grinned, pushed a mop of hair back off his forehead and stuck his hand out. "Michael Brady. Star of the football team. Good to see you. And how come I've not bumped into you before now?"

Brady smiled and shook hands. "Because you got married again, Chris. Made more babies so I heard."

Chris grinned. "So I did. Val Carmichael. I should never have split up with her when I was sixteen. Would have saved me a bloody fortune." He stopped grinning. Looked serious. "I heard what happened, mate. Your wife. We're really sorry. Val sends her best. She says you've got to come round for dinner some time. And bring your daughter."

Brady nodded. "Thanks, Chris. Give her my love. And no, you shouldn't have split up with her. The whole bloody class could see that."

"Come on, then. Enough of the follies of youth. Let's see the house."

Brady put the key in the lock. Pushed the front door. "Welcome to The Crow's Nest," he said.

"The Crow's Nest?"

"Yeah, the house has a name. The solicitor told me. On the original deeds. They stopped using it for some reason. But high up. Overlooking the harbour. It fits, don't you think? Anyway, I'm going to start using it again. And item one. The front door of The Crow's Nest. It's stiffer every time I come round."

"It will be. The wood will swell with the rain. But there'll be more to do than a new door. Let's have a look."

Brady led the way into a hall that still thought it was 1980. "Ouch," Chris said. "Don't tell me. The old lady died, the children wanted a quick sale. The bathroom's going to be avocado isn't it?"

"Two out of three," Brady said. "The bathroom's plum. Or whatever they call that colour halfway between maroon and pink."

Brady turned left. "The lounge," he said. "The best room. The room they used on Sundays."

Chris walked across to the window. "The harbour? The pier? A view like this I'd have used it every day of the week. And twice on Sundays."

He turned round. Looked up at the ceiling. Tapped the walls in various places. "There's a bloody lot of work to do, Mike. Looking at the sketches Tom's done. You're going to use him for the detailed stuff?"

"Yeah. He was Patrick's architect. It seemed the right thing to do."

Chris shook his head. "Bad, bad business. Poor bastard. The sketches, Mike. I've worked with Tom before. He's really good. But I can tell you now, by the time you've bought it and done the work... It'd be a lot cheaper to buy a new house. Nice, sensible four-bed executive home on a new estate."

"But I'm not going to get the view am I, Chris? And I've come back to Whitby. I'm staying. I want to feel part of the town. Part of the town's history. What are we going to do? Give another slice of the town where we grew up to some bloody accountant from Leeds? Besides, imagine looking out of that window. Out across the harbour. And you can see them unloading a whale. Down there on the docks. The whole town's come out to see it."

"You think the house is that old?"

Brady nodded. "The estate agent thinks it's about two hundred years. So 1820. Just as the whaling was coming to an end. So the house has seen that. It's seen the Crimean War. Queen Victoria. It's seen lads march off to fight the

Kaiser and Adolf Hitler. Babies born and grandparents die."

"So you're going to do it justice?"

"No," Brady said. "*We're* going to do it justice. I take your point about money. And I'm not saying money's no object – "

Chris laughed out loud. "Mike, mate, no bugger who was born in Whitby ever said 'money's no object.'"

"Very true. But let's do the job properly, Chris. Let's do something we can both be proud of."

"Bloody right, mate. Give me the grand tour then. Let's see what we're working with. You've got time, have you?"

"Plenty. I'm seeing someone at ten."

Perks of the job. Looking at bones that have been on the Moors for twenty years...

"Come on, we'll start at the top," Brady said. "What my daughter describes as her penthouse suite."

He turned and led the way up the stairs.

Guilt? No, not any longer. Just excitement...

8

She was exactly as Brady remembered her. Wearing what she always wore. Navy cardigan, a red t-shirt just visible under it, black trousers, her trademark red Skechers. The spiky blonde hair losing its battle with grey.

Still looking like a woman who should be on a wildlife programme. Turning and whispering to the camera as the gazelle tiptoes nervously to the water hole...

Julia kissed him on the cheek. Hugged him, then held him at arm's length and looked at him. "You've lost weight, Mike. You need fattening up. You can start by taking me to lunch when we're done here."

"I wouldn't dream of doing anything else. Let me take you down to – "

"There's no need, Mike."

Brady turned. Geoff Oldroyd was at the top of the stairs. "I thought I'd come up from the underworld. Greet our illustrious guest. How are you, Julia?"

"I'm good, Geoff. And good to see you again. Well, assuming the kettle's on."

"The kettle's on. I've shaken the weevils out of the ship's biscuits."

Julia laughed. "Whitby hospitality. Lead me to it. What shall we do, Mike? Give you a call?"

Brady nodded. "If that's alright. I'd like to come down and watch you pick over the bones. But duty calls. Rebecca Kennedy and Alice Simpson aren't the only files on my desk..."

IT WAS ALMOST lunchtime when his phone rang.

"I'm sorry, Geoff. I'll be with you in ten minutes. Make Julia another coffee. I've just been Kershawed."

"You've been what?"

"Ash asked me for some help with her English homework. Creative writing. She had to invent five new verbs. I recommended Kershaw."

"What's it mean then?"

"Simple. To suggest to a subordinate that they'd 'like' to do some totally pointless work. This work will not advance the cause of the company/organisation or the career of the person doing the work, but will show the person doing the asking in a favourable light. So as I said. 'I'll be with you in ten minutes. I've been Kershawed.'"

"GEOFF EXPLAINED," Julia said as Brady tried to apologise. "And it's fine. Besides, any man who can invent a verb without the assistance of alcohol gets a free pass from me."

Brady laughed. Then stopped himself. "How much

humour are we going to need?"

"A fair bit," Geoff said. "We've still got some work to do, but I knew you'd want something as quickly as possible."

"And she's waited long enough to tell her story."

"Something like that. But it's not pretty, Mike. Are you ready?"

"I'm as ready as I'll ever be, Geoff."

He watched Geoff walk over to a corner of the room. Pull back a plastic sheet. Expose the bones.

"Bloody hell, Geoff..."

"I know. A lifetime down here. There are still some things you're not prepared for."

Brady looked at the skeleton.

Half a skeleton. Not even that...

The big bones were there. The ones the scavengers hadn't carried away. Skull, pelvis, the thigh bones. Lower leg.

How many bones are in your foot? Twenty something? If there's half a dozen...

Brady felt a wave of nausea wash over him.

Most of the bones hadn't been exposed. Had lain in the shallow grave in the peat soil. Gradually turned a pale yellow/brown.

The colour tobacco would be if you left it on the windowsill for a year.

Except for the one Paul Jarvis hit with his stream of urine. Bleached white by the sun...

Brady looked down at the small hand. Half the bones missing. Those that were left the colour of faded tobacco. And one stark, white bone completing her middle finger.

He fought down the nausea. Walked over to the tap. Found a coffee cup, ran some water into it. Had a drink.

"I'm sorry, Geoff. Sorry, Julia. I didn't ask you to come over from Sheffield so you could see me throwing up. Or nearly throw up. Twenty years. Hundreds of post-mortems and that's the closest I've come."

"Don't apologise," Geoff said. "I came bloody close myself."

"She looks so – I'm sorry, Geoff, I can't stop thinking of my daughter – she looks so vulnerable. So... there's no other word for it. Naked. Stripped bare. Tell me some cold, hard facts. Some logic. Stop me feeling so emotional."

Geoff glanced at Julia. "You want to tell the grizzly tale?"

Julia nodded. "First things first, Mike. She was naked."

"When she was buried?"

"Yes. There is simply *no* trace of any clothing. Add in what Geoff and Henry found – or didn't find – no jewellery, nothing. And I'd be ninety-nine per cent certain of that."

"Her clothes could have decayed couldn't they? Decomposed?"

Julia shook her head. "No. Joe Average dies. The family dress him in his best suit and tie – personally I'd want to spend eternity in my gardening clothes – stand at the graveside and watch him lowered into the earth. Not much more than a year and any cotton clothes have disintegrated. But come back in a hundred years and there'll still be nylon threads. Maybe all that's left of Joe's

best suit is part of the waistband. Those bones have
been out on the Moors for twenty years. I've never seen a
case where there wasn't *some* fragment of clothing after
that time. There isn't. So there's only one logical
conclusion."

"Is this one of the missing girls, Julia? Has she been
out there for twenty years?"

"Almost certainly. We've sent off for a DNA match.
There's some on file in the national database. Someone
had the good sense to take her toothbrush."

"So which one is it? Alice or Becky?"

"Hang on, Mike. Allow Geoff and me our moment of
drama. Here, look…"

Julia turned back to the remains. Pulled a pen out of
her pocket. Used it to point at one of the bones in
the arm.

Just below her elbow. What am I looking for?

Brady admitted defeat. Had to say it out loud. "What
am I looking for?"

Geoff Oldroyd laughed. "Specsavers, Mike. You'll have
to bow to the inevitable. Shake hands with middle age.
We all do it."

"Here," Julia said. "I don't want to pick the bone up. I
don't want to handle *any* of the bones too much. The acid
in the soil has attacked them. They're starting to
crumble."

Brady bent forward. Squinted at the bone. Vaguely
made out a line, a very faint ridge.

"It's the ulna," Julia said. "One of the bones the walker
found. That faint ridge – the thickening in the bone – is a
break. Not a serious break, but a break all the same. Two

girls? The chance of them both breaking their arm in the same place?"

Brady nodded. "Almost zero. As near to zero as makes no difference."

He looked down at the bones again. Tried to picture her. Laughing, vibrant, the whole of her life in front of her.

Couldn't do it.

"So which one?" he said.

Geoff Oldroyd looked at him.

He looks slightly ashamed. Why?

"We got lucky," he said. "It's Rebecca Kennedy."

"Becky? So why did we get lucky, Geoff? It had to be one or the other."

"Because her medical records are on the file. And like Julia said, someone collected her toothbrush."

"And you're saying Alice's records *aren't* on file? And we've no DNA?"

Oldroyd shook his head. "No. And I suspect the reason's simple. The most common one of all."

Brady nodded. "A cock-up. They were so busy finding Becky's killer they didn't do the basics with Alice."

Ruby was right then. Her daughter had been second-best...

"So Becky Kennedy broke her arm?" Brady said.

"Age six, according to the records," Julia said. "Slipped and fell on some rocks. Landed on her arm. An everyday story of a family day out. And absolutely consistent with what we've got in front of us."

"Everything else adds up?" Brady said. "She's the right age?"

"Yes. Just started puberty I'd say. So yes, I think we've

found Rebecca Kennedy."

Brady exhaled slowly. Started to see the investigation unfolding in front of him. "So she fell and broke her arm. Seven years later someone lays her naked body in a grave on the Moors. And now I'm going to ask you if there's a cause of death. And – looking at your faces – you're going to say 'no...'"

Julia nodded. "I'm sorry, Mike, we are. Based on what we have here there isn't a cause of death. Other than the one we've described, there are no fractures. The skull is intact. Nothing on the bones."

"Nothing on the bones?"

"I had a case a couple of years ago. Down in the West Country. Just the bones to work with. No apparent cause of death. Until we looked closely at the ribs. The faintest nick on one of them."

"So he'd stabbed her? I'm assuming it was a her?"

Julia nodded. "One of the teachers at her school. He'd become fixated on her. Couldn't deal with it when he saw her with a boyfriend. A year before they found the body. But here?" She turned, gestured at what had once been Becky. "Here? There's nothing."

"Strangulation?" Brady said hopefully.

"No. The hyoid bone's not here. A girl of this age, it would only be tiny – a couple of centimetres, maybe – but the bones we do have... I'm talking nonsense, Mike, and I wouldn't say this to someone I didn't know well. All the damage we see here is decay. Decomposition. Not some sudden, violent trauma. You want a hunch? My hunch is a soft tissue injury. But I'm only saying that because you're a friend."

"He could have stabbed her and missed a rib?"

"He could have done. But somehow I don't think so. I know you don't mind me speculating. A violent death? A struggle? This doesn't feel right..."

Brady looked at the bones again. Shook his head. "I was going to buy you fish and chips, Julia. We could have sat by the harbour and shivered. Somehow..."

She laughed. "You're right. I ask myself that all the time. 'Here you are, Julia,' I say. 'You do a job that should put you off food for life.' And yet every Monday morning the bathroom scales tell the same story. And if you think I'm coming to Whitby and *not* having fish and chips you're mistaken, Michael Brady."

Brady smiled for the first time that morning. "It's Whitby in January, Julia. I hope you brought your big coat..."

THEY LOOKED across the harbour and ate their fish and chips. Brady pointed the house out. Told her again to keep her promise and bring Neil for the weekend.

"And how's Ash? How's she doing..."

"Without Grace? You can say it, Julia. Alright, I think. She's a bit moody at the moment. But she's thirteen..." Brady shrugged. "I don't know. Talking to her is difficult."

Julia put her hand on his arm. "It's hard, Mike. There were a couple of years when Neil and Sophie couldn't be in the same room together. Now? They're the best of friends. Go to football together. Weep about the result. She'll come through it."

"I know. Everyone tells me that. It's just that... Sometimes I think she wants to talk to me, and then she stops herself. Like she's making the decision that I'm not going to understand even before she's said anything."

"And you feel guilty?"

Brady looked at her. Nodded. "Yes. How can I not feel guilty? Whatever I say, whatever I do, I can't bring her mum back. And yes, I feel guilty about that. I'll always feel guilty about that."

Brady stood up. Walked over to the bin with the wrappers. Came back wiping the grease off his fingers. "Talk to me about murders, Julia," he said. "They're easier than teenage girls. You definitely don't think he stabbed her?"

Julia shook her head. "No, I don't. God knows I'm not a psychologist but you and I both know this is an organised killer, Mike. Take her there. Bury her. Have the... there's no other way to put it. Have the mental strength to either take her there naked, or to strip the body and walk away with the clothes. I don't see that as consistent with stabbing. That's a crime of passion. *La crime passionnel*. Becky's killer? That's cold blood, Mike. The coldest of cold blood."

"Why there?" Brady said. "That's what's keeping me awake at night. Why that exact spot?"

"I don't know," Julia said. "And I haven't seen where you found her. But from what Geoff said it's remote. Desolate. And you have to walk there. Carrying a body? Neil and I have spent weekends in the Peak District. 'Carry as little as you can for as short a time as you can' is my motto. Or get Neil to carry it..."

"I still think she was killed somewhere else."

"How else does he get her up there? Not willingly. Drugged, maybe?"

"Clearly he didn't want her found. Not for a very long time."

"If ever..."

"So why there?" Brady said again. "And why bury her?" Why not dissolve her in acid? Chop her up?"

"Why not dump the body at sea?" Julia said, pointing at a fishing boat making its way reluctantly to the mouth of the harbour and the waiting January waves. "This is Whitby after all..."

"But you need to own a boat, don't you? Or you need to pay someone who owns a boat. And if our boy is careful enough to take the body up to the Moors I don't think he's going to involve someone else. He doesn't need a fisherman who wakes up one morning and repents. Discovers a conscience and taps on his door."

Brady sighed. Shook his head. "What would *you* do, Julia? You want to get rid of a body. You're the expert. The *ultimate* expert. What would you do?"

"Ah, Mike, the question one of us always asks. The conference is finished for the day. Half a dozen forensic anthropologists are in the bar. Sensible people have over-heard snatches of the conversation. Moved away. And someone *always* asks that question. And every year there's an advance in science that rules out last year's winner."

"Go on then. There's a lot of thought gone into this. We're saying it's not spur-of-the-moment..."

"You're *sure* he doesn't have a boat, Mike? That's still one of my favourites. Wrap the body tightly. Small gauge netting is best so the fish can eat the body – but nothing big escapes to get identified. And plenty of weight, obviously. Twice as much as the physics says. I was talking to an American friend. She said there's a body a week pops up over there because they haven't used enough weight."

"But clearly he didn't have a boat..."

"No. Getting rid of a body is a real problem. Farms are good – pigs, agricultural composting. But for Mr Average in his semi it's bloody difficult. And there's the science, Mike. What we couldn't detect five years ago is commonplace now. You know what you really need if you want to get away with murder? It's not skill or science or cunning –"

"What is it then?"

"It's luck, Mike. Pure and simple luck. Get yourself an alibi, hide the body where you think it might not be found until you're dead – and hope for the best."

Brady looked up to the Abbey. Let his gaze wander across to St Mary's Church. Thought about the graveyard. Where half the headstones were illegible. Where an 18th Century stonemason *had* got away with it. Sold headstones he must have known would fade and crumble with age – but with the confidence that both he and his customers would be safely in the ground before it was discovered.

Was that it with Becky? Was the person who buried her confident he'd be dead before she was discovered? Had he known he only had to be lucky for the rest of his life?

And how long was that? Ten years? Twenty?

9

"You want a cup of tea, Mr Brady? You had some dinner? Can I make you a sandwich?"

He'd said goodbye to Julia.

Driven up onto the council estate. Sat in the car for ten minutes. Tried to work out how to prepare her. Tell Ruby without telling her. Trying to balance the personal – *What if it was Ash?* – with the professional. Tried to work out how to ask if Alice had broken her arm without asking if she'd broken her arm. Had finally given in. Accepted that all he could do was play it by ear.

Hope for the best.

"Tea's fine, thank you, Ruby."

"Yorkshire? It's all I've got."

Brady laughed. "It's all anyone in Whitby's got. When I was a boy the Rington's man used to come round."

"I remember that. Someone said you grew up in Whitby. Where did you live?"

"Just off the Scarborough road. Opposite the cemetery. Then we moved to Runswick Avenue."

Ruby raised her eyebrows. "Posh, then. Here. One sugar, hardly any milk."

"How did you know?"

"Heard you telling that young lad at the police station."

Ruby put a white mug down in front of him. *It's a gin thing,* written on the side.

"Thanks, Ruby. I'm impressed. There's plenty of 'young lads at the police station' wouldn't have noticed that. Or remembered it. You missed your calling in life."

Ruby shrugged. "Took a few wrong turns, didn't I? Too late now."

"It's never – "

She leaned forward. Put her forearms on the table. Looked him in the eye. Stopped the small talk in its tracks. "So have you found her for me, Mr Brady? Now you're sitting at my table with a mug of tea in your hand. Is that what you're going to tell me?"

I wish everyone was this open. This straightforward.

He held her gaze. "Like I said, Ruby. I'm not going to lie to you."

There's plenty I can't tell you though. We lost your daughter's medical records. No-one bothered to call round for a hairbrush or a toothbrush.

"...But right now the answer is 'I don't know.' We've done some preliminary work. But we're waiting for the DNA results to come back."

"But it's Alice. Or the other girl."

Brady nodded. "There's only so much I can say, Ruby. But common sense – "

"Says there's only two girls can be buried up there. When will you get it? This DNA?"

"Monday. They've promised it for Monday."

"So you could have left me in peace for the weekend. Turned up on Monday. Once instead of twice."

"I could, Ruby. I thought about it. But how often do you think about Alice?"

"Ten times a day. A hundred times a day."

Brady nodded. "Me too since Tuesday. So it doesn't matter if it's Saturday tomorrow. You're going to be thinking about her. I'm going to be thinking about her. So tell me about your daughter. Tell me about Alice."

The door banged open. "Hey up, Mam. Whose is that car parked outside? Got yourself a new toy boy? You're getting too old for – oh... Sorry, mate, didn't see you sitting there."

Brady turned. Saw a man in his mid-20s. Tall, rangy, long dark hair combed back, an easy smile, gold earring in his left ear. Overalls that were reinforced at the knees.

A fairground charmer who's given up the Waltzer to fit carpets...

"Jason. My youngest."

Brady stood up, held his hand out. "Michael Brady."

"*Detective* Michael Brady," Ruby said.

"Right," Jason said. "So we're starting again are we? Mam told me, obviously."

Be careful how you answer this. Don't give them false hope...

"You clearly know what happened, Mr..."

"Simpson. But Jason will do."

"I'm just trying to get some background, Jason. If – and right now it's only 'if' – it turns out to be Alice... If we have to re-open the case... Clearly the more I know the better."

Jason stood up and walked over to the fridge. Opened it. "There's a can of Stella, Mam. It's your last one. You alright if I drink it?"

"It's dinner time, Jase..."

"It's Friday, Mam. We're done until Monday morning. Start that big job out at Egton."

"So tell me about Alice," Brady said again as Jason rummaged hopefully in the fridge.

She looked at him. "You're not writing it down? That's what I remember most from last time. Write it down. Write it bloody down. Like if they wrote enough stuff down Alice would walk back through the door."

"I'd rather just talk to you if that's alright," Brady said.

Because I want to be focused on you, not on my notepad...

"You want to know what she was?" Ruby said. "She was a tilly mint"

"A tilly mint? I've heard that – "

"A cheeky little bugger. My grandad was a scouser. Came over here for the fishing. When there was fishing. An' that's what he called her. 'Come here, tilly mint,' he'd say. A cheeky, uppity girl. And that was Alice. Cheeky, uppity, wouldn't do as she was told, skived off school. She was eleven going on twenty. And I loved her with every ounce of breath in my body. Will that do you?"

Brady smiled. "Perfect, at least as far as her character goes. Have you got a photo?"

"What's up, then?" Jason said. "Lost the one on the file have you? Wouldn't surprise me."

You're dangerously close to the truth, Jason...

Ruby didn't hesitate. She picked a spoon up off the table. Flicked her wrist like she was swatting a wasp. Hit Jason across the back off the hand.

"That's for being cheeky. He's doing what he can. An' it's for taking my last can of Stella an' all."

"I've seen the official photos," Brady said. "I want to see one that... shows her character. Helps me get to know her."

"I'll get you one," Ruby said. She disappeared, leaving Brady with Jason.

"Do you remember her?" Brady said as Ruby ran upstairs.

Jason shook his head. "No. I was just turned seven. So not really. Except what Mam says. I remember her being here. I can't picture her. Not without seeing a photo. But – energy. I remember that. She was always running some-where. Even now when I come round, the house seems empty. Seems like there's something missing."

He picked the can up. Drained it. Set it back on the table. "She needs to know," he said. "Mam needs to know where she is. We all do. But Mam especially. That prick in prison. He should tell us. Someone should make him tell us. He – "

Ruby was back, holding a small picture in a frame. "That's Alice," she said. "That's her. That's how she was."

Brady looked at the picture. Understood instantly what 'tilly mint' meant.

Long blonde hair, blue eyes. A mouth that looked like she'd been playing with lipstick and rubbed it off when she heard someone coming. Wearing a grey hoodie with

'Angel' on the front. Half smiling, looking to her right. An expression which very clearly said, 'You don't know what I've done and you're not going to find out.' The photographer had caught it perfectly.

Remember you're here to ask a question. This is your chance...

"She looks lovely," Brady said. "Fierce, determined. You must have been very proud of her."

"Like I said. Every single breath in my body."

Ruby pulled her right sleeve up. Showed Brady the tattoo on the inside of her arm.

ALICE. Always with me

A red rose climbing through the S of 'always.' A single heart at the end.

"Do you mind if I take a photo?" Brady said, reaching for his phone.

Ruby shook her head. "Help yourself. Do whatever it takes, Mr Brady. Just find her for me. Give me somewhere to go on Christmas morning."

Jason stood up. "I need to be off. Got to call in on Uncle Bri. Thanks for the beer, Mam. I'll buy you some more."

Ruby laughed. "I won't hold my breath. Will I see you over the weekend?"

He shrugged. "Dunno. Football tomorrow. Probably have a hangover on Sunday."

He shook hands with Brady. "See you later. And find her for us. For Mam. Like I said. An' you should go and see that bastard in prison. Blake. Maybe he'll talk to someone new."

. . .

BRADY SAT DOWN AGAIN. "It's nice that he comes round to see you."

Ruby shrugged. "He's a good lad really. Calming down a bit now. Talking of moving in with his girlfriend. He needs a bairn. Someone to be responsible for. Make him grow up."

Brady smiled. "You were telling me about Alice. I bet she was always getting into scrapes, wasn't she? My daughter does that. Did that. Not so much now. Climbing trees. Falling over. We were never out of A&E."

Ruby laughed. Smiled fondly. "You're right there. Couldn't get to sleep for her jumping on her bed. Thought it was a trampoline."

"No trips to A&E though? You did well."

"Just the one. Thought she could ride her bike without using the handlebars. Headfirst into a brick wall."

"Ouch. Did she break anything?"

She must have thrown her arm out. Instinctively...

"Chipped her front tooth. Then it fell out a few weeks later. I always remember the doctor. He checked her over. Alice is sitting on the bed. He looks at me over the top of her head. 'She's a lucky girl, Mrs Simpson,' he says. 'Got a guardian angel has this one.' Well, she did have a guardian angel. For about four more years. Then the lazy sod took a day off."

What do I say to that? Nothing. What can I say?

"Ruby. There's something else I need to ask you. When Alice disappeared, the man you were living with was arrested."

"Dennis McBride. The useless streak of piss."

"He wasn't Alice's father?"

Ruby sighed. "No, Mr Brady, he wasn't Alice's father. He's not Jason's dad neither. Just the bloke that was living with me when it happened. And he was questioned, not arrested."

"And released after twenty-four hours. You weren't suspicious?"

"No. He was a wrong 'un and I shouldn't have had anything to do with him. But he wasn't a murderer."

"But the report says he had three hours that Saturday where he couldn't account for where he was."

Ruby laughed. "Like I said, he was a wrong 'un. But he was a bloody good looking wrong 'un was Dennis. And he had a way with him. So I can tell you exactly what he was doing. But I don't know the name of the respectable married woman he was doing it with."

Brady nodded. "So he had an alibi but he wouldn't say so. Do you know where he is now? If I wanted to speak to him?"

Ruby shrugged. "He went back to Scotland. Just outside Glasgow. That's where he was from. So your guess is as good as mine. Maybe he finally found a rich widow. Maybe he ended up back in jail. Either way he had nothing to do with Alice."

Brady nodded. He'd check. Run a search.

But I trust Ruby's judgement.

"What about Alice's father? Are you still in touch with him?"

Ruby closed her eyes. Spread her fingers wide. Leaned back in her chair and tilted her head towards the ceiling. "Only if I've got my Ouija board out..."

"He's dead?"

"Dead as dead gets. Got me pregnant and then went back to Afghanistan and trod on a landmine. Bent me over a gravestone in the churchyard, promised he'd come back and two months later I'm in the queue at the Co-Op. Just found out I'm pregnant and someone behind me in the queue says, 'Have you heard...' And then a month later they tell me it's twins." Ruby laughed out loud. "He was a rifleman. Used both barrels alright. Alice and Ross."

"Is Ross in Whitby?"

Ruby shook her head. "Aldershot. Never knew his dad but went in the army, just the same. Genes will out, eh? Got married and she's expecting. He's the only bloody Simpson that can hold down a relationship. Doesn't get it from his mam that's for sure."

"You've not..."

"What are you going to say, Mr Brady? 'You've not had much luck with men, Ruby?' That's a tactful way of putting it. There's a few men walked through that door. But it doesn't make me a bad person. Like they thought I was twenty years ago. 'She's the local slapper so she won't be right for the press conference.'"

Ruby paused. Finished her tea. Looked across the table. "So I'm relying on you, Mr Brady. Maybe this time a copper will think Alice is worth finding. Maybe you'll give me an' Alice a second chance."

It's impossible not to like her.

Brady stood up. "I'll do my best, Ruby. I promise."

10

It's not as imposing as Patrick's house. But not far off.

He'd phoned ahead. Checked Edmund Kennedy was in. Driven five miles up the Moors road. Turned right.

Brady let the car coast down the hill towards the dozen houses that made up Goldsborough.

It's a hell of a walk from the bus stop. A mile? Maybe more. Overgrown verges. High hedges. Almost no traffic...

Turned left in Goldsborough. Found the house halfway to Kettleness. Sandstone, double fronted. A red tiled roof. A house built for a prosperous farmer, a Jaguar parked outside.

Can I park in his drive? The gate's shut. Maybe not.

There was a gap in the hedge opposite the house. An opening wide enough for a tractor. Brady carefully reversed into it. Locked the car, walked across the country lane and lifted the latch on the gate. Walked the twenty yards to the front door. Paused before he rang the bell.

Sweeping views out to sea.

Or there would be if the sea fret wasn't starting to roll in. What's that pretentious weatherman started calling it? Haar?

Brady remembered sitting in the Geography classroom. Staring out of the window. Watching the fog stealing across the football pitch. The far goalposts swallowed up. The halfway line. The other goalposts would be next. Ten seconds maybe...

Which was usually when a piece of chalk hit me. Phil Ireland. He never missed...

He rang the bell.

Waited. Was on the point of ringing it again when he heard a bellowed "Wait!" Heard footsteps coming slowly towards the door.

"Arthritis. One of my hips." The explanation started as the door opened. "The rugby pitch is but a distant memory. Edmund Kennedy," he said, finally visible, holding out his hand. "Morag's in the garden"

Morag? The update on the file said his wife was dead.

A powerful, thick-set man. In his early 60s, Brady guessed.

A large head, grey hair shaved almost to his scalp. Black glasses. An almost white beard that became more impressive the further south it travelled. The centre of the beard braided, the tip of it tied with what looked like a silver ring.

A retired Viking cast ashore in Whitby...

A large hand enveloped Brady's.

"Professor Edmund Kennedy," he repeated. He looked Brady up and down. Took a pace back and inspected him a second time. "And so it came to pass," he said. "The shepherds said to one another, 'Let us go now even unto Bethlehem.' Or in my case, 'Twenty years had passed and the policemen said, 'Let us go again even unto Kettleness.' Or maybe you are lost on this foggy afternoon, Mr Brady? Just a wandering traveller?"

What's the accent? Is that a faint trace of Northumberland? The Border country?

Kennedy turned his back, leaned on a walking stick and limped along the stone-flagged hall.

"Not all those who wander are lost," Brady said.

"A nod to Tolkien," Kennedy said over his shoulder, "Excellent. You are already a notch above your predecessor. She'll make us tea," he added.

So a housekeeper. Not his wife.

"Your predecessor – Roberts? Something like that – was good at drinking tea. Precious little else."

He turned right into a room that ran the length of the house, that had clearly been knocked through. There was a battered leather Chesterfield in what had once been the lounge. An equally battered armchair. A floor to ceiling bookcase overflowed. And then overflowed some more. Old pictures of what Brady assumed were long dead mathematicians. A graduation picture.

Roughly around the time I graduated.

A set of steps for reaching the books at the very top.

How does he manage with arthritis? Shouts for his housekeeper...

Kennedy waved vaguely in the direction of the Chesterfield. Brady took it as an invitation to sit down.

"Robertson," Kennedy said, sinking into the armchair. "That was his name. A card of a very low order. Which given the average intellect of the British policeman means he's probably Chief Constable now."

"He died," Brady said. "Retired on the Friday and died at the weekend."

Kennedy ignored the comment. "Let us see if you can fare any better, Mr Brady. A promising start but you must maintain it."

Am I back at university? A Monday morning tutorial? Let's hope I've done some work for it...

"I can see you're a busy man, Professor. I won't waste your time."

Kennedy looked sceptically at him. Spread his arms wide in mock amazement. Gestured at a desk covered in papers. "You are here, Mr Brady. You've already started to waste my time."

How many times? How many more times? The contempt. 'I'm too intelligent to be interviewed by the police. I'm too important. Too busy. Too rich...'

"Your daughter, Rebecca, disappeared – "

"Ah, Morag."

Brady turned. Morag – grey hair pulled back in a bun, her reading glasses hanging round her neck – had appeared in the doorway.

"Finally. Some tea if you would. What would you like, Mr Brady? Earl Grey? Lapsang Souchong? Or 'appen tha'd like some Yorkshire, lad?"

The sudden switch into a broad Yorkshire accent caught Brady completely by surprise. He couldn't stop himself laughing.

What is this? A human side to him?

"Earl Grey is fine, thank you."

"And some Dundee cake, Morag. Plenty. If I haven't eaten it all. And if I have could you make some more?"

"You can't live on Dundee cake, Professor."

Kennedy shook his head as Morag went out. "I fail to see why not. But you're not here to listen to my housekeeper chide me on my diet, Mr Brady. Twenty years have passed. Number of visits from Her Majesty's Constabulary? Nil. So very clearly you have finally found my daughter. Or the other girl – whose name also escapes me."

"Alice Simpson."

And yes, it almost certainly is your daughter. But right now I can't tell you that. And I don't want to. Right now I want to talk to the father of a girl who's disappeared...

"If you say so. So which one is it?"

A father who's showing no emotion. Who's treating this like some sort of exercise in logic...

"After all, Mr Brady, there are only three possibilities. You have found Rebecca. You have found the other girl. Or you have found something and you don't know what you've found."

"That is... remarkably logical, Professor."

"I'm a Professor of Mathematics at Leeds University, Mr Brady. I have taught at Harvard and Stanford. Logic is what I do. So which one is it? Or have I forgotten to pay my Council Tax?"

"It's the last one. Two walkers discovered some bones on the Moors. As yet we don't have a positive identification. But the age of the bones appears consistent... Consistent with..."

"With Rebecca's disappearance. You're allowed to say it, Mr Brady."

"Yes. So I need to ask you some questions, Professor."

Morag was back with the tea, and half a dozen slices of cake. Kennedy reached out. scooped one up. Pushed it into his mouth. Paid no attention to the crumbs bouncing down his shirt.

He shook his head. "Have you not read the file, Mr Brady? Do you imagine the passage of time has changed the answers I gave your dull-witted colleague twenty years ago?"

"I'm sure it hasn't, Professor. But what *has* changed is that some bones have been found. So we may have some new evidence. The case may well be re-opened. Not that it has ever been closed..."

"Will that bring Rebecca back, Mr Brady?"

What's he asking me? Will it bring her back? Of course it won't bring her back? He's her father...

"No, Professor. It won't. But the law – "

"The law must take its course? Is that what you were going to say? My understanding was that the law could not take its course as there was not enough evidence. That Norman Blake watches daytime TV in his comfortable prison cell, officially innocent of Rebecca's murder. Presumed guilty but not charged. The past cannot be undone, Mr Brady or, it seems, repaired. But ask away, Mr Brady. And please, drink some tea. Eat some of Morag's Dundee Cake. Don't let both our afternoons be wasted."

'Ask the question they're not expecting, Mike. Ask the obvious question and they have the lie ready and waiting.'

How many times had he relied on Jim Fitzpatrick's advice? More than he could count...

"Do you miss her, Professor? Your only daughter?"

"Do I miss her?"

He's looking at me as though I'm a particularly stupid student. 'How are you even at university, Mr Brady?'

"Do I miss her? You may as well ask if I miss the dog we had when I was a child. My first car. The coffee cup I dropped on the floor. I'm a mathematician. I deal in logic. Basic truths cannot be re-written. Two and two will always equal four. However much we may think that 'five' would be more interesting."

"Two and two will always equal four and..."

"And Rebecca will not walk through the door. Exactly."

"What do you specialise in, Professor? I don't know a lot about maths..."

But maybe I'll understand enough to impress Frankie...

"I specialise in the model theory of groups. Groups in stable and simple theories. The model theory of finite groups. Ah... I see from your expression that I lost you at the word 'specialise.' So maybe you are not going to fare any better than your predecessor after all."

Brady sipped the tea. Broke off a piece of cake.

I need to regain control. Or get control for the first time. Stop this bloody silly game we're playing.

He looked around the room.

"That's beautiful," he said.

Kennedy followed his gaze. Brady was looking at a wooden sculpture. Twelve, maybe 18 inches high. A dozen figures, clearly three family groups of four. Heads and bodies, nothing more. But the relationships within the family groups clear to see. And the social order between the groups.

"Simply beautiful," Brady said again. "May I ask where you got it? Who did it?"

"Two remarkably simple questions, Mr Brady. I got it from my workshop. I did it. Maths and art. Two sides of the same coin. 'The key to maths is beauty.' You've obviously heard that quotation. Beauty, simplicity and no loose ends. *Quod erat demonstrandum* as your classics teacher no doubt told you."

"I went to the local school, Professor. Here in Whitby. *The Odyssey* wasn't something we read. It was the fishing boat Billy Hibbitt's dad worked on."

Kennedy didn't reply. Instead he divided another slice of cake between his mouth and his shirt.

"Let me take you back to the day your daughter disappeared," Brady said.

Kennedy shrugged. "I refer the Honourable Gentleman to the answer I gave a moment ago. The passage of time has not changed the answers I gave your dull-witted colleague."

How much longer are we going to play games? All afternoon if that's what it takes...

"Rebecca was in town when she disappeared?"

"As the notes will doubtless have told you, Mr Brady." Kennedy sighed. "The town. The bus. The walk down the lane. Do you have any *new* questions? Or am I simply helping you with your revision?"

"Humour me, Professor. I may only need another five minutes. When did you first become worried?"

Kennedy spread his hands. "How would I know? When my wife told me *she* was worried, I assume."

"And it was your wife that first contacted the police?"

"I had never spoken to the police in my life, Mr Brady. Not until your predecessor beat a regular path to my door. So yes."

Jim Fitzpatrick, take two. Let's see if it works the second time.

"How did your wife die, Professor?"

Kennedy sighed. "Again, Inspector, there will no doubt be a report. She lost control of her car on the Pickering road."

'Do you miss her?' It's not even worth asking the question. The answer will be the same...

"And since then you've lived alone?"

"As you have seen, I have a housekeeper. Or perhaps Morag's Dundee Cake is a figment of our imagination?"

Brady tried to smile. Thought about making a joke. Realised it would be a waste of time. "I'm nearly finished. Could I ask one final question? How old was Rebecca when she broke her arm?"

"Ah. So you have not only *found* some bones, you have examined them. One of them shows evidence of a break. Rather than wait for DNA the simplest solution is to ask. I applaud you, Mr Brady. Simple logic."

"As you say, Professor, simple logic. So did your daughter ever break her arm?"

Kennedy spread his hands. Looked helpless. Gave Brady the one answer he hadn't anticipated. "How would I know?"

"But surely? She's your daughter?"

"I was away nearly all the time. Lecturing in North America. 'Possibly' is the answer. She may have broken her arm, my wife may have told me. She may have decided there was no point in telling me. Children break bones: bones heal. Unless it is life-threatening it is of no more consequence than – " He gestured out of the window. "The fog. Which has rolled in with the tide and will roll out with the tide."

The conclusion was clear. *It's time for you to roll out with the tide, Mr Brady...*

Brady stood up. Gestured at the graduation picture. "Your son? It can't have been taken long after – "

"After Rebecca disappeared? Once again, feel free to say it, Mr Brady. Eight months. Nine months."

"King's College, Cambridge," Brady said. "I recognise the building."

Brady looked at the picture again. A mother and father, the son – dark haired, smiling shyly – in graduation robes, the unmistakable spires behind him.

A family. A proud family. A normal family celebrating a normal graduation.

"What does your son do now?"

"He stayed in Cambridge, Mr Brady. It is a difficult city to leave. Eric teaches," Kennedy said simply.

Brady passed the Professor a business card.

"If there's anything else you think of, Professor..."

He'll throw it straight on the fire.

"I'll show myself out," Brady said. But Edmund Kennedy was already limping to his cluttered desk.

. . .

BRADY WALKED DOWN THE HALLWAY. Was reaching his
hand out for the door when it opened, almost hitting
him. Found himself face-to-face with Morag.

"Oh, I'm sorry, sir. I just walked down to the village."

Brady smiled. "No, you're fine, Morag. I was miles
away. No damage done."

"Yes, sir."

"That was remarkably fine cake. Thank you."

"You're welcome, sir."

Brady was tempted to wish her luck. Thought better
of it. Walked out into the fog. Could hardly see his car
across the narrow country lane.

*'I just walked down to the village.' Why? The fog's so thick
you can barely see...*

11

"What are you doing on Sunday?"

Brady wasn't optimistic.

She'll be looking after her mother. With her sister. What's the point of six months' sabbatical? It isn't to talk about a murder. Two murders...

"I'm with Mum in the morning. Afternoon? I'll try and find the willpower to go for a run."

"I couldn't persuade you to change the run for a walk could I?"

BRADY PULLED off the road across the Moors and parked the car in a lay-by.

"This isn't it," Frankie said. "We need to be down there. At the bottom of the hill. Just by the bridge."

He nodded. "I know. But I want to talk first. And if we're going to talk we might as well have a view."

He looked through the windscreen. Saw Fylingdales on the top of Snod Hill in the distance. The Moors stretching on either side of them, Goathland to the right, the long march to the sea on the left.

It's taken ten minutes to get here. I live five minutes from the beach. Five miles from the Moors. I haven't been back a year. I couldn't live anywhere else...

"It's beautiful," he said. "It's bleak, it's desolate, it'll be freezing cold but bloody hell, Frankie, it's beautiful."

She nodded. "Bleak, desolate, beautiful... And muddy. You've got your walking boots?"

"Always."

"So what did the reports say?" Frankie said. "I was going to do battle with the GP, you were going to read reports..."

"When did I see you? Tuesday night. So Wednesday morning I went in early. I wanted to read all the reports. I wanted to see Kershaw as well but God knows he's like the Scarlet bloody Pimpernel these days."

"The reports..."

"OK, I started off in Middlesbrough. Sorry, I'm going to be telling you some stuff you already know."

Frankie shook her head. "Go through it anyway. Distance lends enchantment to the view. Let's see if it looks any different twenty years on."

"So Sandra Donoghue is murdered by Norman Blake. Found on waste ground, behind an industrial estate. Multiple stab wounds. A chisel is the pathologist's best guess. Blake gets life, with a recommendation he serves twenty years."

"So he's out soon?"

"You'd think so. I'll get Dan Keillor to check. Anyway, Blake is convicted on a psychologist's report and a confession. No witnesses, no DNA, nothing. But he's convicted, and everyone seems to think he's guilty."

"So what did the report say?"

"Likely to live alone. Not very successful with the opposite sex. Almost certainly had a collection of pornography..."

Frankie laughed. "That's worrying. It fits half the men that have asked me out."

"Right. So *is* Blake guilty? Or did they find one person who fitted the profile and stop looking? Made the facts fit the suspect? Profiling was a shiny new toy back then..."

"...And a lot of pressure to get a conviction."

"Alice and Becky. Or Becky and Alice to get them the right way round. It's what you said to me. All the resources went into finding Becky's killer. And I can see the argument. You find the killer of the first girl, you've almost certainly found the killer of the second girl. But Ruby said something to me. 'They thought I was the local slapper. Not good enough for the press conference.' Words to that effect. And you can see it, Frankie. You can absolutely see how it played out."

"And then Blake drops in their lap."

Brady nodded. "Norman Blake drops *right* into their lap. He's in Whitby on the day Becky disappears. Can't account for his movements. No-one saw him. Case as good as closed. Everyone thinks he's guilty. And twenty years later people don't *think* he's guilty, they *know* he's guilty. 'Ruby Simpson's girl? The bastard that's inside for the girl in Middlesbrough. He'll be out soon. If he comes to Whitby we'll find out where he buried her...' That's pretty much what Ruby's son said to me."

"What did you make of Ruby? Second time round?"

"Honestly, Frankie? I like her. She's strong, she's... I don't know what the word is. Resilient. A fighter. Twenty years on and the pain hasn't dulled. I like that. God forbid anything ever happened to Ash. But twenty years on I'd want to feel like Ruby feels about Alice."

"Did you see Kennedy as well?"

"Did I see him? I'm not sure whether I saw him or whether he thought a particularly stupid student had wandered into the wrong tutorial. I want to talk about the death of his daughter, he wants to play bloody intellectual games. See if I'm brighter than the last copper to cross his path."

Frankie reached out, put her hand on his arm. "You're getting excited, Mike."

Brady laughed. "I am. I know. But if Ruby cares just as much after twenty years, I'm not sure Kennedy ever cared at all. I said, 'Did your daughter ever break her arm?'"

"Why?"

"Sorry, Frankie, I'm getting ahead of myself. One of the bones they found had evidence of a very small break. Maybe done when she was six or seven. So while we're waiting for DNA – "

"Asking the parents if their daughter ever broke her arm is close enough?"

"Right. So Ruby says no, Alice never broke her arm. The medical records say yes, Becky *did* break her arm – "

"So it's Becky they've found. The chances – "

"That's what I said. Except Ruby showed me a picture. Alice looks like the sort of kid who *could* break her arm –

a hairline fracture say – and think it's just a bruise. Here, look."

Brady reached for his phone. Showed Frankie the picture of Alice.

More mischievous every time I look at her...

"So what did Kennedy say when you asked him?"

"He says, 'I don't know.' Shrugs, 'Why would I know?' He's in the States, lecturing – he's a Maths professor. I was going to impress you with his speciality. Sets or something? But it's so complicated I can't remember it. Apparently his wife's under instructions not to bother him with trivialities. 'A bone is broken, a bone heals. Why should I worry about that?' And he excuses it all on the grounds of logic. Christ, Frankie, if I was away and Ash had a nosebleed I wanted Grace to tell me about it."

"What about the meeting with Geoff and Julia?"

"Number one, I came as close to throwing up as I've done in the last twenty years. Number two, the broken arm. Three... Julia said she was naked when he put her in the grave. She gave me a lecture on what happens to your clothes when you're buried. And then told me there was no trace of any fibres. None at all."

Brady paused. Watched the clouds blowing across from the West. Watched the cars going past on the main road.

Going to see mum and dad for Sunday lunch. A drive out in the country. A family walk. Taking the new puppy for the first time. And here we are. Coppers. Sitting in the car talking about a naked teenage girl buried on the North York Moors...

"It doesn't make sense," Brady said.

"Why not?"

"Because the two murders – three if we include Alice – have nothing in common. Nothing at all."

"You don't know that. Did Julia give you a cause of death?"

"No, she couldn't. She gave me a hunch. Does that count?"

"Not in front of a jury. What was it?"

"Becky didn't die a violent death. She said it 'didn't feel' like a violent death."

"But someone took the trouble to bury her on the Moors? That's stretching it a bit, Mike."

"I agree. And that's why it doesn't add up. You kill someone. Then you kill someone else. All the evidence – all our experience – says you're going to do it in roughly the same way. Because you're developing competence. Because – "

"Or that's what works for you. That's what turns you on."

"Right. All of us, we're creatures of habit. Even murderers."

"But we don't know how Becky and Alice died."

"But we know *where* the bodies were found. Two of them. In Middlesbrough the girl is dumped on waste ground behind an industrial estate. That's where she was killed. No question. Becky Kennedy is found on the North Yorkshire Moors. Is that where she was killed? How can it be? So she's been killed somewhere else and taken there. What does that tell us about the killer? In Middlesbrough it could be anyone – "

"You're ignoring the profile?"

"For now, yes. In Middlesbrough there's an argument.

Or he's stalking her. There are – what did the report say? – 'random stab wounds, inflicted with some force.' She dies. She's left there. The killer runs away. He knows she'll be found. He just hopes he's far enough away. Becky's the exact opposite. She dies, her body is taken onto the Moors. 'Random stab wounds?' No. Julia would have found knife marks on the bones."

"How long?" Frankie said. "If it's not a random attack how long does he wait before he takes her on the Moors? A week? Two weeks?"

"Or the next day. But one thing's clear. She's taken there with the specific intention of *not* being found."

"You said the killer in Middlesbrough could be anyone..."

"I did."

"Becky's killer *can't* be anyone. He's got to know the Moors. He's got to be fit. Really fit."

"What would she weigh?" Brady said. "How much did you weigh when you were thirteen?"

Frankie laughed. "Too much. Every thirteen year old girl thinks she weighs too much. I don't know. But Google will."

She tapped the query into her phone. "A hundred pounds," she said. "Forty-five kilos."

Brady shook his head. "It's not realistic is it? What's he do? The girl over his shoulder and a shovel in his hand?"

"It's not far from a road," Frankie said. "I hiked up there with a boyfriend once. There's a perimeter road near Fylingdales."

"So someone pops out from the early warning station

in their lunch hour? 'I might be ten minutes late, boss? Tell the Russians not to attack until I've finished digging?'"

"What else? He'll need a pair of walking boots."

"Brilliant work," Brady said. "We've finally got the killer's profile. Super-fit. Probably an endurance athlete. Used to carrying heavy weights over long distances. Who works for the security services and has a well-worn pair of walking boots."

"You forgot the collection of pornography," Frankie said. "Every profile includes a porn collection."

Brady laughed. "You're right. How could I forget? Come on, Frankie. Enough theory. Time for some practical. Let's go for a walk."

BRADY STARTED THE ENGINE. Drove back onto the Moors road. Followed a camper van down the hill. Wondered for the hundredth time how much they cost.

Me and Archie. Off in our camper van. Drive up to the north of Scotland. Find a deserted beach. But not while Ash is at home...

Drove over the old stone bridge. Pulled off the road on the left. Switched the engine off and climbed out of the car. Shivered in the wind.

" A walk on the Moors?" Frankie said. "You should have brought Archie."

"Don't," Brady said, putting his walking boots on. "I took him on the beach this morning, but I still feel guilty. But we're working, Frankie. Let's get this sorted out. Sunday afternoon inside the mind of a killer."

They waited for a walker with a Labrador to come through the gate from the path. Brady smiled and nodded. "Impressively muddy."

"Aye, he'll need an 'ose down n'all. Should've brought the wife's car."

They laughed and started up the gravel track away from the road.

"You think he parked where we parked?" Frankie said. "Walked up here with the body?"

"He's only got two choices hasn't he? Park there. Or across the road, where the other cars are parked."

"So no-one is going to pay any attention."

"Right. To all intents and purposes his car's invisible in the car park. Or he finds a way to use the perimeter road."

"Which is closer to the grave. Not as far to carry the body."

"But it's a car. In a place where you don't often see a car. So now it is visible. And memorable. And maybe Fylingdales monitor their perimeter road. He doesn't know that. He *can't* know that..."

Brady glanced to his right. The Early Warning Station loomed over them.

"You ever been in there?" Frankie said.

"Fylingdales? No. Plenty of people have though. There's about three hundred people work there. And I met the boss once on a management course. Interesting guy. Trained with the US marine corps."

"And for the last twenty years Becky has been lying on his doorstep."

"That's the problem isn't it? The radar's pointing into

space. Not across the Moors. Looking for a Russian missile. Not someone with a teenage girl slung over his shoulder."

"And a spade in his hand."

The gravel gave way to a grass path. Went gently uphill, a stream off to the left. Brady carried on walking. Was suddenly conscious that Frankie wasn't with him. Turned round to see her ten yards behind him, hands in the pockets of her leather jacket. "What's the matter?"

"We're doing this wrong," Frankie said.

She looks determined. Defiant. The Moors behind her, the breeze blowing her hair. Straight out of 'Wuthering Heights...'

"You want to go inside the mind of the killer, Mike?"

"Yes. I don't like it. You don't like it. But we have to do it."

"So come back here."

Brady walked slowly towards her.

"What did we just say? 'A teenage girl slung over his shoulder.' 'A spade in his hand.' How fit was he?" Frankie said.

"Fit," Brady said. "We've already discussed that."

"Right," Frankie said. "Like you said in the car, *very* fit. We – you – need to know what you're dealing with. He's carrying her body up here, Mike. Forty-five kilos of dead weight."

"What are you suggesting?"

"I want you to carry me."

"What?"

"I want you to carry me. Yes, I weigh more than a teenage girl. But not by much. And our guy's got equipment with him. His spade at the very least. So it's a reasonable comparison."

"Frankie, it's Sunday afternoon. There are other people out here."

She looked straight back at him. "Mike, you walked down a railway line when trains were running. What are you always saying to Dan Keillor? 'To catch the killer you have to be the killer. Think like the killer.'"

"And now you're saying I have to carry you like the killer?"

"Yes, I am. We're saying she weighed forty-five kilos? I'm nine stone. Fifty-seven kilos."

"That's a lot more..."

"Nine stone is not morbidly obese, Michael Brady. Come on, fireman's lift." Frankie played her trump card. "You've tackled Jimmy Gorse at the end of the pier. You can carry a willing victim up a moorland path."

A FIREMAN'S LIFT? Can I even remember how to do one?

She unzipped her jacket and draped it over some heather. Stood in front of him and lifted her arms. "Help!" she said in mock-terror. "Help! Fire."

Brady stepped forward. "Be warned, Detective Sergeant" he muttered. "If I'm at the chiropractor's tomorrow morning this is going on your personnel file. And I'm supposed to put my right leg between your feet. Reach through between your legs. You sure you're OK with this?"

"I'm a woman, Mike. I've had a smear test. So stop

worrying about inappropriate touching of a subordinate officer, DCI Brady. Besides, I'm not back until May..."

Is that a promise? Is she definitely coming back in May?

"Stand still then."

Brady placed his left hand round her right wrist. Crouched down and twisted his body. Reached his right hand through Frankie's legs. Eased her weight onto his back. Used his thigh muscles to straighten up. Brought his right hand round to take her right wrist as he did that. Stood up with Frankie across his shoulder.

"Perfect," she said from somewhere near his left ear. "Now all you have to do is carry me up the hill..."

Brady turned. Grunted. Took a pace forward. Stumbled. Righted himself. Started up the hill.

...And managed fifty yards. Felt his heart thumping in his chest. Eased Frankie down onto the path. Stood panting for breath as she walked back to retrieve her jacket.

"What did we learn?" he said between the gasps.

"I weigh more than a teenage girl. But we already knew that."

"We learned that you're right," Brady said. "He's really fit. Not just the weight, the path, the stones, the mud..."

"He *was* really fit. It was twenty years ago."

"Right. And if he was fit twenty years ago he'll be fit now. We're not talking about a professional footballer here, Frankie. Someone who stopped playing and opened a pub. This is someone who *enjoys* being fit. Twenty years older or not, we're not looking for someone who orders a pizza, drinks a can of Bud and reaches for the remote."

· · ·

TWENTY MINUTES WALKING and they'd reached the top of the hill. Brady looked across at the scene-of-crime tape, fluttering in what little wind there was. "I sometimes wonder if it's a good idea," he said. "Especially somewhere like this. 'Do not cross.' It's an open invitation..."

"Human nature isn't it? 'No-one around, just me on the Moors. Won't hurt to take a look...'"

They walked down the path to the Lilla Cross. "What did he do with her clothes?" Brady said. "Julia says she was naked when she went in the grave. So what's he do about her clothes? Irrespective of the time of day – look at the two guys that found her: out here almost at first light – there's no way he can carry her up here naked. If she's clothed he can maybe get away with it. Just..."

"If he sees someone? 'She's not feeling well. Just carrying her back to the car?'"

"Something like that. You know how reserved people are. Don't like to get involved."

"Except they'd remember that. Becky, Alice... There were a hundred and one news conferences, Mike. 'There's a girl gone missing, love. Remember we saw that chap on the Moors? Said she was ill...'"

Brady shook his head. "It should be a sunny day, Frankie. Early summer. We could sit with our backs to the Lilla Cross. Gaze across the Moors to the sea. Get the sandwiches out of the backpack. Decide there's no better place in England to eat our lunch."

"Except it's January."

"And we haven't got any lunch. And if we'd brought Archie he'd try and eat it."

Brady heard the sound of voices. Looked up and saw

two more walkers coming towards them. At least a hundred yards away.

The wind's dropped. No traffic. The noise travels...

Finally said 'hello' to them. Watched them disappear down the hill.

"They're the answer," Brady said. "Why here? That's what I couldn't work out. Those two walkers are the answer."

"Why?"

"Because if you've murdered someone – I'm assuming the GP's receptionist is still on your hit-list – then you need to dispose of the body. What are the two boxes you need to tick? Safely – and quickly. You don't have a boat. You don't have a farm. But you do have the Moors. We could have seen those guys from half a mile away. And that's what he does. He can see for miles. He's over the hill, out of sight of Fylingdales. All he needs is some soft ground. Somewhere the heather hasn't grown back."

"Yes, he can see for miles," Frankie said. "But it's taken us forty minutes to get here. Forty minutes isn't 'quickly.' And looking at the state of my boots is was *all* soft ground."

Frankie paused. Looked around her. "You don't find this place by accident," she said.

"No," Brady said. "You have to be a walker."

"Or you need to work for the National Parks," Frankie said. "Burning the heather, maybe. They do that in winter."

"Someone could have trekked up here on Christmas Day and dug a grave..."

"Are you absolutely certain she wasn't killed here?" Frankie said.

"I am. Killing her up here is... It's messy, Frankie. It's spur-of-the-moment. It's brutal."

Frankie hesitated. "It's what the psychologist's report says, Mike. It's disorganised. The guy who's described in that report... That's exactly the way he'd have killed her out here."

"But then he'd have left a trace wouldn't he? Broken bones. Clothing. You're not telling me everything decomposed over twenty years. A bracelet? A belt buckle? It's like Julia said. Kill her out here and you *have* to leave evidence. You just have to."

Frankie stared down the path. Looked at the point where the walkers had disappeared over the brow of the hill. "Describe them to me," she said. "The two walkers. Or the guy with the dog."

"Why? Have I missed something?"

"Just describe them. "They *are* the answer, Mike. But they're the answer to 'how?' Not 'why here?'"

"Are you sure?"

"Humour me, Mike. Describe them."

"The guy with the dog then. Black walking trousers. Boots, obviously. Grey jacket. Not a new one. Black beanie hat. Grey backpack. Maybe around forty. Looked like – "

"A backpack," Frankie said slowly. "That's how he did it, Mike. He put her in a backpack. That's how he hid her. What does every walker up here have? He has a backpack. That's how he carried her, Mike. It's obvious. So obvious no-one would notice it."

"Are you saying I wasted my time carrying you up the hill?"

"No, because you found out what you were dealing with."

BRADY LOOKED DOUBTFUL. "It'd have to be a bloody big backpack, Frankie."

She shook her head. "A hundred litres. Maybe one-twenty. You see them all the time. People camping. He could easily do it. And he'd have an excuse for the spade as well. Burying his waste."

Brady stared out over the Moors. Looked back down the path at the way they'd come. Pictured a solitary walker with an oversized backpack. "You're right," he said. "Absolutely right. Remember the MI6 guy. Five? Six years back? The one who was found zipped inside a suitcase?"

"Gareth Williams," Frankie said. "And if you can get a grown man in a suitcase..."

"...You can get a teenage girl in a backpack. Bloody hell, Frankie, it doesn't bear thinking about. He'd need to be *really* fit. Carry her up here. Dig a grave..."

"Think it through, Mike. Maybe he puts a tent up. Like he's been camping overnight."

"That's even more weight to carry..."

"But what do you do if you're out walking and you see a tent? You walk straight past it. You assume whoever's in there is asleep. A two-person tent? There's easily room enough."

'This isn't a crime of passion, Mike. Becky's killer? That's cold blood. The coldest of cold blood.'

"What's to stop him walking up here one night, Frankie? Pitching his tent? Making some tea? Doing some digging, having a rest. Does some more digging. Maybe has a sleep. Once he's pitched the tent no-one's going to bother him. Whatever he's doing everyone is going to walk straight past. And all the time he's got Becky in the backpack?" Brady stood up. Shook his head. Stared at the crime scene. "She's the same age as my daughter, Frankie. I'm not sure I can cope with that image."

"You know what we're saying, don't you?"

Brady nodded. "What we've been thinking all along. This is the exact opposite of the murder in Middlesbrough. It's like Julia said to me. The coldest of cold blood. This is a killer with local knowledge, Frankie. A killer who lives in Whitby."

12

"Come in, come in, Mike. Thank you for seeing me so early. Have you had breakfast? Shall I send someone out for bacon sandwiches?

"Come into my parlour,' said the spider to the fly...' Why do I prefer Kershaw when he's being openly hostile?

"I'm good, thank you, sir. I had – "

"Alan. We don't need to stand on formality. Least of all at eight o'clock on a wet Monday morning. Bring me up to speed. How are we doing?"

'How are we doing?' I can see it now. We solve a twenty year old murder and there'll only be one person doing the interviews. Another photo for your ego wall, Alan...

"Do you want me to go right through it, Alan?"

Kershaw nodded. "From the top. I haven't see you since the funeral, have I?"

No, because the rumour mill says you've been everywhere but Whitby...

"How is Kate doing? That's the most important question."

And you don't really care. So you're going to get a non-committal answer.

"She's doing as well as you'd expect. Dealing with the basics. Looking after her girls. Coping as best she can."

"You know what? We should do something to commemorate Bill. The Bill Calvert Award. See if we can get local schools involved. Outreach, Mike. Broadening our community base. Involving stakeholders. It's never been more important. I'll give it some thought."

Do that Alan, I'm sure Whitby's criminals will be trembling...

"Rebecca Kennedy, sir. Alan, sorry... Alice Simpson. You wanted bringing up to date."

"Yes. Twenty years of peace and quiet and the circus is back in town. We'll need to manage it carefully, Mike. Keep a lid on everyone's emotions. Anyway, tell me everything."

Just the facts. None of the speculation. And no trips to the Moors with Frankie...

"I got a call from Dan Keillor as we were coming out of the church. Went up on the Moors with Geoff Oldroyd the next morning. Spoke to Julia Grey – "

"The forensic pathologist? Anthropologist? I always think she's overrated. Seems to be flavour of the month though."

"She came over last week. We're ninety-nine per cent certain that the body we've recovered – what's left of the body we've recovered – is Rebecca Kennedy. We should get DNA confirmation this morning."

"Nothing found with the body? Nothing to tie it to that pervert from Middlesbrough?"

"No, nothing. Julia thinks that Rebecca was naked when she was buried. There's nothing. No fibres. No jewellery."

Kershaw nodded. *You must surely see that's not consistent with the murder in Middlesbrough?*

"You've spoken to the parents?"

"I have. Kennedy – Professor Edmund Kennedy – was dispassionate."

"No doubt he's moved on. Time heals."

I'm not sure he has anything to move on from. But I'm not going to speculate for you.

"The other parent – Ruby Simpson – hasn't. She's still grieving. It's still raw."

"She was the unmarried mother wasn't she? Didn't notice her daughter was missing until the next morning?"

"That's what it says in the file, yes."

The slim file. The file that shows we lost her daughter's medical records. That shows we didn't bother to collect any DNA.

Kershaw shook his head. "She was the second victim wasn't she? Well, third technically. You've found nothing to contradict that view?"

"That Norman Blake killed the two girls? Strictly speaking, Alan, I've found nothing to contradict it."

Apart from basic common sense. Apart from the fact that the murders of Sandra Donoghue and Becky Kennedy were about as different as murders can be.

"Good. That's the best result for us. The easiest to manage."

"If you go down that route, Alan, we'll need to

manage the fact that Norman Blake is due to come out of prison soon."

"That's a good point, Mike. People are going to be angry. A very good point. We'll need to make sure any anger is directed at Teesside, not at Whitby. I'm assuming he'll go back there when he's released?"

Brady spread his hands. "I have no idea. That's where he's from."

"He lived with his mother," Kershaw said. "One thing I've learned. Always be suspicious of a man that lives with his mother. I'd assume she's dead by now though. Well we don't want him in Whitby. A convicted killer roaming the streets. Especially in the summer season. Not that..."

Kershaw stopped himself. "Like I said, we'll need to manage it carefully. There's no question that Blake's guilty, obviously. Wandering the streets of Whitby all day? Bloody nonsense. Not that there'll be the evidence after twenty years. As I was about to say."

No you weren't. You were going to say something else entirely. But what?

"What time do you expect the DNA report?" Kershaw said.

"Late morning, I think. Geoff said he'd phone me."

"Let me know will you? Ring me on my mobile. I've a meeting this afternoon. Just in case I need to answer any questions. And I can leave it to you to tell the parents?"

Of course. Rely on Brady the Grim Reaper to deliver the bad news...

Brady nodded. "Yes, I'm planning to do that this afternoon. Professor Kennedy is in Leeds Tuesday to Thursday."

"Well, he's not going to cause us any problems. Not based on what you've said. The Simpson woman on the other hand. She should have come to terms with it by now."

And how many children do you have, Alan? None...

Brady didn't reply. Wondered if the meeting was over. Apparently not.

"What do *you* think, Mike?"

Is he asking for my opinion? Or trying to decide whether I'm going to disturb the calm he so clearly wants?

"I think – right now, Alan – that we have no new evidence at all. We have a body, so one family at least can have closure. But neither Julia nor Geoff could suggest a cause of death. So at the moment we've nothing to challenge the conclusions reached twenty years ago."

Kershaw nodded. "Exactly my view, Mike. *Exactly* my view. Let's make sure it stays that way."

The meeting was over. Brady stood up. Wished Kershaw the best of luck with his afternoon meeting. The fly walked out of the spider's parlour.

'Let's make sure it stays that way.' Not if I have anything to do with it...

13

Brady couldn't wait any longer. He pushed the file he was working on to one side. Reached for his phone. "Any news, Geoff?"

"Good God, Mike, you're like my youngest on Christmas Eve. It's half-ten. They said some time around eleven."

"Sorry, Geoff. I know you'll ring me. I'll go and find Dan Keillor. I owe him an appraisal..."

It was quarter past when Geoff rang. "You want it over the phone? Or do you want to come down."

"I'll come down, Geoff."

Dan Keillor made a do-you-want-me-to-go gesture from the other side of the desk. Brady shook his head. "I'll be ten minutes. No more."

He walked slowly down the stairs.

'You want it over the phone?'

No. Because I owe it to her. Because if it is Becky then I should be with her when Geoff tells me. She's been on her own

*for twenty years. She's entitled to some company when we
finally give her a name...*

Pushed the door open. Smelt the unmistakeable mix
of death, decay and chemicals. Remembered the days
when he used to put a dab of Vick's Vapour Rub under
his nose. Wondered how he ever found the time.

"Morning, Geoff. Good weekend?"

"As good as a weekend in January has to offer, Mike.
We didn't have a barbecue, we did have roast beef, I saw
the grandchildren. So yes, good. But – "

"But I'm not here to talk about your weekend..."

"No. You want me to get her out, Mike? You want to
see the bones again?"

Brady shook his head. "No. You and Julia have told
me everything I need to know. And I don't want to embarrass myself a second time."

*One white finger bone at the end of that yellow/brown
hand...*

"I just felt... I just felt she was entitled to some
company. To know someone cared, I suppose."

Geoff nodded. "The DNA report is back. It's definite.
A match with the sample they have on file. Throw in the
broken bone for extra confirmation – as if we need it –
and the answer's 'yes.' The Two Gentlemen of the Moor
found Rebecca Kennedy."

"Last seen twenty years ago. Getting off the bus and
walking down a country lane."

With the whole of her life in front of her...

"Thanks, Geoff. I'll give Julia a ring, just to let her
know."

"What are you going to do now, Mike?"

"Number one, ask you a question. While I remember it."

"What's that?"

"Alice has a twin brother. Is that any good? If I need her DNA at some point?"

"No, not really, Mike. Identical twin, yes. From a DNA point of view your identical twin *is* you. Brother and sister? Being fraternal twins doesn't make a difference. Two eggs. So just a normal brother and sister relationship. They'll share around forty-five per cent DNA."

"Bugger."

"Sorry. So what's next?"

"Run upstairs and apologise to Dan Keillor. Then I've a search to organise. But a limited one. I'm not going to get permission to dig up the whole of the North York Moors. And... I don't think Alice is there, Geoff. He found the place, he dug the grave, he took her clothes off. This guy's so careful, so methodical, that I don't think the two bodies are in the same place. I think he's spread his risk. There's a hell of a lot of Moors out there. I don't think Alice is with Becky."

"So what are you going to do, Mike? Wait another twenty years for a walker to need a pee?"

"Which one is she in, Geoff?"

"What?"

"Becky." Brady gestured to his left.

Lockers. Coolers. Slabs. I hate all the bloody words.

"Which one is she in?"

"Number three."

He walked across. Put his hand on the grey door with the black '3' stencilled on it. "No, Geoff, I'm not going to wait twenty years. That's a promise to both of you. All three of you. I'm going to find the killer. And he's going to tell me where Alice is."

BRADY SAT IN HIS CAR.

Two people to see. A father and a mother. Good news and bad news. The father gets an answer. The mother is left in limbo. No further forward. Twenty years on, she's still looking for somewhere to lay her flowers.

Brady reached for his phone. Made the calls. Started the car. Drove up onto the coast road. Back to the house that had been shrouded in fog.

14

Brady turned right. Pulled on to the dirt at the side of the road. Looked out of the window into a cloudless sky. Saw a hawk hanging motionless over a field.

Kestrel? Sparrowhawk?

Accepted that he knew almost nothing about nature.

Accepted that he knew even less about how Edmund Kennedy would react.

Was it bluff and bluster last week? A defence mechanism? Protecting himself against the fifty-fifty chance that we'd finally found his daughter? Underneath it all he felt exactly the same as Ruby? Maybe he was afraid to show it. Knowing he had to deal with it on his own. Wondering how he'd cope? Apart from his son. He'll have told his only son.

This time it was Morag who answered the door. "I'm sorry, sir, he's busy. On the phone to Eric. He said to show you into the drawing room. He won't be long, sir."

Kennedy must have checked on the broken arm. Or

remembered that he was told about it. He's preparing his son
for the news. He's a normal dad after all...

"Can I get you anything?"

I'm here to tell Kennedy's the bones we found were his
daughter. The bones that were the colour of pale tobacco. No, I
don't feel remotely like eating or drinking. But I can't say no...

"A cup of tea would be lovely, Morag. Thank you. And
– on the off-chance the Professor hasn't eaten it all..."

She laughed. "I've made some more, sir. I don't
wonder I use up Whitby's entire stock of almonds the
amount he eats. But I baked yesterday, so you're in luck."

She left him in a room that was dominated by
pictures of the sea. Sunset, sunrise, the light reflecting off
the water. Brooding cliffs in the distance.

'I must go down to the sea again, to the lonely sea and sky,
And all I ask is a tall ship and a star to steer her by.'

They were the only two lines of poetry Brady could
remember from English. But they matched the mood of
the room. Lonely. A need to find out what was over the
horizon.

There was a battered mahogany sideboard along one
wall, the two sides piled high with yet more books. A
lower section in the middle had a chessboard on it.

Brady walked over and looked more closely. It was
easily the most impressive chessboard he'd ever seen.
Black and white marble, flecks of grey running through
the white squares. But it was the pieces that captivated
him.

Two opposing armies. Vikings and –

Ancient Britons? Picts? Celts?

He reached forward and picked up the Viking king. Turned it over in his hand. Felt the weight of it.

How much time went into this? The detail. The pains someone took to get it right. Hand-carved? It has to be.

He looked intently at the king's face.

"I'm not allowed to touch it, sir."

Brady turned. Morag was standing behind him, a tray in her hands. "That and his papers. The only things I'm not allowed to touch."

She put the tray down on the table. Poured him a cup of tea. "Am I allowed to ask why?" Brady said.

"It's a game he was playing with his son, sir. He's never told me why. I'm only the housekeeper. All I know is the pieces have to remain in those exact positions."

"They're beautiful."

"They're gathering dust," she said, as though she were chiding the chess pieces themselves. "But it's more than my life's worth to move them. So gather dust is what they must do."

She left him with the tea. Told him to help himself to the cake. Brady walked across and looked out of the window. Saw the road sloping down to the village. Wondered again why she walked down the hill in the fog.

Six or seven houses? There can't be a shop, surely? The beach? Driftwood for the fire?

Realised he was still holding the Viking king. Reached across to replace it.

"Do you play, Mr Brady?" Edmund Kennedy said from the doorway.

He was wearing the same red check shirt under the

same navy bodywarmer. The beard just as carefully braided.

"No. I know the moves, obviously. But..."

"But you don't have the time. 'Life's too short for chess' as Byron – the dramatist, not the vastly overrated poet – told us. You should play. Perhaps it would hone your deductive skills."

"Maybe," Brady said, determined not to be drawn into another intellectual sparring match he was certain to lose. "Morag said you liked the board set out in a particular way?"

"I do." Kennedy took a step forward. Glanced down at the board. Nodded. "The king on e2. Where it finished the game. It's a memory, Mr Brady. A snapshot. The first time my son beat me. He looked up from the board. 'Mate in five, father.' My own fault. I lost concentration. And if he could see the moves so clearly..." Kennedy shrugged. Made an 'it's obvious' gesture. "...There was little point in using the board again."

"How old was he?"

"Two weeks short of his seventh birthday. A salutary reminder that we all meet our match sooner or later. But it set my mind at rest. At least it confirmed the boy had a modicum of intelligence..."

"Do you and your son still play? Presumably he comes to visit you?"

"We do, occasionally. Why we play I have no idea. I assume Eric is checking me for signs of senility."

"Is your other board – the pieces – as striking as this one?"

Kennedy shook his head. "Other board? Why do we need another board?"

"Well... I thought you said you still played?"

"We do. We play in our heads. As I said to you, Mr Brady, Eric could see the moves before they were played. So why bother with a board? And when I can no longer finish a game it will be a clear signal. Time for the nurse, the rubber gloves and the commode."

Kennedy sat down heavily in a faded leather armchair. "So, Mr Brady," he said. "We have discussed chess. Wasted enough of each other's time. Ah, but I see you have *not* wasted your time."

He reached forward. Snatched the last piece of Dundee Cake. "You look worried," he said through a mouthful. "But you look worried about the news you are compelled to deliver, rather than the news you *don't* have to deliver. I therefore deduce that Rebecca is dead. That you have found her remains and that you and your muddy-booted colleagues are once more going to trample through my life."

Brady nodded. Sighed. "Yes, Professor, we have. We received the DNA results this morning. They matched the DNA we have on file – taken from your daughter's toothbrush. I'm sorry to have to tell you this."

Kennedy nodded to himself. "Twenty years. And she is found not due to assiduous police work but by an incontinent walker. Where do you go from here, Mr Brady? Presumably to a council estate to tell the mother her daughter has *not* been found?"

"Yes, that's right."

"And then you will re-open the case?"

"Technically the case has never been closed. But this is new information. New evidence, Professor. So yes, I will."

"I can see it in your eyes, Mr Brady. You are what Descartes called 'a seeker after truth.' But what do you hope to find as you seek after your truth? As we said, Blake rests quietly in his cell watching daytime TV. In due course he will be released. What is any of that to me? Or to Rebecca?"

Brady nodded. "I understand that. Nothing will bring your daughter back. But you'll have closure, surely? You can finally have a funeral service..."

'Do whatever it takes, Mr Brady. Just find her for me. Give me somewhere to go on Christmas morning.'

"And you'll have somewhere to go on Christmas morning," Brady said.

Edmund Kennedy frowned. Looked confused.

"Why on earth would I do that, Mr Brady? Do you wish me to buy a tree in the crematorium garden? Festoon it with fairy lights? A nativity scene? You may have gathered by now, I do not react..." He shrugged, searching for the right words. "...As ordinary people react."

"But surely..."

"But surely what, Mr Brady? Rebecca is dead. If you can prove Blake killed her, then you at least will be satisfied. A tick can be placed in your exercise book. But as I said to you before, the past cannot be undone. As for the idea of me donning boots and an overcoat on the morning of a mawkish pagan festival..."

Twenty years. More than that. All that time delivering bad news. I've never seen anyone react like this. No-one has come close...

"I'll have some questions to ask you, Professor – "

"I never doubted it, Mr Brady."

"But for now perhaps I should leave you. No doubt you'd like some time."

Kennedy spread his arms wide in exasperation. "For what, Mr Brady. Do you expect me to drag myself through the five stages of grief? There is but one. Acceptance. Leave me by all means, but leave me to my work. To do something important, Mr Brady. Before that fucking nurse arrives with her rubber gloves and orders me to bend over."

15

Michael Brady sat in his car. Sighed. Knew something was bothering him.

Not the obvious. Not the complete absence of emotion. Something else...

Started to replay the conversation with Edmund Kennedy. Stopped himself.

Don't. What's the point? Let it go cold.

He looked out of the window again. The hawk was gone. He was back in town. Just the seagulls, wheeling, screeching, arguing in the cloudless sky.

Winter. But a winter's day that tells you spring isn't far away. Snowdrops in the park when I walked Archie this morning. A sign of better things to come.

But not before I've delivered the news. How many more times? How many more times in my life will I have to deliver bad news. Maybe there's a job where you only deliver good news? 'Hi, it's Michael Brady. You've won the lottery.'

Not today.

'Your daughter's been murdered. We've found the body.'

'Your daughter's been murdered. We can't find the body.'

One is certainty. Despair. Grief. Pain. But one day, the chance to heal. Not today. Not for Ruby. Twenty years in limbo and she's no further forward.

Brady opened the car door. Walked up the path to Ruby's front door. Sighed again and lifted his hand.

She'd been waiting for him. Opened the door before he could knock.

"I was watching from the window," she said. "Saw you come. You were sitting in the car a long time." She paused. Nodded to herself. "You were sitting in the car a long time, Mr Brady. So it's not Alice."

Fair enough. Your daughter's been missing for twenty years. You're done with small talk.

"No, Ruby. I'm sorry. Really sorry. We've got a positive identification. But it's not Alice."

She had one hand on the door. Nodded again. Brady saw her let the news seep in.

He'd expected her to step to one side. Ask him in. Instead she took a pace forward. Forced him to move to the side. Walked past him and down the path.

Onto the pavement. Bare feet. Oblivious to the cold. Brady followed her. Watched her turn right. Stand at the top of the steps leading down to the harbour. Turn back to him.

Angry. Resigned. Defiant.

Determined not to go to her grave until she knows what happened to her daughter...

"So I carry on, do I? Every time I come out of the house? Every time I walk into town? I look up there onto the Moors road and know she's up there somewhere?

That some bastard in jail knows where she is and he won't say. I'm not having it, Mr Brady. I'm not having it."

She walked back towards him. Said, "You'd best have a cup of tea, I suppose" as she passed him.

Brady followed her into the house. Took his wet coat off and draped it over the end of the stairs.

"He's due out soon," Ruby said as she filled the kettle. "Norman Blake."

"He is. And when he comes out he's a free man. Entitled to live his life."

Ruby turned and looked at him, a brown teapot in her hand. "I like you, Mr Brady. I think you're doing your best. I think you tell me the truth. Or more of the truth than those other bastards. But I want to know where Alice is. And if he knows – if he knows where my Alice is – then I'll tell you this. And I'll say it to your face. I don't care if I swing for it. I don't care if I spend the rest of my life in jail."

She reached behind her. Put the teapot down. Picked up a carving knife. Held it in front of him. "Because I've been in jail for twenty years. And there's no fucking parole hearing for me. So twenty more won't matter. He'll tell me where my Alice is. And I won't take 'no' for an answer."

"Ruby you can't – "

"I can't what? Take the law into my own hands? I – "

Brady heard the door open.

What's this? Jason come to see if his mother's re-stocked the Stella over the weekend?

. . .

BRADY GUESSED he was two or three years younger than Ruby. Tall, lean, pale. Grey eyes, neatly trimmed beard with a hint of ginger, hair combed back, white overalls streaked with maroon paint.

"Bloody hell," Ruby said. "You're meeting the whole family. Des, my little brother."

"It's a big lounge," he said as if he needed to explain. "One of the old houses on Prospect Hill. It can take the colour."

Brady stood up. "Michael Brady," he said, shaking hands.

"Sit yourself down, sunbeam. Do you want a brew? And you'd best behave yourself, Des. This is Chief Inspector Brady. *Detective* Chief Inspector Brady. So piss off back outside and make sure the tax disc on the van's up to date."

Her brother laughed. "Chief Inspector? He'll be too important to worry about a tax disc. What's up, lass? You're not in trouble are you? Or have you found her for us?" he said to Brady.

"No, I'm not in trouble. And no, they haven't found her. It was the other one. The one they wanted to find."

Brady picked his way carefully through the minefield. "You obviously know about what was found on the Moors, Mr Simpson. I came to tell Ruby the remains weren't Alice. We've made a positive identification. And like Ruby says, they're not Alice. I'm sorry. I know what this means to the family."

Des Simpson shook his head. Grimaced. Rang his fingers through his hair. "No, cock, you don't. You don't have a bloody clue what this means to the family."

Ruby put her hand on his arm. "Don't, Des. Don't start."

He shook it away. "No, Ruby. Twenty years and they're re-opening the old wounds. And it's not our Alice. So we're back where we started. Alice Simpson. Second fucking best again. So what are you doing about it?"

You're going to sound too official. Say something stupid like, 'I'm taking a fresh look at all the evidence.' Don't say that...

"I'm taking a fresh look at all the evidence," Brady said.

"But you've no idea where Alice is? Twenty bloody years and we're no further forward?"

"Right now? No, I'm sorry."

Des Simpson shook his head a second time. "Fucking useless. Can you imagine what it's like? For Ruby? For all of us. 'I've been meaning to ask you, mate. While you're painting the lounge. Are you related to that girl that went missing?' Twenty bloody years and they still ask."

Ruby put her hand back on her brother's arm. "Stop it, Des. It isn't going to bring her back. Let him get on with it. I've a good feeling about this one."

Des Simpson stood up. "Let's hope so, lass. Thanks for the tea."

"You don't want a slice of cake?"

"No, I'm in training, aren't I? And I have to get back. Finish up. Bri's off to the cash and carry. Rather him than me. Drive across the Moors in the dark to collect paint. But if he wants to do it let him. We need some more for tomorrow. And maybe some sunglasses. Two walls maroon, two walls Sunburst bloody Yellow. I swear to God we should charge extra for some of the combinations they come up with. I should say it to them. 'You're in Whitby, love. You're not on the bloody telly.'"

He fished around in his pocket. "Good to meet you, Mr Brady. And I'm sorry. Ruby's right. It's always there. Just below the surface. And she's the only sister I've got. So do your best, will you? Not for me. For Ruby."

Brady stood up and shook hands. "I will. It sounds a useless thing to say, but trust me."

Des Simpson nodded. "I will. If you're good enough for Ruby you'll do for me. And here." He passed Brady a business card. "If you ever need a painter and decorator. Me an' Bri, we're good at our job. An' I didn't mean it about Sunburst Yellow, just in case – "

Brady laughed. "Don't worry. I'm white with a hint of blue. Summer Seascape or whatever they'd call it."

"He's a good 'un," Ruby said when her brother had gone. "A bit hot-headed. Like Bri. But the only bloke in my life I've been able to count on. Always there for me."

She stood up and poured herself more tea. Gestured at Brady with the teapot. He shook his head.

"Every other man in my life – they've let me down. 'Course I love you, Ruby. Course I'll love you in the morning, Ruby.' Except Des. He's always been there for me."

"Bri?" Brady said. "That's 'Uncle Bri?' The one Jason mentioned?"

"More than an uncle really. My dad's younger brother. Brought me and Des up. Well, half brought us up."

"What happened to your parents? Not that it's any business of mine."

"No, I don't mind telling you. Mam died giving birth to Des. Some bloody junior doctor not paying attention. I don't know…"

"So your dad coped on his own?"

"Dad and his fancy women. I'd just find one I liked and he'd be home with another one. Then he died. I was ten. Des was seven. Just had his birthday. Dad bought him some football boots. The next day he's gone."

"What happened?"

"Silly bugger lost a bet," Ruby said. "He was down at the harbour. Started drinking with some Norwegian sailors. Apparently it turned into a right session. The Ship. Dad staggers out of the pub and bets them he can swim across the harbour. Calm night. Full moon. Except he's had nine or ten pints of heavy. Someone tries to stop him but he's down the steps and out of his clothes. He made it to halfway…"

"So Brian – your uncle – took you in?"

"He did. I don't know whether it was love or guilt. He was drinking with Dad and the sailors. But it was him or the children's home. And he was good to us. Especially Des. Stopped him running wild. Taught him a trade. Took him into the business."

"Was Bri married? He must have had some help?"

"He was. Then she left. Think that was enough for him. Des the same. Not Ross and Jason though. They're good lads. An' like I say, Ross's wife is expecting. I just wish she wasn't three hundred miles away."

.   .   .

BRADY STOOD UP TO GO. Thought better of it. Gestured at the teapot. "Can I change my mind, Ruby?"

"Course you can. I can make a fresh pot if you want." She looked at him. "You've got that expression all men have when they want something. Not what men usually want though. What is it?"

16

"I'm a police officer, Ruby. But I'm a dad as well. So officially you know what I'm going to say about Norman Blake. Unofficially... unofficially, I'd feel the same. *Want* to feel the same. Not that I can begin to understand. But there's something I need you to explain to me."

"What's that?"

"Why you're so convinced it was him."

Because I'm not. And the more I think about it the less convinced I am.

"The more I learn, Ruby. The more I know – "

"The more chance you have of finding Alice." Ruby nodded. Drank some of her tea. "I had my doubts," she said. "He didn't seem the type. Then he *did* seem the type. Because there's something not quite right about Norman Blake. And if you ever meet him you'll know it, Mr Brady. An' that bollocks about wandering round Whitby that day. When it was blowing a gale and pissing down? What did he do? Eat six lots of fish and chips?

So like I say, I wasn't convinced. Then I *was*

convinced. 'Cos the killings stop don't they? And if he's a serial killer – like they said he was – well, if it was someone else then the killings *wouldn't* stop, would they? And then I think to myself, why did he kill *Alice?* Why my Alice? Thousands of other girls to choose from. He could have stopped in Loftus, or Sandsend. Or Skinningrove. But he doesn't. He carries on to Whitby and he picks on Alice. My Alice. And all I can think is why? Then someone says to me one day, 'why not?'"

Don't interrupt. Maybe this is the first time she's put it all into words...

"Elaine Tanner. I see her in town and she tells me her husband's got cancer. And I say, 'Why Ted, he's such a good man?' And she says to me, 'Why not Ted? There's none of us got a guardian angel, Ruby.' And I think, she's right. 'You're just unlucky, Ruby,' I tell myself. 'You and Alice. Just unlucky.'

And then I get logical. And I think, 'Two girls in Whitby. And all the girls he's driven past to get here. So there's a connection between them. And I tell myself, they're clever people. They'll soon work out what it is. But no, every time they knock on the door they tell me there's no connection. 'She's a young lady is Rebecca, Ruby. How could she possibly know a scrubber's daughter from a council estate?' They don't say that. But they do say it, if you know – "

"Yes. I do know. And I'm sorry. Did they say anything about the body?" Brady asked gently. More gently than he'd ever asked any question.

Ruby shook her head. "No. All this time I'm thinking, 'they'll work out the connection. And then they'll find the body. And Blake can't hold out for ever. He'll tell them where the bodies are. Then I'll have Alice back. And I can lay her to rest. Go and talk to her on a Sunday. Tell her how I'm getting on. But they *don't* find the body, Mr Brady. And then they tell me they've stopped looking. 'Manpower and resources, Ruby' they say. 'They're not infinite, Ruby.' And then I open the paper and see they've spent another million quid on that McCann girl."

"I don't know what to say, Ruby..." Brady reached across the table. Put his hand on hers. Squeezed.

"You don't have to say anything, Mr Brady. You asked me a question, I answered. I suppose I want you to understand, that's all. I want someone who can do something about it to understand. And stop me hurting. 'Cos it doesn't heal. They say time heals but it doesn't. Not when someone takes your child. 'She'd be sixteen' you think. Eighteen. Then she's nineteen. I was nineteen when I had her. She – "

Ruby shook her head. Blinked. Fumbled in a pocket for a tissue. Managed to smile at him. "There, you bastard. You've set me off. Twenty years and I thought I had it under control." She took a deep breath. Tried to compose herself. "She was a wild one. She'd have caused me any amount of trouble. Boys? Bloody hell. She'd have made me look like a nun. But she was my wild one. So when he comes out we'll be waiting. And you don't need me to tell you that 'cos you're a bright boy and you can work it out for yourself. Coming up to twenty years. So we don't have long to wait. An' he'll tell me will Norman Blake. 'Cos I won't take no for an answer."

I should caution her. Make it clear she can't do anything.

But if it was Ash... And maybe you'll need her. Because she's a lot more use than the police file.

Brady smiled at her. Made a conscious effort to lighten the mood. "Thank Des for the card. I might need him – "

"Des and Bri? Like he said, they do a good job. And you've bought that house. Spending a few bob I hear."

Brady laughed. "Whitby, eh, Ruby? The town without secrets. Yes, I might. What's Des do? He said he was in training."

Ruby raised her eyes to the ceiling. "He's a daft bugger. Goes to the Lake District. Chases other daft buggers up hills. Fell running or summat. Every bloody weekend. No wonder he couldn't stay wed..."

BRADY STOOD UP. Thanked Ruby for the tea. Promised he'd keep her up to date. Walked down the path. Saw a white van pulling up outside the house.

Simpson and Nephew. Painters and Decorators. What's this? Des changed his mind about the cake?

The van eased into a gap between two cars. The door opened and a worn, faded rock star climbed out. Tall and lean like Des, the same white overalls. Thin lipped, his face not so much lined as creased. Long hair, parted over a frown.

The bass guitarist who's been forced to go on one last tour. The guy in 'Love Actually.' Billy Mack?

Brady held out his hand. "Michael Brady."

"Aye, I heard. Brian Simpson. Come to check if she wants anything collecting for the weekend."

"Des said you were going for paint."

"I am. But it's not the only wholesalers up there. Our Ruby's not averse to a slab of Stella."

Brady laughed. "Last time I was here Jason finished the last one. I'll leave you to get on."

He climbed into the car. Needed to go straight home. Clean the kitchen while Ash was at Bean's.

Changed his mind.

17

He put his key in the lock. Pushed hard on the front door. Pushed even harder...

'The wood will swell with the rain.' Any more of Whitby's rain, Chris and I won't be able to get it open...

He walked slowly up the stairs. Breathed in. Not for the first time felt he was breathing in the history of the house. "Don't worry," he said out loud. "I'll do it justice."

Brady pushed the bathroom door open. Shook his head sadly. The suite was still plum...

'Have a word with the neighbours, Mike. We're going to need a bloody big skip. And there'll be more than one load.'

He walked into what had been the main bedroom.

'It's seen babies born and grandparents die.'

It has. And mostly in this room...

Crossed carefully over to the window. Looked out over the harbour, the light fading.

'You'll need to put steel in to support the walls?'

'We will. Plenty.'

'So we can carry it on? Make a balcony?'

Chris had nodded. Mentioned the four-bed exec on the new estate again. But only as a joke...

Brady turned, walked up to the top floor. Almost tiptoed across to the window.

'*She'd better not be planning any parties, Mike. Not until we've replaced some of these floorboards...*'

He was starting to learn the ones that creaked ominously.

Brady leaned forward. Ignored the dust. Rested his arms on the window-sill. Watched a fishing boat making its way reluctantly to the harbour mouth.

'*Why did he kill Alice? Thousands of other girls to choose from. He could have stopped in Loftus, or Sandsend. Or Skinningrove. But he doesn't. He carries on to Whitby and he picks on Alice. Why does he kill my Alice...*'

And the conversation with Frankie...

'*Are you absolutely certain she wasn't killed here?*'

'*I am. Killing her up here is... It's messy, Frankie. It's spur-of-the-moment.*'

'*It's what the psychologist's report says, Mike. It's disorganised. The guy who's described in that report... That's exactly the way he'd have killed her.*'

'*But then he'd have left a trace wouldn't he?*'

'*A backpack. That's how he did it, Mike. He put her in a backpack. That's how he carried her. It's obvious. Maybe he puts a tent up. Like he's been camping overnight. You know what we're saying don't you?*'

'*This is the exact opposite of the murder in Middlesbrough. This is cold blood. The coldest of cold blood. This is a new killer. A local killer.*'

He turned and looked around the room that would be his daughter's bedroom.

'She's the same age as my daughter, Frankie. I'm not sure I can cope with that.'

That's tough. Because you're going to have to cope with it. And the next step is obvious.

'There's something not quite right about Norman Blake. And if you ever meet him you'll know it.'

I need to find out for myself. Rule him in or rule him out. First thing tomorrow. Speak to the prison governor. Do the paperwork. Arrange the visit. Go and see if he matches the profile. See if twenty years inside have changed him.

The decision was made. Michael Brady walked carefully across the worn floorboards. Down the stairs of his new house. Out to his car. Remembered he had a kitchen to clean...

18

The walls of the interview room were a dirty cream. Half-hearted attempts at graffiti: equally half-hearted attempts to paint over it.

He'd completed the paperwork. Re-stated the purpose of his visit, handed his phone over. Been escorted to the interview room. Waited for ten minutes. Gradually felt the numbness creeping up his spine.

These are the chairs schools buy. Their sole purpose is to cause you pain on speech day. Will this bloke ever stop talking? Will I ever be able to walk again? At least they're not bolted to the floor...

The door opened. Brady got stiffly to his feet.

Norman Blake shuffled in, a warder a pace behind him. Jeans, a sweatshirt that might have been dark blue before it went through the prison laundry a hundred times.

And a fluorescent orange vest. Brady was irresistibly reminded of a football substitute warming up. Knew the vest allowed a watching warder to instantly identify the prisoner through the frosted glass screen.

"I'll be outside if you need me," the warder said.

"Thank you."

"And not too long, Norman, alright? He's got better things to do than listen to you all afternoon."

He's forty-two. Forty-three at the end of the month...

Greasy brown hair, brown eyes, a wispy goatee that looked more like he started shaving and got bored than a conscious decision to grow a beard.

He looks puzzled. Like he still can't understand why he's in here...

"Thank you for seeing me," Brady said.

Blake nodded his head three or four times. "I haven't had a visitor. Not for a long time. My mum came. Then she died."

"I'm sorry," Brady said, gesturing for Blake to sit down. "I saw that in the file. I'm really sorry."

Blake looked at him. Eyes wide, still puzzled. "They let me go to the funeral. But I had to stand with Mr Harris all the time. Because I was handcuffed to him. And my Auntie Irene was there. But Mr Harris said I couldn't give her a hug."

"Norman – you don't mind if I call you Norman?"

Blake shook his head. "No. That's my name. Mr Harris said I had to call you Mr Brady. He said you were an important policeman so I had to call you Mr Brady."

Brady laughed. "I don't know about that, Norman. Let's just talk shall we?"

"Yes. I'd like that, Mr Brady."

Twenty years in jail for the murder of Sandra Donoghue.

*The whole of Whitby convinced he murdered Becky Kennedy
and Alice Simpson...*

*'Because there's something not quite right about Norman
Blake. And if you ever meet him you'll know it, Mr Brady.'*

*You might be right, Ruby. But I've spent sixty seconds with
him. And I'll tell you now, he didn't murder your daughter.*

"Norman, I don't know if Mr Harris told you what I
wanted to talk about." Blake opened his mouth to speak.
Brady held his hand up. "Let me finish, Norman. I want
to talk about what happened. Just tell me in your own
words what happened. Right from the beginning. If I ask
a question you don't understand, tell me and I'll ask it in
a different way. And never mind what Mr Harris says. If it
takes all afternoon it takes all afternoon."

The eager nod again.

"You lived with your mum?"

"And my sister, Mr Brady. But then she got married
and moved away. To someone in the south. So she went
to Portsmouth."

"So just you and your mum after that? And you lived
next door to Sandra Donoghue's grandmother?"

"Lauren was my girlfriend, Mr Brady. But her
grandma didn't like me."

"Lauren was Sandra's sister? She was eighteen?"

"She was eighteen on the first of July, Mr Brady. But
she didn't invite me to her party."

"Why didn't Sandra's grandma like you, Norman?"

"Because I went fishing, Mr Brady."

Brady shook his head. "I don't understand. Just
because you went fishing?"

"I went fishing. In the river. And I caught some fish.

And I wanted her to like me 'cos I wanted Lauren to be my girlfriend."

"I thought you said she *was* your girlfriend?"

"She wasn't my girlfriend then. She said she'd be my girlfriend at two-seventeen on November the eighteenth."

"So you gave her grandmother the fish before that?"

"Yes. I left her some fish on the doorstep. We went to Greece on holiday once and I saw people do that. They grow things and they leave them on their neighbour's doorstep. I thought that was really kind. So I did that for Lauren's grandma. But she said it was a hot day and the smell had gone inside the house. Something like that. So she didn't like me."

Brady tried not to laugh. "It happens, Norman. Sometimes you do kind things and people, well... they misunderstand. So Lauren's your girlfriend?"

"She was. I asked her to be my girlfriend. And she laughed and said, 'Of course I'll be your girlfriend, Norman.' And then I said if she was my girlfriend we should go for a walk. And she said, 'Not today, Norman.'"

"And then what happened?"

"I kept asking Lauren when we were going for a walk. Every time I saw her. 'Cos she was my girlfriend and she wouldn't tell me when we were going for a walk."

"And in the end she complained."

Blake nodded. Looked even more confused. "A policeman came round. He said I had to stop asking her to come for a walk. He called it something. I can't remember. And I explained that he didn't understand, she was my girlfriend. And he laughed. He must have thought I'd made a joke and he said, 'Yeah, right. In your dreams, old son.'"

Brady pushed his chair back. *Give him some space. Don't go too quickly. Like you said: all afternoon if that's what it takes. And gently…*

"And then they found Sandra?"

"They came in the morning, Mr Brady. At six twenty-two. I said I hadn't taken Mum her cup of tea. I said, I always take her a cup of tea and a slice of toast at seven o'clock. And the policeman who'd come before laughed again and said she'd have to get used to making her own tea."

"So you were arrested?"

"They put me in the police car. And handcuffed me. And she was standing outside."

"Who was?"

"Sandra's grandmother. And other people. Mr and Mrs Sellers. And Mrs Sellers was crying. And she shouted at me."

"Mrs Sellers shouted at you?"

"No. Sandra's grandma shouted at me. 'Fuck your fish' she shouted. 'There's no fishing where you're going.' And people were looking out of the window."

"So they took you down to the police station and questioned you?"

"No. They didn't ask questions. They told me what I'd done. And I said I hadn't. And they said I had. And they described it to me. They said because Lauren wouldn't be my girlfriend I'd… done bad things to her sister."

Norman Blake looked at Brady.

Eyes wide. Still not understanding. Pleading.

"But Lauren *was* my girlfriend, Mr Brady. Why would I hurt my girlfriend's sister?"

"Then what, Norman?"

"Another policeman came in. He said he'd been going through my bedroom and he'd found... He'd found my pictures. I liked looking at pictures. And he said, 'he fits, boss. Fucking pervert. Lives on his own or with his mother.' And the one he called 'boss' laughed and said it was like shelling peas."

"What's your solicitor doing while all this is going on, Norman?"

Blake shook his head. "I didn't have one. I didn't know until afterwards. I was on my own. And they kept telling me what I'd done. And this policeman – not the one who came to see me and laughed, a different one – kept shouting at me and saying, 'What have you done with her blouse?' And other things. Worse things."

"And eventually you confessed?"

Norman Blake looked down. Put his hands in his lap. Spoke to Brady with his head bowed. "I need the toilet, Mr Brady."

"You need the toilet? Now?"

Still with his head bowed. "When I'm nervous or frightened, Mr Brady. It's worse. And I hold on as long as I can, but..."

Brady walked across to the door and knocked on it. "He needs the loo," he said to the warder.

"Yeah, right. Course he does. The more time he wastes with you the less time he spends in his cell. Come on then, Norman. Time for a tinkle."

Brady stood and waited. Stared at the cream walls. Saw Norman Blake being questioned.

No idea what's happening. A detective across the table working his way through the profile. Steadily ticking off the boxes...

'Miss Donoghue's blouse was missing. The taking of clothing as trophies is well known. The killer may have discarded the blouse – however, when you search his home you will certainly find other 'collections.'

In summary, you are looking for someone who lives alone – or perhaps with his mother: who has an unhealthy interest in pornography; who 'collects' things: who is unsuccessful with the opposite sex, who lives locally and – based on the severity of the attack – is likely to lose his temper if he does not get his own way.'

He ticks all the boxes. 'Like shelling peas?' It would have been. If you'd made your mind up in advance...

THE DOOR OPENED. "There you go, Norman. And no more wasting our time. We weren't born yesterday."

Brady smiled at him. "OK? You alright if we carry on talking?"

The eager nod again. "Yes, Mr Brady. If it's helping you. That's what they say, don't they? 'Helping the police with their enquiries.'"

Brady laughed again. "They do, Norman. Let me just take you back a minute. When you lived with your mum – around the time Lauren became your girlfriend – did you have a job?"

"I had a job at the supermarket, Mr Brady. Emptying

boxes. And taking stuff off lorries. But there was some-one... He kept calling me names. And I lost my temper. And I hit him. So they said I had to leave."

"And that was it?"

"No." He shook his head vigorously. "Mr Sellers said I could work for him. He did people's gardens. But someone shouted at me. She said I'd let her dog out. And I hadn't. He was at the back gate. And it was obvious he wanted to go out. So I opened it for him. And then Mr Sellers said there wasn't the work. He could manage on his own..."

Brady smiled. Did his best to smile. "Let's talk about the day in Whitby, Norman. You remember, the day you went to Whitby to go fishing?"

Norman Blake nodded. Smiled. "That's what I'm going to do when they let me out, Mr Brady. 'Soon,' Mr Harris says. 'Not long to wait now, Norman old son. You and me will have to be pen pals. Tell me all about your fishing.' Except I'm not very good at writing."

"That sounds like a nice plan, Norman."

Blake looked confused again. "It's not a plan, Mr Brady. It's what I'm going to do. I'm going fishing and nothing is going to stop me. The day after they let me out of prison I'm going fishing at Whitby."

Where Ruby and half her family will be waiting for you...

Brady sighed. "That day, Norman. You caught the bus to Whitby? But you didn't go fishing? The weather was bad that day?"

"It was raining. And really windy. But Mum had booked the trip for me, for my birthday. So I still went. They were doing something on the boat. I told them that

I'd come for the fishing trip and they laughed. 'Come back when it's calmer,' they said. I didn't understand why they were laughing. But that's what I did. I waited in Whitby."

"All day?"

"Well obviously. Where else would I go? Because I was waiting for it to get calmer, like they said. And I went back – "

"Where?"

"To where the boat was. But there was no-one there. And then it got dark so I caught the bus home."

"You just wandered round Whitby? All day?"

"Yes. With my fishing rod."

"Why did you take your fishing rod? I thought – when you went out on a boat – I thought they gave you rods and bait?"

"Because it was *my* fishing rod. Because my grandad gave me it before he died. 'There you are, Norman,' he said. 'That there is a lucky fishing rod.'"

"Why didn't you... I don't know. Find somewhere to leave your fishing rod? At the bus station, maybe?"

Norman Blake finally managed to look Brady in the eye. "Don't you understand anything? Because I didn't know when the weather would change. They said 'when it gets calmer' but they didn't tell me *when*. So I went back. To ask them. 'When will it get calmer?' But they'd gone home."

'The ring of truth.' How many times did Jim Fitzpatrick say it? 'They'll say something. It might make them look stupid. It won't show them in a good light. But you'll know it when you hear it, Mike. The ring of truth.'

Everything the poor bugger's said has had the 'ring of truth,' Jim...

Brady sighed. "We've nearly finished, Norman. I hope it hasn't been too painful."

Blake shook his head. "No, no, Mr Brady. I've enjoyed talking. And you're the first person who's ever listened to me."

"Let's just go back to the police station, Norman. When they're asking you questions. You remember they were asking about Sandra's blouse?"

"They kept shouting at me, Mr Brady. 'Where's her blouse? What have you done with her blouse?' I didn't know what they were talking about. What could I do? And... And..."

"And what, Norman?"

His head was down again. His hands back in his lap. "I needed a wee, Mr Brady."

"So they let you go to the toilet?"

"No. And I asked again. And the one who was shouting at me laughed and said I couldn't go to the toilet until I signed his piece of paper. So..."

Norman Blake hunched forward. Slowly brought his forehead down to the grey prison table. Whispered. "I wet myself, Mr Brady. And he said I was disgusting. So I signed it."

He straightened up. Brady slowly exhaled.

"So I signed the paper, Mr Brady. Then they let me go to the toilet. But it was too late. And then I did have a solicitor and he told me I wasn't guilty but they said I was and I'd signed the paper to say so. And then all these people stood up in court and said what I'd done. The policeman – the one who'd been through my bedroom – he said he'd found pictures of girls. The man at the supermarket said I was violent. And Lauren was there. She said she wasn't my girlfriend. She said she didn't even like me. 'He makes my flesh crawl.' That's what she said, Mr Brady. It made me cry."

"One last question, Norman," Brady said gently. "I don't suppose – twenty years later – I don't suppose you can remember the policeman who was asking you the questions? The one who was shouting at you? What his name was?"

Because maybe I can talk to him. Make some sense of it all. See if they had any other leads...

Norman Blake looked up and smiled. "I can remember names, Mr Brady. I can remember everyone's name. Everyone in my class. In my class there was Paul Allen, Clive Clarke, Valerie Dennis, Martin Hartley, Valerie King, Angela Miller. Valerie and Angela – their birthdays were on the same day. But they weren't twins 'cos they lived in different houses."

"The policeman's name, Norman?" Brady said.

"The policeman who came to the house talked to him. When he said it was like shelling peas. He said, 'They won't all be this easy, Alan.' And then an older man came in and said, 'Good work DS Kershaw.' So that was his name, Mr Brady. Alan Kershaw. And if he'd been in my class he'd have sat next to Valerie King. Because that's how we sat. Alphabetically. So Alan Kershaw, Mr Brady. Between Martin Hartley and Valerie King."

Brady thanked him. Promised he'd talk to him again. Told Norman Blake to take care of himself. Stood up and shook hands. Knocked on the interview room door. Watched the man in the fluorescent orange vest shuffle back to his cell.

'Alan Kershaw, Mr Brady. Between Martin Hartley and Valerie King.'

Brady reached for his phone. There was someone he needed to talk to.

19

"So what can your tame psychologist do for you this time, Mr Brady?"

"I thought we were on first name terms now?"

"We are," Susanna Harrall said. She was exactly as he remembered her. An inquisitive, intelligent face, blonde hair falling to her shoulders. A navy trouser suit this morning, a cream open necked blouse, two gold chains round her neck.

"I'm sorry, Mike. I've just come out of a formal, depressing, call-the-Samaritans management meeting. Not enough money, too many patients, not enough people with stethoscopes, *way* too many people with opinions."

Brady laughed. "Let me guess," he said. "The vast majority of those opinions were wearing suits?"

"How did you know? Because you've been in the same meeting. What can I do for you?"

"I want – I'm sorry, I would like – to understand something, Susanna. Autism. And Asperger's. What's the difference? How does it impact behaviour?"

"In relation to crime? Criminals? You're a man who deals in practice, not theory."

Brady smiled. "Of course. I need to rule someone out of an investigation. And before I do anything rash... Well, I want to be certain. As certain as I can be."

Susanna raised her eyebrows. "You realise you've strayed into my specialist subject? Did you bring sandwiches? A flask of coffee? Reading material?"

"Would it be simpler if I asked questions?"

"Almost certainly."

Brady nodded. "I was talking to someone – "

"We're talking someone on the autistic spectrum here?"

"I think so. Insofar as I understand what the autistic spectrum is. I've done some reading. Looked online..."

Susanna nodded. "But you wanted the tutorial not the text-book? Autism is a label that's tossed around with gay abandon these days. Not least by so-called experts on TV."

"And is it different to Asperger's? Are they two different things? Or is it – "

She smiled. "Is it just another stop on the same line?"

"Yes, I suppose so."

"Asperger's is part of the autistic spectrum. Really intelligent people at one end, learning disabilities at the other. I often think – this is a simplistic way of putting it, so don't quote me – I often think if you're on the autistic spectrum you get lucky or unlucky. Genius at one end, a life in care at the other."

Or a prison cell. Public acclaim or public enemy...

"But it's not that straightforward," she said. "At one end of the spectrum you're going to find extreme intelligence. But you might find that in a person who say, can't follow an Ikea diagram. Or maybe can't even tie his shoelaces. And at the other end there's someone who has a learning disability – who's perhaps never going to be able to live independently."

"You keep saying 'he.'"

"I do. Which I shouldn't. But there are between four and five boys with autism for every girl. That seems to be a broadly-accepted ratio now."

"Are there any examples?"

"Are you talking about famous people? You've heard the saying, 'Genius is one per cent inspiration, ninety-nine per cent perspiration.' Sometimes the perspiration is obsession. And very often that's autism. Einstein? Newton? There's plenty of speculation. Barnes Wallis – "

"The bouncing bomb?"

"The very same. I have my pet theory about Bill Gates. Watch him rocking backwards and forwards. And then there are the people who've been diagnosed. Woody Allen. Anthony Hopkins. Hans Christian Andersen. Lewis Carroll."

"So a lot of creative people?"

She spread her hands. "Isn't that a reasonable definition of genius? Creativity plus hard work? Plus obsession?"

"But that doesn't help my guy. Who's not a genius. Who leaves dead fish on someone's doorstep because he thinks they might like fish for tea."

"And someone opens the door and finds a dead fish that's been in the sun all day, and doesn't quite see it that way? We're on to specifics?"

Brady nodded. "Yes. He said he'd asked a girl out. Asked her to be his girlfriend. She'd laughed and said, 'Yes, but not today.' Words to that effect."

"So saying no in the gentlest possible way?"

"To you and me, yes."

"But the person you spoke to took it literally. Kept asking her when they were going out?"

Brady nodded. "Exactly that."

"That's absolutely text-book behaviour. Taking everything literally. A woman says that and most men will understand what she's really saying. Well, some men... But to someone on the autistic spectrum 'maybe we could have coffee' means 'we *will* have coffee.'"

"And they'll ask about it every time?"

"Very possibly. Like I said, obsession. Having an obsession – maybe more than one – is another sign. I had one client – sadly he's dead now, so I'm not breaking any confidences – who had an obsession with silence. So if he went for a walk and there was someone playing music – teenagers in a park or a car at traffic lights with the window open – he'd shout abuse at them. Yell at them to turn the music off."

"So taking things literally. Obsessive behaviour... Are there any more of these 'classic signs?'"

"You can list them, Mike, but in many ways they're different sides of the same coin. People on the autistic spectrum struggle with empathy. Non-verbal communication. And when the communication *is* verbal yes, they take it literally. They don't see other people's point of view. So they're argumentative. They're unlikely to sustain a relationship. Unless they've a partner who really understands. And I mean *really* understands."

More boxes. And Norman Blake ticks them all. But these are the boxes that should have seen him acquitted...

Brady nodded. "What you said about being argumentative... Supposing someone's being questioned. Accused of something they haven't done..."

"By questioned you mean questioned by the police?"

"Yes. Or in court. Being cross-examined."

"Either way," Susanna said, "The argument is going to escalate. The person you're describing will get more and more frustrated at not being believed. In many ways their reaction... Let me put it this way. If the person who's doing the questioning doesn't understand their behaviour, he's going to interpret the answers as confirmation of guilt."

"And the same for a jury?"

She nodded. "Watching the behaviour? Yes. I can't believe there are many jurors who recognise the signs of autism."

So the more they question him, the more guilty he looks...

Brady stared out of the window. Saw Norman Blake being questioned. Saw Kershaw smiling. Accepting the congratulations.

Self-satisfied. Job done.

"Can I ask one last question, Susanna? You mentioned obsession. The person I'm talking about is a prisoner. He's due for release soon. There's something he's determined to do when he's released. *Absolutely determined to do."*

"If he's in prison, Mike, that obsession – determination – might be the only thing that's got him through. Take it away and... well, there's a risk that he'd become unstable. Dangerous. To himself or to other people. Or both."

Brady walked across the hospital car park in the fading light.

'I'm going fishing, Mr Brady. I'm going fishing and nothing is going to stop me. As soon as I'm out of prison I'm going fishing at Whitby.'

'And if he knows – if he knows where my Alice is – then I'll tell you this. And I'll say it to your face. I don't care if I swing for it. I don't care if I spend the rest of my life in jail.'

Norman Blake in his cell, dreaming of Whitby. Ruby waiting for him to come out.

Both determined to get what they want.

'There's a risk that he'd become unstable. Dangerous. To himself or to other people.'

So the solution's simple.

I have to find the killer...

BRADY OPENED the tailgate of his car. Reached for the battered plastic chair.

Probably even less comfortable than the one in the prison. But that's what you get for taking a cast-off from the police canteen...

He said a small prayer of thanks for two days of dry weather and opened his front door easily. Used the torch on his phone to walk upstairs. Remembered he needed to speak to Chris.

If he's starting work he might want the electricity switching back on...

Walked across the landing. Pushed the door of the lounge open. Or what would eventually be his lounge...

Saw the lights of the harbour through the window. Heard the seagulls screeching.

A flock of geese fly over your house and they're at ease with each other. Chattering, sharing the latest gossip. Seagulls are angry. Always angry, always hurling abuse at one another. Seagulls don't even like other seagulls.

He shivered as the January wind blew through the distorted window frame. Ignored the cold. Put the chair by the window and sat down. Was surprised by how much light from the harbour shone into the house.

I used to go on the Moors to think. Or on the beach. Now I'm here. In my two hundred year old house. Maybe it has ghosts. Maybe I've bought a house with ghosts. Not the sort of thing the estate agents tell you...

But sitting on a battered plastic chair in the dark, looking out over the harbour, watching the lights reflected off the water shining, rippling across the roof of his lounge, Michael Brady felt at home. At peace. Welcomed. If The Crow's Nest had ghosts they were friendly ghosts. At least for now...

How much time have I got? Ten minutes. I should have gone straight home. But it's not home. Somewhere we pay rent. A stop-gap. This is home. Or it will be. Eating breakfast on my balcony. Watching the sun rise out of the sea. Assuming you get the electric turned back on and they can start work.

'The DNA report is back. It's definite. A match with the sample they have on file. What did Geoff call them? 'The Two Gentlemen of the Moor.' They'd found Rebecca Kennedy.

Murdered...

Is Frankie right about the backpack? How else did he get her up there? And a tent? Is that what he did? Dug for an hour. Stopped for a rest. Drank a cup of tea? Sat there and ate a bloody Kit-Kat? Did he talk to her? Before he started digging again? Before he finally rolled her naked body into the grave...

How long between Becky dying and being carried onto the Moors?

And why kill Alice?

'Thousands of other girls to choose from. He could have stopped in Loftus, or Sandsend. But he doesn't. He carries on to Whitby and he picks on Alice. My Alice. And all I can think is why?'

Because she knew something, Ruby. Because you're right. The person who murdered Becky is the person who murdered Alice. But it wasn't Norman Blake. He might have ticked every box on the profile. He might not have done himself any favours in the witness box. But he didn't do it. You should let him come to Whitby. Enjoy his fishing trip. But you won't. No-one will. Not unless I find the killer.

The girls knew each other. They must have done. Otherwise nothing makes sense.

But they didn't prove it. Did they even try? Alice's friends will still be in Whitby. Becky's... everywhere but Whitby. But the school will have a record. And once I've found one friend Facebook will do the work for me... Maybe I could co-opt Ash. She'd have it done in twenty minutes.

Ash...

He'd dropped her off at Bean's that morning. A hockey tournament. An overnight stay in Durham.

She'd seemed quiet. Pre-occupied. As if there was something on her mind. Then she asked him about his plans...

'Will you be alright while I'm away, Dad? What are you doing? Watching football? Falling asleep?'

'There's no football on, Ash. And if there was I wouldn't be watching it.'

'Why not?'

'Because I'm going out to dinner.'

'What? You didn't tell me.'

'I'm sorry, sweetheart, I didn't know you had to approve all my meetings.'

'Where? Who with?'

'Aren't you due at school, Ash? Do you have time to check up on my social life?'

'You don't have a social life, Dad. Besides, it's Science first period. Or staring out of the window as it's known. Are you seeing someone, Dad? Is it a date?'

'No, I'm not seeing someone, Ash. And no, it's not a date. I'm having dinner with a friend, that's all.'

'Which friend?'

'You're not getting out of the car until I tell you are you?'

Ash had smiled at him. Her butter-wouldn't-melt look.

'Finally, Dad. The message gets through...'

' I'm going to someone's flat. She's cooking me a meal.'

'Who?'

'Frankie.'

The last thing she said on Sunday. 'You're still alright for dinner? Just so I know whether to buy two boxes of bread sticks...'

Ash had paused before replying.

'Frankie, Dad... Is that DS Thomson? Or is that Frankie, who was at our house that night I came home unexpectedly? Who I now realise was looking hot. In both senses of the word...'

'It's Frankie Thomson, Ash. My friend and – when she comes back to work – my colleague. Nothing more, nothing less.'

Another smile. Conspiratorial this time.

'So you'll be taking flowers. And wine. How long is she on sabbatical for, Dad?'

'Until May. Now get out of the car. Good luck in the tournament. Take care of yourself. And I'll see you tomorrow night.'

Ash had surprised him. She'd leaned over and kissed him. Then she winked.

'Don't drink too much, Dad. You don't want to fall asleep on her. Or disappoint her...'

MICHAEL BRADY SMILED at the memory.

I need to talk to Frankie. Bring her up to date. See what she makes of Edmund Kennedy. And Ruby.

And I need to buy wine. And flowers...

He stood up. Left the battered plastic chair alone with the reflections from the harbour.

20

Brady looked in the bathroom mirror. His favourite navy shirt. Ash called it his grandad shirt. "Technically, sweetheart," he'd corrected her, "It's known as a half-placket shirt. Pullover shirt if you must. But less of the 'grandad.'"

He'd had one as a teenager. Missed it ever since. He folded the cuffs back twice, so the sleeves ended just below his elbows. Opened the bathroom cabinet. Pushed his shaving cream out of the way. Reached for the bottle.

Hesitated...

A birthday present. One of the last birthday presents she gave me. Tom Ford.

I haven't worn after-shave since she died.

What would Ash say if she were here? 'What do you tell me, Dad? Do it properly or don't do it at all. And you're wearing your best shirt...'

Brady took hold of the black bottle. Flicked the top back.

Walked downstairs. Told Archie to be good. "Beth from next door has a key. She'll be round to let you out.

Stare at her with those big brown eyes, Archie. You'll get a hundred biscuits. And I won't be late."

He ruffled the top of Archie's head. Reached for his coat. Picked up the wine and opened the front door. Took two steps down the path. Shook his head in disbelief. Went back for the flowers...

Ignored the parking space outside Frankie's flat. Parked a hundred yards further up the road so he could look across the harbour and see The Crow's Nest.

I can barely pick it out in the dark. Maybe I should leave a light on so I can see it from this side of the harbour. So get the bloody electric turned back on...

He walked back along the pavement.

Why am I not as nervous as I expected to be?

Christ, you're having dinner with a friend. What did you say to Ash? 'A friend. Nothing more, nothing less.' So why should you be nervous at all?

Reached the door. Pressed the buzzer for Flat 3.

"I've left the doors open, Mike," her voice said. "I can't open them. I'm making pasta."

Making pasta? I'm impressed. Do I know anyone who makes their own pasta...

Brady's phone rang. Wine in one hand, flowers in the other. He pushed the door open. Put the wine on the windowsill. Fished the phone out of his pocket just as it stopped ringing.

Recent calls.

There it was in red.

Bean.

Remembered the conversation.

'Ash, I need Bean's number.'

'She's my friend, Dad. Besides, don't you think that's, well... a bit pervy?'

'No, I think it's a bit sensible. Suppose there's an emergency? Suppose I need to contact you one day and your phone's out of charge? Bean would be a good bet. And make sure Bean's got my number as well. Emergencies aren't a one-way street.'

Brady bent down. Put the flowers on the floor. Tapped 'Bean.' She answered almost immediately. "Bean, it's Mike Brady. You rang me..."

Knew the answer he wanted to hear.

'Did I, Mr Brady? I'm really sorry. I had my phone in my pocket. Sorry again...'

Didn't get it.

"Oh, Mike. Mr Brady. Thank you – "

"Bean what is it? Is Ash hurt? Why are you ringing me? Why you and not the school?"

"No. I'm sorry, Mr Brady, I'm flustered. I'm – "

"Bean. Calm down. Take a deep breath. Tell me what's happened."

"It's Ash, Mr Brady. She's... I think the teachers will ring you. You'll have to come and get her. I'm sure you will – "

"Bean. What's wrong with her? Is she ill?"

"No, she's not ill. I'm sorry. Like I said, I'm flustered."

"Take another deep breath, Bean. Just tell me what's happened. Why do I have to come and collect Ash?"

"She's... I'm sorry, Mr Brady. Ash has punched someone."

. . .

BRADY WALKED SLOWLY up the stairs to Frankie's flat.

'Ash has punched someone.'

No Bean hadn't seen it. Hadn't had chance to talk to Ash. But thought he should know.

'Who, Bean? Who has she punched? And why?'

'Another girl on the trip. Shelley Clarke. And why? I thought Ash would have told you.'

He knocked lightly on the open door. Pushed it gently. Was greeted by the smell of pasta sauce.

No, not pasta sauce. Deeper, richer. Something that's been cooking for a long time...

He stepped into the hall. The kitchen door was open. Frankie had her back to him. Engrossed in the cooking. Music playing. She hadn't heard him come in.

He remembered the first time he'd seen her. Bill's birthday party. She'd reminded him of a warrior princess in *Lord of the Rings.*

Dark hair pinned up. Grey eyes. Looking determined.

The sort of girl that ignores her father's pleas and straps on armour...

Brady knocked on the kitchen door. Slightly louder. Frankie turned round, wooden spoon in her hand. Smiled. "Mike, I'm sorry, I was miles away. Possibly singing out loud. In which case I apologise some more." She saw his face. "What's wrong? You look like something dreadful has happened. Is Archie alright?"

"I brought you some flowers," Brady said. "To say 'thank you.'"

Flowers. Wine. Worrying about after-shave. All irrelevant...

She stepped forward. Took them from him. "They're

lovely. Beautiful. Thank you. And let me take the wine. Spare you another speech. And then tell me what's wrong. Because something clearly is wrong."

Brady sat down at her kitchen table. Looked at his phone. At his recent calls.

Like I'm checking the conversation really took place.

"Bean phoned me," he said. "Ash's friend. Two minutes ago, just as I was ringing your doorbell."

"So what's happened?"

"My daughter has punched someone. On the school trip."

"You mean she's been in a fight?"

Brady shook his head. "No. Well, I don't think so. Bean said, 'I'm sorry, Mr Brady. Ash has punched someone.' And one of the teachers will be ringing me – "

"And have they?"

"No. Not yet. And..."

Brady looked at her. The warrior princess didn't have her hair pinned up. Definitely wasn't wearing armour.

"...And. You're wearing a dress, Frankie."

Pale lilac. Small white spots. Wrapped round her. V-neck. Cap sleeves. Belt loosely tied.

"I am, Detective Chief Inspector. Clearly I should apologise again. I see you're in shock."

Brady laughed. "I'm sorry, Frankie. I'm just so used to seeing you in jeans. Working clothes. You look..."

Can I say this to another woman?

'Do it properly or don't do it at all, Dad.'

"You look lovely, Frankie."

You look beautiful. And I want to stand up and wrap my arms round you. Hold you. But my daughter needs me.

She leaned forward. Put her hand on his. "Thank you. But you don't look like a man who's staying for dinner."

Brady shook his head. "I don't know. Until someone rings me I don't know. Bean said she didn't see what happened. Only that Ash had punched someone. And she sort of implied I should know why."

Frankie reached behind her and turned the gas off. Turned back to him. "Did she say who, Mike?"

"Who she punched? Only a name. Shell – "

His phone rang. A number he didn't recognise. But he knew who it was.

"Michael Brady ... Miss Gibson. I wasn't expecting a call from one of Ash's teachers ... May I ask why ... Well surely Ash must have given you a reason ... With the greatest possible respect, Miss Gibson, that sounds like a vague platitude from a badly-worded handbook. We're talking about a thirteen year old girl here ... I'm sure you *are* acting in accordance with school procedure, Miss Gibson, but presumably Ash isn't the only one involved in this ... so I'm the only parent being asked to drive ninety miles on a dark, wet January night ... supposing I'd been drinking, Miss Gibson? And I couldn't drive? What would you do then? Or is that not covered by school procedure ... No, Miss Gibson I am not being abusive to you, I am simply asking a logical question ... Frankly, Miss Gibson I don't give a toss about your procedures. I have a lifetime's experience of inadequate people covering their own ar – back. I'll see you in two hours. And remember you have a duty of care to my daughter."

Frankie raised her eyebrows. "You, er... You may not

have won Tactful Diplomat of the Year there. What did she say?"

Brady shook his head angrily. "She said that Ash punched one of the other girls. Apparently for no reason. When they were having dinner. Apparently this other girl said she wished Ash 'good luck for the game tomorrow' and Ash stood up and punched her. 'In front of children and teachers from other schools, Mr Brady. We have the good name of the school to think about.'"

"And what does Ash say?"

"She told this bloody jobsworth incompetent teacher that the other girl had been bullying her. For two weeks. Christ, Frankie, she never said anything to me. Surely she'd tell me? This girl said something to Ash. It was the final straw. Ash lost her temper and thumped her."

"Did she say what this other girl said?"

"Ash refused to tell her. 'From which we have to conclude, Mr Brady, that nothing at all was said. That Ashley is simply seeking to excuse her own appalling behaviour and in accordance with the school fucking handbook – which all parents receive, Mr Brady – I must ask you to come and collect Ashley immediately.' And some bullshit about the latest Ofsted report. Which says the school doesn't have a bullying problem."

Frankie laughed. "Or that anyone who might report it was given the day off. What are you going to do?"

"What the bloody hell can I do, Frankie? Drive to Durham. Find out what happened. Bring her home. Prepare myself for the usual bureaucratic bullshit from the school."

"Do you want me to come with you?"

Do I want you to come with me? Yes. Yes, I do. Because you'll stop me saying, or doing – or both – something stupid. Because Ash would talk to you before she'd talk to me. Yes, I do.

"No, Frankie. I can't ask that. Thank you, but no. She's my daughter. I'll have to deal with it. And two hours is long enough to calm down. No, I can't ask that. I've already – "

Brady gestured at the pan on the hob. "It smells wonderful. Like you've been cooking all day. And – "

"And I'm wearing a dress? Don't worry, the planets are in line again in a hundred years. The dress will keep until then..."

Brady stood up and smiled. Walked across to her. Put his hands on her shoulders. "I'm genuinely sorry," he said. "Can I re-book the table? Next week, or the week after? As long as you cook whatever-it-is-you're-cooking again?"

She brought her hand up. Touched her index finger to his lips. "Yes. But go and get Ash. And if she wants to talk to someone who's not her dad, I'm here."

"Thank you. Thank you, Frankie, I really appreciate that. I'll call you tomorrow, let you know what happened."

Brady picked his keys up off the table. "Across the Moors in the middle of January. Just what I need."

"Drive carefully," Frankie said. "And keep calm."

Brady nodded. Apologised to her again. Turned to go. "Mike, one question."

"What's that?"

"Did they tell you the name of the other girl? The one Ash hit?"

"Shelley. Shelley Clarke."

"I thought so when you said 'Shell.' She's been in trouble before. And you know her mother, Mike. She runs a bed and breakfast. She's Ruby's cousin."

21

'You want to talk to your children?'

He remembered the conversation. Sitting in the canteen in Manchester. He was 30, just been promoted to sergeant. Ash was still a toddler. Two older uniform guys at the next table. 'You want to talk to them? The only way to do it is to put them in the car.'

'Or take them for a walk. But it's got to be with the dog.'

'No,' the first one said. 'I want to talk to my lad the *only* way is in the car. Something about not looking at each other. And the road. Works every time. Sit him down at the table and say 'we need to talk, Damian' and he clams up. Road trip. Definite. It's the only way you can talk to a teenager.'

Does Durham to Whitby count as a road trip? We'll soon find out...

"You sure you've got everything?"

"Dad, I only brought a sports bag. And a hockey stick. We were only here one night."

Brady started the car. Turned the wipers on. Drove out of Durham. Didn't say anything for the first ten minutes. Didn't want to rush it. Started off low-key. "We should be home in an hour and a half hopefully. There won't be much traffic round Middlesbrough. Archie will be surprised to see you."

Archie. I should have seen this coming What was it? A week ago?

'You alright, Ash? You don't usually volunteer to take Archie out in the rain.'

'I'm fine, Dad. I just... I like being with Archie. We're good friends. We talk.'

'The only thing Archie wants to talk about is where the next biscuit is coming from.'

'You're wrong, Dad. Archie's a good listener. You could learn a lot from Archie.'

She'd turned and walked out of the room, Archie scampering after her. Brady had spent half an hour wondering what he'd done wrong. Was still wondering when a very wet Ash and an even wetter Archie came through the door.

ASH WAS CURLED up on the seat. Legs drawn up, arms round her knees.

Foetal position? Protecting herself?

Brady glanced across. Saw his daughter's jaw.

No. Still angry...

"What did she say?" Ash said. "Gibson. I assume you had to talk to the Witch of the East before she signed my release papers."

Brady couldn't help laughing. "I thought she was called Bellatrix?"

"Only on a good day."

Do I edit it? Try and gloss it over? Or just tell her the truth?

Brady went for the last – the only – option. "You want it word for word, Ash? Pretty much what she said to me on the phone. You punched Shelley Clarke. You say because she'd been bullying you. Shelley Clarke denies it. No-one overhead the conversation. So she thinks – "

"*Everyone* overheard what she said. But no-one will admit it because they're all scared of the fat freak."

The same old story. Everyone sees. No-one speaks.

"What about Bean?"

"She was late. She wasn't there."

"Bean's OK? This isn't going to rebound on her?"

Ash shook her head. "Bean's fine. She texted me. So what did Bellatrix say?"

"What you'd expect, Ash. It's the same bullshit in every organisation. She waffled on for about five minutes about school policies and not tolerating violence. Said the school didn't have a bullying problem and said I'd need to discuss it with the headteacher. The new one presumably."

"She's a liar."

"I thought that's what you'd say. Hang on, let me just get on the A1. Then tell me your side of the story."

Brady drove round the roundabout. Accelerated to overtake a lorry as he joined the motorway. Glanced across.

"Ash? You want to tell me your side of things?"

Ash didn't reply.

"Ash?"

"She's been bullying me." So quietly Brady could hardly hear her.

"Shelley? How? And for how long?"

"Two weeks. Since you found that girl's body on the Moors."

'Shelley. Shelley Clarke.'

'I thought so when you said 'Shell.' She's been in trouble before. And you know her mother, Mike. She runs a bed and breakfast. She's Ruby's cousin.'

So she's related to Alice Simpson. Second cousin, something like that. But part of a tight-knit family. And she's seen the chance for revenge...

"What has she been saying Ash?"

"That you're a pig. That all coppers are pigs. Which makes me a pig. I'm only in the hockey team because I'm your daughter."

"Anything else?"

"That you've been pissing on her family for twenty years. Now it's her turn to piss on me. That she's going to find me one night. Put me where you'll never find me."

"And what have you said?"

"Nothing. Just told her to leave me alone."

"Except you hit her..."

"Yes."

"Why?"

"Because we were eating dinner. She leaned over my shoulder and spat in my food. Then she said..." Ash started sobbing. "Everyone saw it but no-one did anything. Then she said..."

"What did she say, sweetheart?"

"She said, 'Tonight's the night, bitch. You're a long way from home and your lovely daddy's not here to protect you.'"

Brady braked, indicated, slowed down and pulled over onto the hard shoulder. Turned the hazard warning lights on. Came to a stop. Unfastened his seat belt. Unfastened Ash's seat belt. Pulled her to him and hugged her. Wrapped his arms tightly round her and hugged her some more.

Held her until she'd stopped sobbing. Asked the question he was frightened to ask.

"Why didn't you tell me?"

Ash pulled away from him. Blinked back the tears. "Because you're never there when I want to talk, Dad. Because since that girl's body was found... You're there but you're not there. You're on the Moors. You're more interested in girls who died twenty years ago than you are in your own daughter. So I go to Bean's."

She could have shouted. She didn't. Which makes it worse...

"I thought Bean was your friend?"

"She is. She's my best friend. But I don't want to live at her house. But... but..."

"Say it, Ash. Say what you're thinking."

Even though it's going to stab me through the heart.

"But... I'm lonely, Dad. There's no other way to put it. I come home and you're not there. And I give Archie his tea. And I love him. But he's a dog. He's the best dog in the world, but I can't talk to him."

Michael Brady let go of his daughter. Put his hand

under her chin. Tilted her head up. "Not any more, Ash. Not any more. I'm sorry. Never again."

"WHAT ARE we going to do about school?"

"You know what, Ash? Fuck school. I'll see the head-teacher and I'll get it sorted out. They're not going to mess you around. And for Christ's sake, they're not the only school in North Yorkshire."

"No," Ash said. Shook her head. "No," she said again.

"No?"

"No, Dad. If you're talking about me going to a different school – Fyling Hall or in Scarborough – the answer is no."

"I wasn't... I mean, I hadn't even started to think about it."

"Don't. Don't think about it. This is the first big challenge of my life and I'm not going to deal with it by running away."

Brady indicated left and turned off the motorway. Glanced across at his daughter. "I know this isn't what you say to your thirteen year old daughter. I know you're not the right age for an emotional father. But bloody hell, Ash, I love you. And I'm proud of you. And... this *definitely* isn't the question a responsible parent should ask – especially if he's read the school handbook. But I need to ask it."

"What?"

"How hard did you hit her?"

Ash curled her right hand into a fist. Blew nonchalantly on her knuckles. "Hard enough. And – don't tell anyone – I got lucky. She was so surprised someone had finally stood up to her she stepped backwards. And she tripped over a chair and ended up on the floor."

Brady nodded. "So you were following the family motto? Do it properly or don't do it at all. I repeat. I'm proud of you. And I'm assuming you haven't eaten? We'll stop for fish and chips. Christ, Ash, I love you so much I'll even let you put vinegar on them and stink the car out."

Ash smiled at him. "Archie likes the smell, Dad..."

22

"Ash, sweetheart?"

Brady put his head round the bedroom door. Thought he heard, 'I'm asleep' come from somewhere under the quilt.

"Ash, on the assumption you can hear me I'm going out. Not because I'm working, not because I don't want to have breakfast with you. I'm going to sort something out. I'll be about an hour. So get up, have a shower and *don't* have any breakfast. We'll go out. That café in Sandsend. And then we'll take Archie for a walk on the beach. And yes, you can slip him your sausage when you think I'm not looking."

A muffled, "OK, but I'm still asleep."

Brady walked downstairs and picked up his car keys.

Eight o'clock on Saturday morning. Let's hope she's up. And if she isn't I'll bang on the door until she is...

IT TOOK ten minutes to drive to her house.

Ruby answered the door with a cup of tea in one hand. She was wearing a black t-shirt that finished halfway down her thighs. As far as Brady could tell, nothing else.

"Mr Brady. What can I do for you at stupid o'clock on Saturday morning? You're not here to tell me you've found her?"

"No, Ruby, I'm not. If I was here for that I might have waited for a more civilised time. What can you do for me? You can let me in, make me a cup of tea – or I'll make a cup of tea while you get dressed – and you can talk to me for ten minutes. Or you can listen while I talk to you."

Ruby stepped back to let him in. Walked towards the kitchen. "I've just got out of bed," she said over her shoulder. "If you want to talk to me you'll have to take me as I am." She switched the kettle on and reached for two mugs. "You want a slice of toast to go with that?"

"No, I'm fine thanks, Ruby. I'm taking my daughter out for breakfast."

Ruby put two slices of bread into a battered looking toaster. Pressed the handle down. Pressed it half a dozen times before it finally admitted defeat and stayed down.

"How come you're taking your daughter out for breakfast?" Ruby said. "She's away isn't she? My cousin's girl – "

She saw the look on Brady's face. "That's why you're here," she said.

"Right," Brady said. "And 'that's why you're here' means you know the background. So make your toast, Ruby, and let's talk. I want this sorted out."

"You sure you don't want a slice?"

"Stop playing for time, Ruby, it's not like you."

Ruby put a mug of tea in front of him. Another one for herself. Two slices of toast with thick-cut orange marmalade. Not so much spread as plastered. She saw him looking. "I like this marmalade," she said defensively. "Reminds me of my dad."

"Right. You're a close-knit family. So you know your cousin's daughter, Shelley. And you know what she's like."

"What's she done? And what's it got to do with me?"

"I suspect you know what she's done, Ruby. I suspect you knew the minute you saw me at the door. Anyway, next time you see Shelley she'll have a black eye. My daughter thumped her last night."

Ruby stared at him. Put her toast down. Started to laugh. "She thumped Shelley? Seriously? Fuck me, I take my hat off to the girl. That takes balls. Christ, that's the best laugh I've had in ages."

Brady shook his head. "Stop it, Ruby. It's not funny. Your cousin's daughter has been bullying Ash for two weeks. And I can see by your face that's not a total shock to you. So last night Shelley took it too far and my daughter thumped her. As a result of which I had to drive to Durham to collect her. That took me maybe four hours."

When I was planning to have dinner...

Brady looked straight at her. Tapped his middle finger hard on the table. Four times. "Four hours wasted, Ruby. You might begin to see a connection."

"So you're threatening me. You're saying it has to stop or you'll stop looking for Alice."

Brady shook his head. "No, Ruby. I'm not threatening

you at all. I'm just making some observations. And explaining the realities of my life. And the reality is that on Monday morning I'll have to go into school and play stupid political games with a headmaster who cares far more about a bloody Ofsted report than he cares about my daughter. Who's going to say Shelley can't have been bullying Ash because they don't have bullying at the school. That's bollocks, Ruby. And to quote you the other day, 'I'm not having it.'"

"What do – "

"Just be quiet and listen to me. I'm not having the blame put on my daughter so the school can lie to Ofsted. Let me be blunt with you, Ruby. I don't give a shit about the Ofsted report. I do give a shit about my daughter. Now I've sat here at your kitchen table and I've seen the way your son and your brother defer to you. So I'm prepared to bet the rest of your family is the same."

Ruby shrugged. "They might do."

"They *will* do. So you go round to your cousin's today. Or tomorrow. Just make sure it's before Monday morning. And you tell Shelley two things. One, the bullying stops. And it stops now. And never starts again. And two, Ash didn't thump Shelley. She tripped over. And because the headmaster wants a spotless Ofsted report he'll believe that complete crap. And we can all be friends."

"Supposing she says 'no.'"

Brady sighed. "Oh, for Christ's sake, Ruby. Tell her some home truths. Tell her what she did was threatening behaviour. Tell her – tell her bloody nosy mother as well – that she doesn't need me for an enemy. This is my daughter we're talking about, Ruby. I'm not going to take prisoners."

"It's my daughter as well, Mr Brady," Ruby said quietly. She reached her hands up, ran her fingers through her hair.

"Right. It is. Which is why you and I need to be friends."

"So you're going to find her for me?"

"I'm going to do my best."

"How?" Ruby said. "How are you going to do it. That other girl – "

"Was only found because we got lucky. Because a walker needed a pee. That's not how I'm going to find Alice. I could pay a hundred walkers to piss on the Moors for a hundred years and they'd still not find her. There's only one way I'm going to find her. You know what it is. I know what it is."

"Find the killer," Ruby said quietly.

Brady nodded. "Right, find the killer. So help me out, Ruby. Two things. Tell Shelley what I've told you. So I'm not pissing my time away at school. And two, Alice's friends. Think back to when she was at school. Some of them must still be in Whitby?"

"Some. Some had the good sense to get out. But yeah, a few. I still see them round town. Half of them on their second husband by now."

"Anyone in particular? That Alice was really friendly with?"

Ruby pursed her lips. Looked thoughtful. "That's still in Whitby? Two. Mandy Jamieson, Tamara Prince. No. Tamara got married. Moved away. And you'll have to be quick if you want to talk to Mandy. Last time I saw her she was the size of a house. You might need to talk to her between deep breaths."

"Thank you."

"I haven't got addresses or anything."

"Don't worry. We'll find them. And I'll find your killer, Ruby."

Ruby pushed her chair away from the table. Leaned back in it. Brought her hands together. Laced her fingers. Looked at him. "You will, won't you? You're a determined bugger, I'll give you that. I like a man that knows what he wants..."

She stretched her arms slowly up over her head. Brady saw the black t-shirt ride up her thighs. She held her arms there. Now very clearly not wearing anything under the t-shirt. "Do you not get lonely, Michael Brady? There must be other things you want. Since your wife died..."

Brady stood up. Reached forward and picked up his mug. Finished his tea. "I want three things, Ruby. To find Alice for you. What we've talked about. And breakfast with my daughter."

Ruby kept her arms above her head. If anything stretched them even further. Held his eyes.

"Let me know when you change your mind."

Brady smiled. "I'm a copper, Ruby. And like you said, a determined bugger. I'll find her for you. But I'm going to have breakfast with Ash."

She laughed. Finally brought her arms down. "I'll see what I can do. Enjoy your bacon and eggs, Mr Brady."

23

He hadn't wanted to disturb her. Didn't know if she'd be with her mother. She phoned him in the middle of the afternoon. "So how did it go?"

"You want the truth, Frankie?"

"It's usually a good place to start."

"I drove to Durham. Endured a five minute lecture from Bellatrix Gibson – "

"Bellatrix?"

"Her nickname. Ash says when she has a bad hair day she looks like Bellatrix Whatever-her-name-is out of Harry Potter."

"Lestrange. But you got Ash back?"

"Yes."

"And had she thumped her?"

"In a word, yes. But I've sorted it out. Think I've sorted it out."

"How?"

"Spoken to the head of the family."

"Ruby then. You make her sound like a Mafia godfather."

"So long as she makes Shelley an offer she can't refuse I don't care. But there's something more important than that."

"What?"

"Long answer or short answer? You want the short answer. I fucked up. I moved to Whitby to be a good dad and here I am repeating all the mistakes I made in Manchester. Except this time it's my daughter paying for it."

"You're being too hard on yourself, Mike."

"No, Frankie, I'm not. I'm being honest with myself. I'm so bloody determined to prove I'm right. And... other people pay the price."

"So what are you going to do about it?"

"I'm going to be there for her. I'm going to finish work when I should finish work and I'm going to cook us a meal. And I'm going to listen. Maybe I'll get 'I'm listening' tattooed on my forehead. I don't know, Frankie. But I've only got her for another five years. I'm not going to make the same mistake again. We went for a walk on the beach this morning and..."

"And?"

"It was perfect, Frankie. Just bloody perfect. Cold, crisp, the sun shining off the sea. Clear. You could see for miles. Just a perfect winter's day. And we talked. Just talked and talked. Ate breakfast and talked some more."

"About what happened with Shelley?"

"No. Everything but that. About Whitby. About life, school – in general, not in particular – about responsibility, facing up to challenges. It was just... It was a privilege, Frankie. Once, just once, I felt like a competent father."

"That's brilliant. I'm really pleased, Mike. Can I... Can I just talk to the competent copper for a minute?"

"Yes, of course. What is it?"

"We might have wasted our time on Sunday."

"Walking up to the Lilla Cross? Why?"

"Because you can get to it another way."

"From the Scarborough road? That's about three miles. Closer to four. He couldn't carry the body that far."

"No, check your OS map, Mike. You can park the car at May Beck. Walk through the woods."

"How far is it?"

"Two miles? Two and a half? But it's flat. Relatively flat."

'I'm going to finish work when I should finish work. I've only got her for another five years. I'm not going to make the same mistake again.'

But she's with Bean. Helping with her photography project.

"What are you doing tomorrow?"

She laughed. "Walking through the woods? But bring Archie this time. You're not the only one who feels guilty."

24

No money in school budgets? Maybe I chose the wrong career...

Brady looked round the headteacher's room. "I don't like to use the word 'office,' Mr Brady. 'The headmasters office.' It has such negative overtones. Anyway, thank you for coming to see me."

Less than a year since he'd brought Ash to see the school. They'd listened to the head extol the virtues of the school – and explain that she was ready to retire.

Her office had been retired with her. Battered leather armchairs had given way to a low, black sofa along one wall, under a huge picture of Whitby. Clearly painted by one of the students, abstract but not so abstract you couldn't tell what it was. Sculptures on the windowsill. A desk that was simply a table, the obligatory minimalist Mac on top of it. Not a drawer or a filing cabinet in sight.

A room for talking, not working...

And here we are again.

Brady spread his hands. "Clearly this situation needs resolving, Mr Oswald."

Dark-haired, smiling, navy suit, royal blue tie, Martin Oswald looked like he'd stepped out of a building society advert. Earnest, eager-to-help, the sort of man who'd listen intently to your problems. And then the director shouted, 'Cut!' and the man in the suit explained that, regretfully, they'd exhausted all the options. 'A duty to our shareholders, other borrowers, procedures and policies in place...'

"I appreciate you must be busy. But – as you and Ashley must understand – this is a serious matter. Not just the physical violence, but I have read Miss Gibson's report. There appears to be a difference of opinion, to put it politely. Do you wish to say, anything, Mr Brady? Ashley?"

Brady turned to his daughter. "Just give me two minutes, Ash. Wait outside."

Ash looked questioningly at her father. Even more questioningly at Oswald. "Just do it, Ash," Brady said.

She stood up. Walked hesitantly to the door. Left Brady alone with Oswald.

"You're relying on Miss Gibson's report are you?" Brady said as Ash closed the door.

Oswald looked confused. "Why would I not rely on it? She's an experienced teacher. Head of year – "

I can't be bothered. I just can't be bothered to tiptoe through this crap...

"You've got an Ofsted inspection coming up, Mr Oswald."

"We have. But I don't see what this episode has to do with it."

Brady smiled innocently.

I'm going to look bloody foolish if Ruby hasn't delivered. But I haven't misjudged her. And I've two cards to play.

"What episode, Mr Oswald?"

The head looked even more confused. "The incident on Friday night. The reason Ashley had to be sent home. And... I must say, Mr Brady, in all my years as a head-teacher – and before that – I have never known a parent act in such a... such a cavalier manner."

"Well, there's a first time for everything, Mr Oswald. And the last two weeks has been the first time my daughter has been bullied. And she's been bullied by Shelley Clarke. As well you know."

Here we go. More bluff, bluster and bullshit. Kershaw's twin brother...

"You no doubt read the latest Ofsted report before your daughter came to the school, Mr Brady. We don't have a bullying problem. We neither condone it nor tolerate – "

"Because you don't record it. There wouldn't be a problem with knife crime if the police didn't record it. I don't know, maybe we should stop recording domestic abuse? And I had some spare time yesterday..."

Because it was hammering down all day so I couldn't go to May Beck. Because Frankie's mother tripped and broke her wrist. Because Rabbie Burns' best laid plans o' mice and men and coppers went spectacularly agley.

"...So I went into the office. Checked through our records. Maybe, Mr Oswald..." Brady smiled at the headmaster, "The police should stop recording pupils arrested outside school gates for selling cannabis?"

Brady watched the air, the certainty, the pomposity leak out of Martin Oswald. "That was a one-off. A total one-off. A pupil who was only at the school for six months."

Brady nodded. "I'm sure it was. And I'm sure Ofsted would see it that way. But..." He smiled again. "It's probably best not to risk it. Why don't you ask Ash to come back in, Mr Oswald? And Shelley Clarke as well? We're both busy men. Let's get this misunderstanding sorted out shall we?"

Oswald reached for his phone. Hesitated. Looked at Brady.

"I don't want special treatment, Mr Oswald. I'm not expecting you to make Ash head girl. I just want my daughter treated fairly. So I suggest you press nine. Or whatever number you need for the school secretary."

Oswald made the call. An uneasy silence settled between them. Brady let it lie there. Watched Oswald check his desk, look round his office.

...Desperate for some paperwork to hide in.

There was a tentative knock on the door. Shelley Clarke walked in first. Looking flustered. A white top, tracksuit bottoms. Someone who'd been dragged out of a PE lesson. Lank blonde hair, braces on her teeth, a bad complexion, slightly overweight...

'Fat freak' was a bit unkind, Ash.

...And the shadow of a black eye.

Ash glanced at Brady. An expression that said, 'I think

it's going to be alright but I've no idea how it's going to be alright.'

Trust me, sweetheart.

Oswald gestured at the settee. The two girls sat as far apart as it was possible to sit. Shelley glanced nervously at Brady. He smiled back.

Thanks, Ruby. I'm in your debt.

"Shelley," Oswald said. "This – as you may have guessed – is Mr Brady. Ashley's father. I'm trying to ascertain what happened on Friday night. On the hockey trip."

Shelley looked coolly back at the headmaster.

How many times have I seen that look? Challenge, defiance, the declaration of innocence. Inevitably followed by 'You can't prove it.' You're thirteen or fourteen, Shelley. It's not a look that ends well...

"Nothing happened."

Oswald shook his head. Squinted at Shelley. It was hard to tell whether he was more surprised by the words or the outright challenge to his authority.

"What did you say, Shelley?"

"Nothing happened, sir. I stopped to wish Ash luck in the hockey. She stood up to say the same to me. There was someone from another school behind me. I tripped over her foot and fell."

"And banged your eye?"

"Yes, sir. On the corner of a chair, sir."

Brady had to admire her. *Thieves, burglars, conmen... I've heard them all. You're right up there, Shelley.*

"Did you? And what do you say to that, Ashley?"

Ash nodded. "That's as I remember it, sir. Shelley and

I have always been good friends. Haven't we, Shell?" she said from the far end of the sofa.

"And what do you both say about Miss Gibson's report? About the reason Mr Brady drove ninety miles on Friday night? "

"If you'll allow me to interject, headmaster," Brady said. "We see it a lot in the police. A crowded room. You only see part of the picture. It's very difficult for us. Almost impossible. Mistakes are easy to make, even for the most seasoned observers. And witnesses – even reliable people like Shelley – realise afterwards that they've made mistakes."

Oswald stared at his open laptop. Looked up at the two girls. "So it would seem. Well as you're both such good friends, why don't you go back to your classes?"

Oswald watched the girls walk out. Looked at Brady across the table. "I'm not quite sure how you managed that, Mr Brady, but let me say – "

"No," Brady said. "There's nothing to say, Mr Oswald. There's nothing to report. No bullying, no fighting, no drugs being sold outside the school gates. And nothing to worry Ofsted about. I'm sure an intelligent man like you has read *The Seven Habits of Highly Effective People*. This is what the late Mr Covey would describe as a 'win/win,' isn't it?"

Oswald nodded. Let his gaze drift up to the ceiling. Brought it back to Brady.

"I have, Mr Brady. And you're clearly a man I can speak openly with. I've also heard the expression that it's better to have certain people inside the tent urinating out than outside... Well, you get my drift." He stood up and held his hand out. "Would you be willing to come and speak to some of our students? The older ones who are making career choices? I think they could learn a lot."

Brady smiled. Stood up and shook hands. "I'd be delighted, Mr Oswald. Just let me know a time. Anything I can do to help the school."

25

"Do you mind?" Mandy Jamieson gestured at her left breast.

"No," Brady said, "I don't mind at all. If you're OK with it."

There's a first time for everything...

"He's going to be like his dad is this one. Always hungry, always thirsty. Always bloody horny n' all but one accident is one too many."

She half turned away from Brady. Lifted the baby to her breast. Bent forward and kissed him on the forehead. Murmured, "I didn't mean it, sweetheart." Held the baby with one arm and put a cushion behind her back with the other. "What do you want to know?" she said, twisting her head towards him.

"Alice Simpson," Brady said. "But you guessed that. I'm sorry to be back asking questions after twenty years."

"You're not," Mandy said.

"Not what?"

"Not 'back asking questions.' No-one ever talked to

me. So you're the first. My best friend disappears and not a copper came near me. So ask away. And maybe you'll get better answers than they would have done all that time ago. There's a lot of time passed. I can see things more clearly now."

"How well did you know Alice?"

"How well do you know anyone when you're eleven? We were best friends. What my daughter calls 'bezzies.' Started little school together, went to big school together. Walked home together. But like I say, I can see it more clearly now. Alice was outgrowing me."

"How? In what way?"

"She was eleven going on nineteen. I was eleven going on twelve. Have you got a daughter?"

"Yes, I have. She's thirteen. And like you say, going on fourteen one day. Going on God knows what the next."

"So you know – ouch, you little scallywag, gently with Mummy. There's plenty, don't worry – you know what I'm talking about. Alice was growing up faster than me. She was confident, I was shy. We were best friends at eleven. By twelve she'd have found someone new. Someone older."

"What was she into? What did she like?"

Mandy laughed. "Alice? Anything that scared her. She was a real – I don't know, she'd be called an adrenalin junkie these days – but whatever we shouldn't do, Alice did. But it came easily to her. She was one of those girls... You know, no-one can climb that tree. Alice could. No-one's brave enough to do that. Alice was."

"Did she have any other close friends?"

"Everyone," Mandy said. "She was everyone's friend

was Alice. It's a girls' thing. There's always one girl in the class everyone wants to be friends with. That was Alice. But like I said, she was growing away from me. Growing away from everyone in our class."

"What did you do? When you weren't in school?"

"What did we do? Hung about mostly. Down on the seafront. Sat on the railings. Ate chips. Talked to boys. Ate more chips. Wondered why anyone came to Whitby for their holidays."

"So what teenage girls do?"

"Yeah. Teenage girls and girls that can't wait to be teenage girls."

I'm not getting anywhere here. She's not telling me anything I couldn't have guessed from speaking to Ruby. Or from talking to Ash. Teenagers' behaviour, human nature. Nothing changes...

"And Alice just sat on the railings with you?"

"Mostly. Sometimes she'd take herself off. Just walk across to another group of girls. She dared me to go with her one time. She just walks across. 'Hi, I'm Alice' she says. Five minutes later she's known them all her life."

"But no other close friends?"

"The other girl that disappeared."

"What?"

"Maybe. Like I said. No-one ever asked me." Mandy shifted in her chair. Turned to face him. "Bugger it, I can't talk to you like this. It's killing my neck. Sorry if I'm embarrassing you."

"No, you're fine. It's..."

I used to watch Grace feeding Ash. Just sit and watch them both...

"It's absolutely fine. And you're serious? You think she knew Becky?"

Mandy nodded. "Like I say, maybe. She had one friend she talked about. Honestly, I didn't know if it was true or if it was Alice in fantasy land. She called her Posh Spice. Said she went to a posh school. Said they used to go up to the graveyard together. St Mary's Church – you know, where all the Goths go now to have their photos taken."

"She didn't mention a name."

Mandy shook her head. "No, she thought Posh Spice was really clever. It's like, everyone in our class sort of looked up to Alice – like they wanted to be Alice. The way she spoke... Alice wanted to be this Posh Spice girl. Like she'd finally found someone as... As mad as her."

Don't jump to conclusions. Don't...

"So it wasn't necessarily Becky Kennedy? There's no proof?"

"Except... This is what I mean about looking back. After that other girl disappeared Alice was... She was different. Quieter. Not so confident any more. Not so sure of herself."

"Hi, sweetheart. Everything alright?"

Ash looked at him. Nodded. "Yes, Dad, thank you. An interesting day at school. Shelley Clarke appears to have appointed herself my bodyguard. Two or three teachers gave us suspicious looks and *very* wide berths. And Bellatrix Gibson waited until it started pouring down and then asked 'Miss Brady and Miss Clarke' if they'd mind moving the hockey goals to the other side of the pitch."

Brady laughed. "Right. I should probably apologise for that last one."

"You're fine," Ash said. "And Shelley likes to talk. She says Bellatrix is having an affair with Jonny Banks."

"Who's Jonny Banks?"

"The other PE teacher. Shelley says – "

"Stop it, Ash. You're a scurrilous gossip. I've got a question to ask you."

"Am I going to Bean's? No. Do I want fish and chips? Yes please."

"It's Monday. No-one has – "

"Does my stomach know what day of the week it is, Dad? Do I need less calories on a Monday? You've lost, Dad. What was the question?"

"Alright, answer me this. Then I'll go out into the cold and the dark. Remember to put some plates to warm. Do you have friends at other schools? Girls you've met in Whitby, say?"

Ash shrugged. "Friends? There are some girls I know. Cross-country, hockey. It's the same people every week. So I sort of know them. But they're not friends, no."

"Oh..."

"Why? Did you want me to have a friend? Does Bean not count any more? She's got a friend if that helps. I think she's at school in Scarborough. Do you want me to ask her?"

"No, no. How did she meet her?"

Another shrug. "I don't know. Photography maybe?

Bean says she's really good. Between you and me I think Bean's a bit jealous."

"So it happens. Thanks, sweetheart."

"Dad?"

"Yes, love?"

"Don't forget Archie when you're getting the fish and chips. He says he could manage some scraps."

26

For the third time in three weeks Brady parked the car in the entrance to the field. Walked across the road and knocked on Edmund Kennedy's front door.

Third time lucky. Maybe this time I'll get my questions answered.

Didn't have to wait long for it to be opened.

"Detective Inspector Brady. Come in. I'm still not sure... With the Professor being away..."

"Like I said on the phone, Morag, it's you I want to talk to."

...To get some background. To try and understand. Because you must have learned something. Overheard some conversations...

She led him through to the kitchen. Made coffee, pushed a plate of home-made biscuits towards him, invited him to sit at an old kitchen table overlooking the garden.

"No Dundee Cake?" Brady smiled.

She sighed. "Inspector Brady, let me be blunt. If Hell

exists it's a place where I make Dundee Cake every day.
But he's back on Friday, so I have no choice. And 'yes' is
the answer to your next question."

Brady laughed. "You know what it is then?"

Her hair was tied back. She was wearing a long
sleeved navy t-shirt, the sleeves pulled up to her elbows.
She looked brisk, business-like, organised.

And much less deferential when he's away...

"You were going to ask me if I enjoyed the breaks,"
she said in her soft Scottish accent. "Mid-week when he's
away in Leeds. Yes, I do. The house is mine. I bake, I
clean, I read, I do the accounts, I walk on the beach."

"Are you not lonely?"

Morag shook her head. "I am not lonely, no. I was an
only child, Inspector Brady. I was married for ten years.
We couldn't have children, sadly. Then... Ah well, it's an
old story. I'm sure you don't want to hear it."

"And you came down here? It's a long way from home.
You must have started some time after the Professor's
wife died?"

"Six months after poor Eilish. I did wonder at the
funeral how he would – "

"At the funeral?" Brady did his best not to sound
surprised. Failed hopelessly.

She looked at him. An expression which clearly said,
'didn't you know?'

"Of course. Why would I not be at my cousin's
funeral?"

Eilish. Morag. Two Scottish names. Hardly a coincidence.
How did I not work out there was some connection? Because I

saw her as a housekeeper. Because I wondered how she coped with him. Not how she came to be here...

"So the Professor asked you to come down?"

"No, I suggested it. He'd lost his daughter. Five years later he loses his wife. I didn't know him that well... but family is family. And my husband had left. The company I worked for had gone into liquidation. I needed... Today they'd say I needed some space. Time out. I wanted a break, a change of scene. A summer on the Yorkshire coast while Edmund sorted himself out seemed ideal."

"But you've been here ever since?"

She nodded. "I have. Three months became six months. Six months became a year. The beach in winter captured me. Eat a biscuit with your coffee, Inspector. It does me good to hear someone say 'thank you.'"

Brady looked at her. Raised his eyebrows. "Yes," she said. "He's difficult. Irascible to use an old-fashioned word. The trick is to stand your ground."

Like all bullies...

"And one day it became a formal arrangement?"

Are you sleeping with him? Why don't you come out and say it?

She nodded. "It is. We do have a formal arrangement. Which suits both of us. The university takes care of him for three days a week, I take care of him for four. And there's always some conference giving me a week or two's respite in the summer."

"Morag, I couldn't have some more coffee, could I?"

Because you've completely thrown me. Because I need some thinking time.

"Of course." She stood up to get the cafetiere. Was

interrupted by a knock on the door. Glanced at the clock. Picked up a Tupperware container from the worktop. "You'll excuse me a moment, Inspector."

Brady heard the door open. A man's voice. A dog's yelp that sounded almost like Archie. A conversation he didn't catch. The door closing. Morag came back without the container.

"I'm sorry. You wanted more coffee."

"If you don't mind. It's really good."

"I drink a lot. I'm a bit of a coffee snob. And me with a Presbyterian upbringing. It's almost certainly a sin."

She's his wife's cousin. She must have known the family. Stop wittering about bloody coffee and get this back on track...

"Morag, you obviously know about the bones we found. Rebecca..."

She nodded. "I do. I heard you talking. And news travels. Even to this remote outpost."

"So we have a body. The popular belief has always been that she was killed by a man named Norman Blake. He was convicted – "

"For the murder in Middlesbrough. I read about it."

Do I tell her the truth? That I have doubts? No.

"But never convicted for Becky's death. Or for Alice Simpson. Both cases are still open."

"And that's why you're here? You think you can find some evidence?"

Maybe not the evidence you think, but yes...

Brady smiled. "I'm a copper, Morag. I don't like unsolved cases. And the more background you can give me – "

"The more chance you have of closing the file." She nodded. Looked at him.

The same look Ruby gave me. Weighing me up. Making a judgement.

"You put me in a difficult position, Inspector. I am obviously obliged to answer your questions – "

"Your Presbyterian upbringing again?"

"Possibly. So ask your questions. But clearly I have a duty to Edmund. To his privacy. The confidence he has placed in me."

And to your life here, Morag. 'I bake, I clean, I read, I do the accounts, I walk on the beach.' Yes you do. And no, you're not sleeping with the Professor. Because that was your boyfriend at the door. A widower down in the village I'd guess. Whose Spaniel gives the same excited yelp Archie gives when he sees someone he knows...

"I appreciate that, Morag. But you must have known the family. Seen the children growing up? What was Rebecca like as a child?"

She shook her head. "Not really. They were down here. I lived in Aberdeen. My husband worked offshore. On the oil rigs. So maybe a wedding and a funeral. Eilish and I wrote letters. Real ones. With stamps on the envelope."

"Is there anything you remember about Becky? Even from those brief meetings? Anything Eilish said in her letters?"

"She was considerate, Inspector. She knew I couldn't have children, so she didn't say much – if anything – about her own. Nothing of consequence. What do I remember? A wedding. A pretty girl in a red dress. The funeral? She was older. Withdrawn. Funerals are not occasions for children."

"I don't suppose by any chance you have a photo, do you? Anything would be a help."

She stood up. "Of Rebecca? The honest answer is I don't know. When I... When I sold the house in Aberdeen I brought some stuff down here. But I'm not a sentimentalist, Inspector. Especially where that chapter of my life is concerned. Most of it went to the charity shop. Or into a skip. But I'll look for you."

She walked out of the kitchen. Brady heard the noise of her going upstairs. Looked around the kitchen. Neat. Well-ordered. An equally neat and well-ordered garden through the window. Raised beds for the vegetables. What looked like a summer house to the side.

A summer house? Or a workshop? 'I got the sculpture from my workshop. I did it. Maths and art, Mr Brady. Two sides of the same coin.'

And the chess set. I need to see the chess set again.

She was back. A faded photo album in her hand. "I found one," she said. "I don't know if it's much use to you. Another cousin's wedding."

She opened the album. Held it away from Brady as she turned the pages.

Doesn't want me to see all the blank pages? Her ex-husband?

Finally put the album down on the table.

The bride's family. Or the groom's. Two dozen smiling people in front of what had once been a Scottish castle and was now a hotel. 'We'll have the photos taken at the reception. Such a lovely setting.'

"The bride or the groom?" Brady said.

"The groom. Angus. They're divorced now."

There, on the front row. What is she? Seven? Eight? 'A pretty girl in a red dress.' Standing in front of her mother. Looking impatient to be off. To find a friend. Someone to chase round the gardens.

Morag was on the far left, standing with a dark haired man in a kilt.

Standing next to him but apart from him. The writing already on the wall...

Edmund Kennedy was halfway between Morag and the bride. The grey hair was darker, the beard younger, less impressive.

But you can sense the irritation. 'Why am I wasting my time?' 'What is a family wedding to me?'

Eilish was on his left, a tall, gangling teenager on his right.

"Do you see much of Eric?" Brady said. "That is Eric, I assume?"

"It is. And there – " Morag reached forward, pointed at a stooped figure on Eric's right. "That's Oswald, the Professor's father. You think Edmund is a force of nature. You should have met his father."

"Eric must be married now? With a family? Does he come up to visit? Surely the children would want to see their grandfather?"

Morag shook her head. "He's very busy. A lot of research work at the college."

'What does your son do now?'

'He stayed in Cambridge, Mr Brady. It is a difficult city to leave. Eric teaches.'

Eric teaches? Teachers don't do 'research work at the college.'

And teachers have long summer holidays. Surely, a grandad by the sea...

Brady didn't pursue it. Asked Morag if he could take a photo.

First Alice, now Rebecca. All I'm doing is taking photos...

Brady looked again at Rebecca. Blonde hair, a pale complexion.

Not blonde. What do they call it? Strawberry blonde?

Standing in front of her mother. Her father and brother to the side of her. All of them dark-haired...

'Do you miss her, Professor? Your only daughter?'

'Do I miss her? You may as well ask if I miss the dog we had when I was a child.'

Brady looked across the table at Morag.

Finally, for the first time in this case. Finally I stumble on the truth.

"Rebecca was adopted wasn't she?"

She shook her head. "I can't – "

"You can't give away family details? Not without speaking to the Professor? Of course you can't. But we can soon check. You haven't denied it, Morag. Children or no children, Eilish must have told you about it in the letters."

"He doted on the boy. Said he had a son and heir, that was all he wanted. Told Eilish she'd done her duty. And the birth had been difficult. She... There, Inspector Brady. I've said enough. What Eilish went through is no concern of yours."

You don't need to tell me, Morag. I can guess.

Brady stood up. "I've taken up enough of your time,

Morag. Thank you for everything you've told me. And for the biscuits. I've just one more question."

She looked at him warily. Nodded. "What might that be, Inspector?"

Brady smiled. "Nothing important. I just wondered if I could see the chess set again? The one in the other room."

She stood up. "You want to check if the pieces have moved?"

Brady laughed. "As if I could tell. I wasn't lying when I said I know the moves and not much more. Like the sculpture in the other room, it's beautiful. Did the Professor make it himself?"

She nodded. "A labour of love. You may have noticed, we don't have a television. I read in the evenings. He sits at his desk. Or disappears to his workshop."

She led the way into the drawing room. For the second time Michael Brady bent forward and picked up the Viking king. Felt the weight of it. Admired the craftsmanship. Looked closely at the king's face. At his braided beard.

No family resemblance in the wedding photo. But plenty in a chess piece...

"DAN, can you do something for me?"

"What's that, boss?"

"It's fifteen years ago, so you'll need to do a bit of digging. Becky Kennedy's mother – Eilish – died in a car crash. She went off the road. Up on the Moors – the bend, just as you're coming down the hill from Fylingdales."

"Fifteen years ago, boss? Will we still have the records?"

Brady nodded. "For an RTA? There'll be a paper record. Chances are it'll be stored off-site somewhere. Have a word with the traffic guys. Tell them you need it ASAP. Don't take 'no' for an answer."

27

Durham last week, almost to Harrogate this week. Brady shifted uneasily in the driver's seat. Wondered if it was time to change the car. Wondered how much the smell of wet dog would knock off the trade-in value...

A pre-war semi on the outskirts of the village. A row of six houses that looked like they belonged in a town rather than the West Yorkshire countryside.

Andy Boulding answered the door. "Paul just rang. Says he'll be about five minutes. Some problem at school."

Let's hope it's covered by the handbook...

Brady sipped his tea. "Thanks for this. And to answer your first question, we're still not sure when the inquest will be. To answer your second, yes, we've formally identified the remains you found. Rebecca Kennedy, who went missing twenty years ago. And if your third question is 'why do I need to see you again?' I'm trying to understand. Trying to see what happened up there."

Andy Boulding shook his head. "Poor lass. Alone up there. All that time. Paul says he's still embarrassed."

Brady nodded. "In the long run, he did her – everyone – a favour."

"Except the other family," Paul Jarvis said from the doorway. "Sorry I'm late. And I might have done one family a favour. Didn't I read two girls went missing around the same time? What about the other family?"

You're right. Ruby. A weekend's hope after twenty years and then it's taken away. The law has to take its course. And sometimes it leaves casualties by the roadside.

"You did," Brady said. "But for now I'd like to focus on Becky. Specifically, where she was found. And walkers..."

"There are walkers in Whitby, Mr Brady. Why us? Apart from us being the ones that found her?"

"Something you said. You've walked that route three or four times. You know it well. And you're experienced walkers. And good guys. My guess is you want to see justice done."

Paul Jarvis spread his hands, "Who doesn't? Like I said, I'm still embarrassed. Every time I go to the bathroom..."

Dog walker finds body. The headlines always focus on the body. The investigation. No-one thinks about the dog walker. Who can't set off for his early morning walk without thinking about it. Or in this case, go to the bathroom...

"Have you spoken to anyone?" Brady said. "It's not something I'm an expert on but it's a recognised condition. Traumatic grief."

Jarvis shook his head. "I was brought up... my dad

was old school. Get on with it. Stiff upper lip. Do your duty."

Brady nodded. "Mine too. But I think times have moved on. There's a psychologist I know. I'm sure she could recommend someone. Or start with your GP. But don't keep it all inside, Paul."

Jarvis nodded. "I'll see. Thanks for the advice."

"Or get back on the horse," Andy Boulding said. "Maybe that's the answer. Do the walk again. Straight past the Lilla Cross with nowt on our minds except blisters."

"Tell me about it," Brady said. "You've done the Lyke Wake Walk what? Three times? Four times?"

Andy nodded. "Yep. Three for me. Four for Paul. Or it would have been."

"Tell me," Brady said. "Why do people do it?"

They both laughed. "Why do we do it? Because we're mad buggers."

Where have I heard that before? Ruby. Talking about Des. 'He's a daft bugger. Goes to the Lake District. Chases other daft buggers up hills. Fell running or summat...'

"Or because we like being on the hills," Andy said. "Watching the sun coming up over the next ridge. And you're the only one seeing it. Then the mad buggers are the ones that are still in bed."

"How fit are you?" Brady said.

They looked at each other. "Serious answer?" Paul said. "Pretty fit. Not as fit as I was when I was younger. But fit enough. Fitter than most men my age. Hill walking is bloody good exercise, Mr Brady. Heart, muscle tone, mental health. I know it was walking that made me find that girl. And I take your point about talking to someone. But if I have problems, it's walking that'll cure them. Not some tablets that I'm on for the rest of my life."

"How much weight do you carry when you're walking?"

Jarvis shrugged. "It depends, doesn't it? Good rule of thumb is twenty per cent of your bodyweight if you're camping. Ten per cent if you're just out for the day. So say I'm eighty kilos. The maths is simple."

Becky weighed forty-five kilos. So fifty percent of the killer's body weight. Maybe more. So he didn't carry her far. But we knew that already...

"Why the Lyke Wake Walk then?"

"Well number one, it's on our doorstep. Number two, it tests you. People say 'forty miles in twenty-four hours. Less than two miles an hour.' But you're up and down hills like a bloody yo-yo in the first ten miles. Then there's the weather. Get on top of the Moors and you can go through four seasons in half an hour. Then it gets boggy. Somewhere along the way you have to sleep. And then you get to the Lilla Cross. And it's all downhill. Or it used to be."

"Physical and psychological," Andy said. "You should do it, Mr Brady. You need to do it to understand it."

Brady laughed. "No, I'm too old to start."

"You're never too old to do it. Plenty of people in their eighties have walked it. One bloke's done it more than two hundred times. His dog's getting a bit knackered mind you..."

This time they all laughed. Finished their tea. Brady realised he'd wasted his time.

Nothing I couldn't have learned online. Or worked out for myself. One last question...

"What's the history?" Brady said. "Lilla's been up there for fifteen hundred years so presumably people have been walking the route for a long time?"

"The official walk goes back about sixty years. There's a Lyke Wake club," Paul said. "Lyke means corpse. And then the Wake. That's where the name comes from. Supposedly they carried the monks' bodies across the Moors. You get that in a few places. You'll find a few Corpse Roads on the Ordnance Survey maps."

"Why? Why carry a body across the Moors?"

"Like I said, the monks. They wanted to be buried at Whitby Abbey I suppose."

"But the walk ends at Ravenscar..."

Andy Boulding shrugged. "They didn't have Sat Nav. Who knows? But it's a good story. And people do it now. Carry a coffin across the Moors for charity. Some undertakers did it a few years back. Push a bed, carry a coffin. What's the difference?"

"Boss?"

"What can I do for you, Dan?"

"That report you asked me to get?" Dan Keillor passed Brady a Manila file, a case number stamped on the front of it, half a brown ring where someone had rested a coffee cup 15 years ago. Brady flipped it open.

Like I said to Dan. Coming down the road from Fylingdales.

Where Frankie and I walked the other day...

'We estimate the car was travelling at between 50mph and 60mph when it hit the bridge. The vehicle sustained considerable damage from the collision. One witness reported that the vehicle overtook her travelling 'like a bat out of hell.' The witness said that she did not see brake lights come on as the vehicle travelled down the hill.'

Where she'd have to slow down – slow down drastically – to go right and left across the bridge...

'The witness put the time of the crash at 19:07. PCs James and Dallas arrived at 19:19. Fire and Rescue arrived at 19:25. The sole occupant of the car – Dr Eilish Kennedy – was pronounced dead at the scene. Subsequent examination of the vehicle suggested that Dr Kennedy was not wearing a seat belt at the time of the crash.'

Going too fast. Far too fast. Failing to brake. Not wearing a seat belt. None of that proves anything...

Brady reached forward. Tapped 'committing suicide by car crash' into Google. Found a lot of speculation. And then a report from Finland. Started to read.

Nearly six per cent could be classed as suicides. Half that in the official figures. One suicide in a hundred is a driver suicide. Fifty per cent by men between fifteen and thirty-four.

'The victims had often suffered from life-event stress, mental disorders and had alcohol misuse problems. The cases were usually head-on collisions between two vehicles with a large weight disparity.'

Not a truck, a bridge. But the same result. 'Life-event stress.' Yep, I'd say your teenage daughter disappearing constitutes 'life-event stress...' Especially if you suspect your husband is the reason she disappeared.

28

Hair pinned up. Jeans and a sweatshirt. No pale lilac dress today, no ragu simmering slowly on the hob. But the second time I've been to her flat in a week...

"Thank you," Brady said. "I know you're busy. How is she today?"

Frankie shrugged. "The same as every day. I tell you, Mike, how people do this on a long-term basis – full-time carer with no end in sight except someone dying – I have no idea. Not a clue. Anyway, you're not here to listen to my woes."

She looked at him. "And you've some news to tell me. I saw it before. When you finally worked out who killed Gina. You have a glint in your eye, Detective Chief Inspector. Your body language has changed. You're suddenly pro-active, not reactive. You're more animated."

"Thanks, Frankie. Remind me not to play poker with you."

"Late night game in the police canteen? It wouldn't be the first time. Anyway, you want coffee? And I've some week-old ragu in the freezer if you're hungry. Some bloke turned up. Took one look at my cooking and made an excuse..."

Brady laughed. "No, I'm good. I'm fine thanks, Frankie. And that's not fair."

"Did you sort it out?"

"I did sort it out. Except that I'm now in debt to Ruby. I owe her one."

"Over and above finding Alice?"

"Yes and no. I told her to get Shelley under control."

But it was my daughter. And I'd do it again...

Brady looked round the flat. A wooden floor, two matching rugs, Frankie sitting on a leather sofa.

One leg tucked under her. Like the night she came round to tell me about Gina Foster...

A tapestry on the pale peach wall, the window looking out over the harbour.

"This is a lovely flat, Frankie."

"Don't tell me you're going all *Ideal Home* on me, Mike."

"I'm not. I haven't even thought about it. Ash knows exactly what she wants. She'll give the builder explicit instructions. I haven't got any further than white with a hint of blue. Seascape or whatever it's called."

Frankie laughed. "Not off Whitby in the winter. Grey with a hint of greyer. You have a theory to tell me..."

Brady nodded. "I do. It ticks all the boxes. But tell me if I've gone mad."

"You're a copper. A copper with a law degree. You could be earning three times what you earn *and* sitting in a nice warm office. No need to fight Jimmy Gorse on the end of the pier. No need to listen to Kershaw's endless bullshit. Of course you're mad."

"OK. Point taken. But hear me out. A child is murdered. Who's the most likely killer?"

"A parent. We both know that."

"Right. More so when the child is younger but still… the best starting point we have. Who do you put your money on, Frankie? A random stranger or a parent? A parent. Where was Becky Kennedy last seen? Getting off the bus. Walking down the lane that led to her house. Have you seen that lane?"

Frankie nodded. "I know it, yes. And if I didn't then all the lanes off the Moors road are the same."

"You don't go there by chance, Frankie. You simply don't. So it's not a random killer. Or are we suggesting a stranger has followed Becky all the way from Whitby? The only way he can do that is on the bus."

Frankie shook her head. "No. Supposing he follows the bus? He's in a car. She's walking down the lane. That's plausible."

"But then we're back to square one. He's got her in the car somehow. He's killed her. He has to keep the body. Store it. Take the body up to the Moors. We're right back where we started. How did he kill her? How long does he keep the body? Where does he keep it? Why Becky? Why bury her where he buried her?"

"And you're saying her parents answer all those questions?"

"Parent. Singular. I'm saying Edmund Kennedy killed her. Buried her on the Moors. Forced his wife to keep quiet. Five years later the strain, the constant bullying, is too much for her. She unclips her seat belt and drives into a bridge at sixty miles an hour."

Frankie stood up. Walked into the kitchen. "I'm going to make you a coffee," she said. "I've bought a new machine. You're a policeman, so I'll confess. I've spent some of my mother's attendance allowance on a Gaggia. So I'm my own barista. Whitby's answer to Billy No Mates. Frankie One Coffee. Or Frankie far-more-coffee-than-she-should-drink."

"But it tastes good?"

"Yes. And it makes all the right coffee machine noises. Soothing. My equivalent of being in the womb. So I'll make some..."

Brady smiled at her. "Do that. And I'll try and convince you."

"Becky gets off the bus," Brady said, coffee in hand. "She walks home. There is no random stranger. No Norman Blake lying in wait. In a car or otherwise. She goes home, she's killed."

"How?"

"I don't know."

"Why?"

"I don't know."

Frankie nodded. "OK. As foreman of the jury I'm not *quite* convinced. Not yet. Carry on."

"I was out at the house yesterday."

"I thought you said Kennedy wasn't there through the week?"

"He isn't. That's why I went. I wanted to talk to

Morag."

"The housekeeper?"

"No, not just the housekeeper. I swear to God, Frankie, I get more stupid with every year that passes. His wife's called – was called – Eilish, his housekeeper's called Morag. Two traditional Scottish names. They're cousins." Brady shook his head. "I go into that B&B. Then I see Ruby. I make the connection. This time all I see is bloody Dundee Cake and Kennedy's behaviour."

"Let me get this straight. His wife dies. Her cousin turns up as housekeeper?"

"Not originally. She comes to help out. 'Just for three months until Edmund sorts himself out.' Then three months become six months, six months become a year..."

"And she's never gone back?"

"No. She said her husband left her. No children. What has she got to go back for? She told me she fell in love with the beach. 'The beach in winter captured me.' And one day she meets a lonely widower who's walking his dog... Anyway, that's not the main thing."

"So what is?"

"Rebecca was adopted."

"You're sure?"

"I'm certain. I asked Morag if she had a picture. There she was, a blonde seven year old with her dark haired parents and an equally dark haired brother. Morag didn't deny it. I had Dan Keillor check the records this afternoon. Adopted when she was two years old."

"Which explains – "

"Which explains a lot. Why Kennedy was so callous.

Something else I should have noticed. He always called her Rebecca. Never 'Becky.' Never 'my daughter' or 'our daughter.' I suspect his wife persuaded him. Morag said she'd had a hard time with the birth – maybe Eilish couldn't have any more children – but she wanted a daughter."

"And he didn't?"

"Morag told me that Eilish had 'done her duty.' She'd given him a son and an heir. Those were the words she used."

"That seems... I don't know. Not so much misogynistic as... I think 'creepy' is the word I'm looking for. Medieval. But it doesn't make him a killer."

Brady stood up and walked over to the window. Looked out over the harbour.

How long until Norman Blake turns up with his lucky fishing rod in his hand? Not long. I have to find the killer. And this is the only theory that fits...

He was conscious of Frankie standing next to him. She reached up. Put her hand on his shoulder. "This one is getting to you isn't it?"

Brady nodded. "You want an honest answer? Yes. It's not just the girls. Becky and Alice. There's a guy in jail who I think is innocent. Who's the copper that was prepared to let Blake piss himself to get a confession? Alan bloody Kershaw – who casually asks me, 'How's it going, Mike?' And there's being in debt to Ruby. You want me to be completely honest? Right now I feel like an incompetent father and an even more incompetent copper."

"Come on then, Mike. Let's get to the bottom of it."

She turned. Walked back to the sofa. Brady watched her.

Hair pinned up. Two stray strands escaping...

Remembered her tongue, darting and dancing across his. Saw her slowly, deliberately, undo the buttons on her shirt. Saw it fall open.

Remembered hearing Ash's key in the front door.

Concentrate on the bloody case...

"Mike?"

"Sorry, Frankie, I was... Sorry, like you said, it's getting to me."

"Tell me the rest of your theory, Mike. Becky got off the bus. Walked home. Her father's murdered her. Persuaded – "

"*Forced* his wife to keep quiet. Coercive control, Frankie. Threats, intimidation."

Frankie shook her head. "After he's killed their daughter? Come on, Mike..."

Brady was insistent. "I've seen him, Frankie. He's not just a bully, he's... manipulative. Every conversation is an exercise in proving he's more intelligent than you. That you can't keep up with him."

"So you're saying he killed her – for whatever reason – and then buried her on the Moors? Carried her up there in a backpack? You're still not answering the basic questions, Mike. Why there?"

Brady stood up again. Walked over to the window for a second time.

Why am I doing this? Staring out of the window? Because what I'm going to say next is so far-fetched that I daren't look at her when I say it.

"I don't know why there. And I don't think he used a backpack either," Brady said quietly, still with his back towards her. "He used a coffin. And he carried it with his son."

He turned round. Finally looked at her.

"You understand what you're saying, Mike? And you know who his son is? Eric Kennedy?"

"I Googled him. He's a Cambridge professor. Emmanuel College."

"Mike, he's not just a professor, he's *the* professor. What Stephen Hawking is to Physics, he is to Maths. And more. He's... he's not a genius, he's whatever comes after genius. And you're suggesting he went hiking across the Moors carrying his dead sister in a coffin?" She shook her head. "I'm not going to laugh because – whatever you might think – you're a bloody brilliant copper. But no, Mike. Just no."

Brady did laugh. "A brilliant copper? I wish I was, Frankie. But supposing the son *is* involved? Supposing Eric murdered her? How old is he when she's killed? Twenty? Still at university."

"So now you're saying the father is protecting the son? And that's why the wife keeps quiet? Alright, Mike, it's slightly more credible, I grant you that. But where's Alice in all this?"

"She knew Becky. I saw one of her old schoolfriends. Someone the police never bothered with twenty years ago. She said Alice had a friend 'at a posh school.' She called her Posh Spice. Looked up to her. Admired her."

"So you're saying Becky and Alice did something – saw something, heard something maybe – and that was enough to get Becky killed? And the same for Alice a month later?"

"What I'm saying, Frankie, is that it's the *only* theory that fits the facts. The schoolfriend said Alice was changed after Becky died. Maybe she doesn't know what's happened to Becky. Maybe she's worked out what happened. Maybe she even goes out to Kennedy's house?"

Frankie shook her head. "Forget Alice for a minute. Go back to the coffin. This is something to do with the Lyke Wake Walk?"

"Yes. I went to see the two guys that found her. They were telling me about a group of undertakers that did it. Carried a coffin to raise money for charity. I've Googled it – "

Frankie laughed. "Is this official policy now, Mike? Google has replaced police records?"

"I'm serious. Where's the one place in the world – outside a funeral – you can carry a coffin and seem normal? The Lyke Wake Walk. 'Afternoon, we're doing it for charity.'"

"So Edmund Kennedy – who's what, about forty at this point?"

"Slightly older. But still fit. And he's a big guy."

"Edmund Kennedy and the man who's going to make Stephen Hawking seem average carry a coffin across the North York Moors? With Becky in it? What else is in there, Mike? A spade? A tent? Some cheese and tomato sandwiches?"

"So give me another theory, Frankie."

"Elvis? Martians? I understand what you're saying,

Mike – and I understand how much you want to solve this – but you're putting two and two together and making five. Not five, fifteen. And we're starting to argue." She paused. Looked at him. "Sit down. You're like a caged animal. Sit down and let me ask you one simple question."

"What's that?"

"Where does Kennedy get a coffin from? Last time I looked – "

Brady held his hand up. "Don't. I know what you're going to say. Sainsbury's didn't have them in stock. He made it, Frankie. He's got a workshop. Tools. He carves. You're not telling me he couldn't make a simple coffin. What is it? Six? Eight pieces of wood? And cheap wood would decay quickly. There'd be no trace of it."

"Nails? Screws?"

"Wooden dowels."

She shook her head again. "No, Mike. It's..." Frankie stood up, faced him. "Look, Mike, I want this solving as much as you do. If you can find a way to nail that prick Kershaw while you're doing it so much the better. But listen to me. Four months' time and I'm going to be calling you 'boss' again. Maybe I shouldn't say this. But I'm going to say it while I'm your friend. You're wrong. You've spoken to Morag, you've spoken to Alice's best friend, you've spoken to the two walkers. And you've come up with this theory. And... I don't know how to put it into words, Mike." She paused for breath. "I do know how to put it into words. But I don't want you to walk out. And I don't want you to make a fool of yourself."

"So say it, Frankie."

She looked straight at him. "You're up your own arse, Detective Chief Inspector Brady."

Brady laughed. "Thank you, Frankie. But I wish you'd say what you think. Stop sitting on the fence..."

"Sorry. But cast your mind back, Mike. Three months ago, four months ago. We're in your house. I've come round to tell you that Gina Foster is Gina Kirk. We *know* we've found the answer. It feels right. It *is* right."

"And this doesn't?"

Maybe she is right. But it's all I've got. So I have to run with it.

"Maybe you're right, Frankie. But Blake's coming out of jail. He's coming to Whitby. Ruby and her family will be waiting. And the only thing that's going to stop them is me finding the killer."

FRANKIE PICKED up the coffee cups. Walked into the kitchen. Turned the machine on again.

She's right. It is comforting. Or maybe just having someone around is comforting...

"What's next?" she said from the kitchen. "What are you going to do?"

Brady stood up. Walked across and stood in the doorway. "What else can I do? I've got one theory, I've got to go with it."

"So you're going back to see Kennedy? Ask him if he carried her up onto the Moors? Stripped her naked before he buried her? Christ, Mike, I can't believe anyone would do that."

"Neither can I, Frankie. Neither could any rational

person. But we're coppers. We've seen it before. And it's all I've got. But no, I'm not going to see Kennedy. Not that one anyway."

"So what *are* you going to do?"

"I'm going to Cambridge. I'm going to see Eric."

"On a whim? Supposing he's not there?"

Brady shook his head. "I did think of that. Not forewarned is not forearmed – or whatever the saying is. And if it had been Leeds I might have risked it. But it's two hundred miles. And Becky Kennedy isn't the only file on my desk."

"So you're going to ring?"

"I am. And I'm going to bet that simply saying who I am will be enough."

"He'll want to know what you know?"

"I think so. More than think so. And the more willing he is to see me..."

"The more guilty he is?"

"Something like that."

"Can I give you something to think about?" Frankie said. "Something different? While you're trying to remember where the speed cameras are on the A1?"

"Of course you can."

"Supposing we've got this totally wrong, Mike? Supposing it's the other way round?"

"How?"

"The assumption we're making – the assumption everyone has made for twenty years – is that Alice was killed because of Becky. Either the killer got a taste for it and picked Alice at random – "

"Or he killed Alice because of what she knew. *Kennedy* killed Alice because of what she knew."

"Supposing it's the other way round, Mike? Supposing Alice was the target?"

"I thought about that, Frankie. I even discussed it with Archie on the beach yesterday morning. But I just don't see how that works. Alice disappears a month after Becky."

Yes, I thought about it. And a two hundred mile drive? Four hours. Four-and-a-half. This case is all I'll think about...

Brady stood up. "Thanks for everything, Frankie. I need to collect Ash. But thank you. I really appreciate it."

She put her hand on his arm. "Drive carefully. And revise your maths. You want to make a good impression. Drop quadratic equations into the conversation."

Brady laughed. "What's a quadratic equation? But don't worry. I'll do some homework."

29

Homework? A slight exaggeration. One phone call.

Brady listened to the clicks as the call pinged its way round the world to be answered 20 miles up the coast.

Or maybe not.

Is that the sea I can hear? It sounds slightly more tropical than Saltburn...

"Detective Chief Inspector Brady. How are you? What is it? Four months? Five months since we spoke?"

"Four, maybe?"

"Marko Vrukić. What did I say to you? 'He who sups with the Devil must use a long spoon. He who sups with Marko Vrukić must use a *very* long spoon. Attached to the end of a very long stick.' It seems you managed to do that, Michael. I congratulate you."

"Thank you. I – "

"You need my services again. You need me to rifle through a virtual filing cabinet for you. Whose dirty secrets have washed up on Whitby's beaches this morning?"

"It's not specifically information. It's background. I'm going to see someone. I'd like – "

What the hell is that noise? It sounds like water lapping against a boat.

"– Am I allowed to ask where you are, Mozart? All I can hear is the sound of a tropical island."

Mozart laughed. "That's because I *am* on a tropical island, Michael. A working holiday. My client has some secrets. He flew me out to make sure they stay secret. And that – "

"That's as much as you're going to tell me."

"It is. And it's warmer than Whitby. But you could have guessed that. What can I do for you?"

"Like I said, it's background. Someone I'm going to see. Someone who I should be able to find info about online. But... there's just a lot less than there should be. Or it seems that way."

"So your question is do I have a spare hour or two for research?"

"Essentially, yes."

"I suppose I could postpone my snorkelling for someone I now consider a friend. Who is it, Michael?"

"He's a professor. A maths professor at Cambridge. Eric Kennedy."

There was silence. Broken by the noise of the ocean. The cry of a seabird.

Softer, gentler than Whitby's seagulls...

"No," Mozart said. "I'm sorry, Michael. Eric Kennedy? No."

"You can't do it?"

The sigh was audible down the phone.

Not exasperation. Regret.

"It's not that I can't do it, Michael. I *won't* do it. Even for someone – as I just said – I now consider a friend as well as a client. Professionally... It's just somewhere I can't and won't go."

Don't push him. Don't ask for a reason.

"OK, I respect that. Thank you for being honest with me. Enjoy your break."

"I will. Thank you. I'll be back in a month. In time for spring. You should come to dinner."

"I'd like that. Thank you."

Not that my lounge will ever look as elegant as yours...

"Enjoy Cambridge, Michael."

Brady pressed the red button. Ended the call.

'It's somewhere I can't and won't go.' Just saying that tells me something. And 'Enjoy Cambridge.' Was that information as well? Does Mozart know Eric Kennedy?

30

'You have reached your destination.'

"Thanks very much," Brady said out loud. He wound the window down, reached out and took a ticket for the car park. Glanced at the clock.

Why? Just why? Collect Ash from Bean's and I can barely get there on time. Drive from Whitby to Cambridge and I'm an hour early...

He found a space and parked the car. Walked down the stairs and out through John Lewis. Fleetingly wondered how much shopping he'd need to do for the new house. Saw the entrance to Emmanuel College diagonally across the road. Crossed St Andrew's Street, turned left instead of right and found a café. Drank a flat white. Tried to work out what he was going to say. Accepted that he had no idea.

Play it by ear. As usual...

. . .

HE WALKED SLOWLY BACK to the College. Past the students' bikes chained to the College railings. Presented himself at the porters' lodge. Wood panelling, pigeon holes lining one wall, a square clock above the fireplace, old college photos on the wall. A sense of history you could touch.

Three men in dark jackets, white shirts, black ties.

The latest in a long line.

'Whatever it is, we've seen it before. Murdered his sister? Didn't one of the old Masters do that? Seventeen something...'

"My name's Michael Brady. I'm here to see Professor Kennedy. Eleven o'clock."

"He's expecting you is he, sir?"

The accent was more East End of London than he'd expected.

"He is."

One of the porters nodded. "Give him a ring will you, Dave? Tell him we're on our way." He lifted a flap on the front desk. "If you'll come with me, sir. I'll take you up. From the Government are you, sir?"

THE PORTER LED the way up the stairs to the first floor. More wood panelling. Worn stairs. Walked ten paces along a corridor and knocked on a door, waited a respectful twenty seconds and opened it.

Study? Office? What will it be?

It was neither. A room, bigger than most people's lounge. Crossed rowing oars above the fireplace, tipped with navy and pink.

The college colours?

A battered leather Chesterfield, two leather

armchairs facing it separated by a coffee table. The floor covered in an assortment of rugs. A trolley with a kettle, cups, tea and coffee. The inevitable bookshelves.

But none of his father's chaos. Someone who doesn't shout for help when he needs to find something...

Eric Kennedy had his back to Brady. Sitting at a surprisingly modern desk in front of the window. Two computer screens covered in what looked like code. A view out across the immaculate lawn to the College clock tower.

"Thank you, George. One minute, Mr Brady."

He minimised the screens, turned to face Brady.

Black glasses, a mop of dark hair that looked like it was brushed with his fingers. A vaguely worried expression.

Tom Baker in 'Doctor Who.' But with glasses.

He was wearing a cricket jumper. A navy scarf with two pink stripes round his neck.

Definitely the College colours.

He ran both hands through his hair. Blinked and shook his head.

Stood up. The tall, gangling teenager from Morag's photo even taller.

Didn't make eye contact. Spoke to someone to Brady's left.

...And standing two yards behind me.

"Mr Brady. I've been expecting you. You or someone like you. Ten years? Fifteen?"

No point in small talk then. I needn't have paid for so long in the car park...

"You know why I'm here then, Professor Kennedy?"

"A policeman from Whitby? My sister's death. What other reason could there be?"

None of the bombast, the bullying of his father. Simple logic...

"Where would you like to start, Professor?"

"Where would *I* like to start? My understanding is that you ask the questions, Mr Brady."

His hand gestures don't fit what he's saying. Exaggerated, random gestures. Like he's weaving a spell. Like I'm speaking to a ridiculously intelligent wizard...

"I asked your father a hundred questions, Professor. And I got nowhere. I don't want to waste your time. Why don't you just tell me what happened?"

"What do you want to know?"

Still talking to the person behind me. He's got children. How does he relate to them if he can't look at them?

"I'd like to know how she died. Why your father buried her on the Moors. I've a hundred other questions – "

"But those two will do to start with?"

"Yes."

"Good. That's good. I used to interview students, Mr Brady. Admissions, every December. We take about one in four, one in five of the students who apply to us. We're not looking for brains. You don't come for an interview at Emmanuel unless you have *some* brains. We're looking for an ability to learn. To be stretched. If you like, to ask the right questions. As you've done."

So ask the question...

"How did Rebecca die, Professor?"

Brady saw the effort it took. Eric Kennedy dragged his

eyes away from the other person. Forced himself to look at Brady.

"I killed her," he said.

"*You* killed her?"

"Yes."

How many times have people confessed to me? 'I killed her, but...' 'I didn't mean to...'

Never this. A simple, straightforward confession.

"What happened?" Brady said.

This is madness. A professor. Sitting here in his study. Wearing a cricket jumper. Cheerfully telling me that he killed his sister. Not cheerfully. But with no hint of remorse. How the hell am I going to describe this to Frankie?

Eric Kennedy put his head on one side. Went back to speaking to the person behind Brady.

"Drugs. We had a pharma party. Just the two of us."

"A pharma party?"

Eric Kennedy spoke in a flat monotone.

"Pharma party. Pill party. Fruit salad party. I lived in a house round the corner." He waved a hand at the window. "Park Terrace. Seven of us. So the rules were simple. We each had to get hold of three prescription drugs. Tablets. We threw them into a bowl. So twenty-one tablets. You took three at random. Any three from twenty-one. One thousand, three hundred and thirty different combinations. Washed them down with alcohol. Cheap vodka from Sainsbury's. The results were often spec-tacular."

"And you did that at home? With your sister?"

"Only ten tablets. Far fewer combinations, obviously. Being at home in Whitby when you've been in

Cambridge... We had an electrical engineer in the house. A computer scientist. We built our own internet, amused ourselves by hacking into Government databases. Some students watch football, we read classified FBI files. Where was I? Whitby. It wasn't just boring. It was survival. A challenge to survive."

"So to relieve the boredom you had your own pharma party. And you had it with Becky?"

"She was curious. Adventurous. Wild. Wanted to take risks," Eric Kennedy said. "And she died."

Did you call an ambulance? Try and revive her? What happened when your parents came home? What do I ask him next?

"Why didn't you call an ambulance? Try and save her?"

"I was incapable of doing anything. My own combination of pills... I passed out. My parents came home and found me unconscious. And my sister dead. A bit of a mess, you might say..."

"But surely then... Then they'd have phoned the ambulance? The police?"

Eric Kennedy shook his head. "Why? What could they do? Revive her? You've met my father, Mr Brady. He made a decision. For my father an entirely logical decision. What he believes to this day was a completely logical decision."

"And that decision was to take Becky up on the Moors and bury her? How can that possibly be a logical decision?"

Brady told himself to keep calm. Completely failed.

"For Christ's sake, Professor Kennedy, how can

burying her be logical? How the hell can walking two miles with your dead daughter in a backpack be anything other than the decision of a madman?"

"Mad? No. Different? Yes. Eccentric by conventional standards? Quite obviously. But mad? No, my father wouldn't see himself as mad."

Brady looked down. Looked back up at Eric Kennedy. Tried to make eye contact with a man who wouldn't make eye contact with him. Shook his head. "As your father has no doubt told you, Professor, I'm just a simple policeman. Explain it to me will you? How does wasting police time, obstructing the course of justice, letting the blame fall on an innocent man... How does that make it a logical decision? Please, Professor, in simple words, tell me."

Because I don't have a bloody clue. Because I've tracked down killers, I've arrested them and I've interviewed them. And not one of them has ever told me it was a logical decision.

Kennedy spread his hands wide.

Finally, a gesture that ties in with what he's saying.

"Two wrongs don't make a right?" Kennedy said. "No. The greatest good of the greatest number."

"I'm sorry, I don't follow you."

"My sister was dead, Mr Brady. That was obvious. I had killed her. Equally obvious. Not deliberately, but I was responsible. My sister no longer had a life. I did. So my father made the logical decision. Nothing could be done for my sister, my life could still be saved. I was in my final year." Another wave at the window. "Here, as you know. My doctorate studies were already arranged. It was obvious that I had... talents, abilities. Possession of drugs.

Causing Rebecca's death. What was the point of me going to jail when I had so much to offer the world?"

"So that was it? A simple transaction? What about the police officers who spent time investigating the case? The local people who were questioned? Who lived in fear. The blame falling on someone else? And for God's sake, what about your mother?"

Brady stood up. Looked past Eric Kennedy and out of the window, across the perfect lawn to the clock tower.

"And killing Alice Simpson," he said. "That was an entirely logical decision was it? That was your father, I assume?"

Kennedy forced himself to look at Brady for a second time. Looked completely baffled.

"Who is Alice Simpson?"

A wizard? I'm in some sort of 'Alice in Wonderland' story. 'Killing people is fine as long as it's logical.' Forgetting who you've killed – who your father has killed – that's fine as well.

"Surely you don't need me to tell you that?"

Eric Kennedy nodded. "I do, Mr Brady. As you've no doubt guessed, I am just as far along the autistic spectrum as my father. I can tell you the position of all the chess pieces on the board when I first beat my father – he's cheated by the way. His position was far worse than the board shows. I'd taken his bishop as well – but I cannot remember names. My wife is called Rachel. My children are Isaac and Sophia. My wife's parents? My children's teachers? Please, enlighten me. I don't have a clue."

"Alice Simpson was the girl who disappeared a month

after your sister died. The Whitby girl. Your father murdered her. Buried her body somewhere."

Eric Kennedy frowned. Forced himself to look at Brady for a third time.

"Why would he do that? He's not a murderer. It's not... It's not logical, Mr Brady."

Is he telling me the truth? He can't be.

"It's entirely logical, Professor. If your father was prepared to bury your sister on the Moors to protect you – because you had so much to offer – then killing a girl from a council estate who somehow found out what had happened... That must have been a simple decision to make. After all, what did Alice Simpson have to offer the world? Your father said it to me. Talking about someone else. 'A card of a very low order.' What was Alice Simpson? The two of clubs? Nothing compared to you. The ace of hearts he'd do anything to protect."

"You're wrong," Kennedy said. "I don't know what else to say to you. Yes, I was responsible for Rebecca's death. Yes, my father took the decision... That we'd deal with it ourselves. But Alice Simpson? I had nothing to do with that. Neither did my father. You've wasted your time, Mr Brady."

He's telling me the truth. The bastard is telling me the truth.

Brady felt himself drowning. Clutched at the only straw he could cling on to.

"You realise, Professor... Irrespective of what you say about Alice Simpson... You realise what you've told me means you and your father have committed a criminal offence? Several criminal offences. Obstruction of justice, wasting police time. Preventing a lawful burial. It doesn't matter who you are, Professor. No-one is above the law. And – "

Bloody hell, I sound like Dixon of Dock Green.

"The law must take its course."

"No," Eric Kennedy said.

What the hell is it with these people? First Mozart, now this one. He can't say 'no.'

"Professor, I'm not sure you've understood what I've said. You – and your father – have committed a series of criminal offences. You're going to be arrested. Questioned. Almost certainly charged. Both of you. The fact that it's twenty years ago doesn't make it any less serious. I'm sorry, but as I said – "

"The law must take its course?"

"Yes."

"No, Mr Brady. The law must not take its course. It won't." He glanced at his watch. "And you'd know why by now. But it seems the Cambridge traffic has got in the way."

BRADY STARED AT HIM. "PROFESSOR, YOU – "

There were two sharp knocks on the door. It opened immediately. Brady turned, saw a man of his own age. Fair hair, a neatly trimmed beard. Freshly pressed jeans, a pale blue button down shirt, a navy jacket. Six foot maybe, an open, smiling face. But eyes that were wary. That had seen their share of troubles.

Out of the combat zone and into a catalogue for upmarket

clothes. Blazers for three hundred quid. But a man who could slip back into combat fatigues tomorrow.

He held his hand out. Smiled again. "Michael Brady. Good to meet you. I'm Simon Butler."

An expensive accent. A man used to giving orders. A man I've seen before? I don't know...

Brady shook hands. "I wasn't expecting company, Mr Butler."

"Simon. We're the same age. Give or take a few months. And... Let's not waste time. You can work with me or you can work against me, Mike. I strongly advise the former."

Brady glanced across at Eric Kennedy. The lines of code were back on his computer screen. He'd lost interest in the policeman from Whitby.

31

"Walk with me, Mike."

Simon Butler led the way back downstairs. "One minute."

Brady saw him disappear into the porters' lodge. Heard him say, "Thanks, George, I owe you one." Saw him reappear with two takeaway coffee cups. "Flat white, no sugar," he said, handing one to Brady and gesturing towards the clock tower at the same time.

Brady looked up at the clock. Gold Roman numerals on a blue background.

Half past eleven...

Butler gestured at an archway under the clock. "There's a seat in the gardens. We can drink our coffee. And fifteen eighty-four," he said. "You were wondering when the College was built. By Sir Walter Mildmay, Elizabeth's Chancellor. You know what he said to her?"

"No, I have no idea."

"I have set an acorn, Ma'am. Which when it becomes an oak God alone knows what will be the fruit thereof.

Well, Mike, Eric Kennedy is the fruit thereof. And it's my job to protect him. There, the seat on the right. By the duck pond."

"SO WHAT ARE YOU?" Brady said. "Home office? Special branch? MI5?"

Simon Butler smiled his easy smile again. "All of them," he said. "None of them. Do you want a reference?"

He reached for his phone. Scrolled through his contacts. "Here," he said, offering Brady the phone. "Phone her. I'm one of six numbers she'll answer immediately."

Brady looked at the phone. At the name of the Home Secretary. "So it's important," he said.

Butler nodded. "Yes, it's important – "

So important you've had me followed. Because that's the only way you know it's a flat white with no sugar. And you don't mind me knowing...

" – But you're entitled to an explanation. Because you'll have to go back to Whitby and forget about Rebecca Kennedy."

As if I hadn't worked that out...

"So you found Professor Kennedy, Mike. You know he killed his sister."

"What he said was true?"

Butler nodded. "He doesn't tell lies. I'm not sure he knows how to lie. But can you go back to Whitby and arrest Kennedy Senior? No. If that was... what you'd been expecting then I'm sorry. It's not going to happen."

"I'd still like an explanation. Several explanations. I

can't go back to my office and push Rebecca Kennedy's file quietly to one side. There are – "

"Procedures. Of course there are. But there's also a bigger picture, Mike. A much bigger picture. Let me – ah, Emma's ducks."

Whatever the explanation was it would have to wait. Six ducks with teal green heads waddled sedately across the path in front of them. "The college ducks, Mike. Mallards mostly, but occasionally there are a few more exotic visitors."

Brady watched the ducks wander off. Thought sitting in the sun watching the ducks after a tutorial seemed an idyllic education.

Maybe Ash could come here...

"Five minutes that way," Butler said, pointing across the pond. "And you come to King's College. Beautiful. Beyond beautiful. And in nineteen thirty-one King's welcomed an undergraduate. One Alan Turing. Well, you know the story. How many lives did Turing save in World War Two? A million? Two million? I've seen one estimate that puts it at twenty million. Eric Kennedy is today's Alan Turing, Mike."

"But we're not at war – "

"With the Russians and the Chinese? Not officially. Do you use e-mail, Mike? Of course you do, everyone uses e-mail. You know what ransomware is?"

"Vaguely..."

"Right. Here we are sitting in a Cambridge garden. A crisp, clear day in early 2016. A hundred yards from St Andrew's Street. People strolling around, living their lives, happy in the knowledge that the local council is taking care of public services. That if they get sick the NHS will take care of them. Meanwhile down in Westminster our elected leaders hive off another part of the UK's infrastructure to the Chinese. What's the preferred career option for bright boys in Russia? Computer hacker. And not Ivan the nerd in his lonely bedroom. Organised gangs. State sponsored gangs. So while our political masters bugger about and talk about diplomacy, the Russians and the Chinese go to work. And one day the local council *won't* be delivering services. One day the hospitals *won't* be open. One day the national grid will just close down. Because some eager young civil servant has responded to the wrong e-mail. Because the Government has opened the front door to diplomacy and something very nasty has crept in the back door."

'He's not just a professor, Mike. He's the professor. What Stephen Hawking is to Physics, he is to Maths. And more. He's not a genius, he's whatever comes after genius.'

"And the reason you're telling me this is Eric Kennedy?"

Simon Butler nodded. "The reason I'm telling you is Eric Kennedy. Who leads a team. A very specialised team. Who right now – as far as the defence of the realm is concerned – is just about the most important man in the country."

"So what he did twenty years ago – "

"What he did twenty years ago doesn't matter. Not one iota. We know about it. We don't care. We all make mistakes when we're twenty and Eric Kennedy has paid for his a thousand times over. You may not approve of what his father did. You may believe in crime and punishment – "

"I do – "

Butler shook his head. "I'm sorry, Mike. You'll just have to live with it. You take any action against Edmund Kennedy, by implication you're taking action against his son. You take any action against his son – "

"And you'll be knocking on my door." Brady laughed. "I thought I was supposed to be warned off by a six foot thug with a broken nose? Not someone... I don't know. I suspect I could enjoy a pint with."

Butler nodded. "I suspect we could. But appreciate that I'm the velvet glove, Mike. There *is* an iron fist. I cannot overstate the threat to our country. I cannot overstate the importance of Eric Kennedy. Forget his sister. Right now Eric Kennedy could bugger the Queen at the state opening of parliament and we'd take no action."

Brady laughed in spite of himself. "Answer me one question."

"What's that?"

"What do you know about the death of Alice Simpson?"

Butler nodded again. "The question you had to ask. Nothing. Except for one small detail."

"You say that in a tone of voice that suggests I'm not going to like it."

"Probably. When Eric Kennedy first appeared on our radar – the radar of the security services – we checked. Did a lot of checking. We knew his sister had disappeared. Knew a local girl had disappeared a month later. We did far more checking than your predecessors. And I can tell you that Edmund was out of the country when Alice went missing. If you want proof, I'll make sure you get it."

"And Eric told you about his sister?"

"Yes. Not me, I wasn't involved then. But yes."

"And you took the decision to protect him?"

"We did. Kennedy and his team. They might be odd, they might be bloody difficult to talk to, they might be so far along the autistic spectrum that they've dropped off the far end. But they're bloody geniuses. And Eric Kennedy is whatever comes after genius."

Brady laughed. "You're the second person to say that to me."

"Maybe it's true then. Have you got time for that pint? Or is the Great North Road calling you?"

"Maybe another time. I've a daughter waiting for me. And – "

"A twenty year old murder to solve?"

"Yes. And two hundred miles to think of what to say to my boss. Tell him why I'm closing the case I've just re-opened."

Butler shook his head. "Don't worry. That'll be taken care of. Official channels. One other thing."

"What's that?"

"I've read your file. You're a tough bastard. That business with – Gorse, was it? I admire that. But even tough bastards need help occasionally. "

Butler fished in his pocket. Handed Brady a card. He glanced down. *Simon Butler*. A mobile number. Nothing else.

"Thank you," Butler said. "And trust me, on this one it's better to be inside the tent."

The second time someone's said that as well...

"Ring me if you think I can help. Any time."

Brady nodded. "I will." He shook Simon Butler's hand. Took one last look at the duck pond and walked back to his car.

'A tough bastard?' There's a woman on a council estate who's lost her daughter. And I don't have a bloody clue who did it. She's a tough bastard as well. She'll need to be.

32

Brady knocked on Alan Kershaw's door.

Not often the great and good are in this early...

Pushed it open. Glanced out of the window. Checked for the tenth time that his new house wasn't visible from Kershaw's office.

You're an adult. Why does it matter? I don't know. It does...

"Good morning, sir."

"Alan, remember. We really ought to be less formal with each other, Mike."

Kershaw glanced down at a sheet of A4 on his desk.

What's that? An e-mail he's printed?

"It looks like we're singing from the same hymn sheet, Mike."

'Don't worry. Your boss will be taken care of. Official channels.'

Simon Butler's been as good as his word.

"So we can let Rebecca Kennedy rest in peace, can't we? Tell me what happened in Cambridge, Mike."

How much do I say to him? As little as possible.

Brady shook his head. "It was bizarre, sir. Alan, sorry. I saw Eric Kennedy. Professor Eric Kennedy. Who told me – plainly and simply, without emotion or remorse – how his sister died."

Kershaw nodded. "I'm given to understand it was a drugs overdose. Or an allergic reaction. Not that we'll ever know after twenty years. And that... We are to consider the case closed. No further action. As you can probably guess, I had a call – *and* an e-mail – from the Chief. Who in turn had received a call... Well, you know how it works, Mike."

"I do."

"And you had the same message?"

Brady nodded. "Delivered while I drank a coffee and admired ducks in a Cambridge college. But yes, the same message."

Kershaw nodded. Looked happy with the outcome.

'That's the result I wanted.' Not your most difficult expression to read, Alan...

"So case closed," Kershaw said. "Life returns to normal."

"It still leaves Alice Simpson, sir."

Kershaw shook his head. "It leaves her relatives, Mike. Who have been unnecessarily stirred up by recent events. The best thing for us..." Kershaw put his hands together in front of him. Interlocked his fingers. Studiously rested his chin on them. "Is to let things calm down. Let time do what time is supposed to do. Heal all wounds."

"Except that Norman Blake is coming out of jail. And he's coming to Whitby."

'That was his name, Mr Brady. Alan Kershaw. And if he'd been in my class he'd have sat next to Valerie King.'

Is there any way Kershaw can guess what Blake told me? No. He's written him off. Dismissed him as an idiot. An idiot who was useful...

Kershaw shook his head. "And you think there'll be some sort of vigilante posse waiting for him? Piss and wind, Mike. Take it from me. People in Whitby are all talk. Then it comes to doing something and they've gone for a pint. So if you're worrying about *The Wicker Man* at low tide you can forget it."

As little emotion as Eric Kennedy...

"I don't know, Alan. Last time I saw Ruby's brother he seemed fairly determined. He seems to think he owes it to her."

"No, trust me, Mike. I've been here the best part of twenty years. Getting drunk, getting divorced. Moaning there's not enough tourists. Then moaning there's too many tourists. That's all they do."

"So your advice..."

"My advice is to let Alice Simpson rest in peace. Wherever she is. Review the file once a year, and it'll gradually die down. And we can both get on with things that are far more important."

'Find her for me, Mr Brady. I know she's dead. I know I'll never see her again. But find her. Give me a place to go on her birthday. Christmas Day. Somewhere I can take her teddy bear. Lay flowers. Find Alice for me. Please.'

I'm not sure anything's more important, Alan. I can't leave it like that...

"Except that... When that walker found the body he

re-opened the town's old wounds. We can't allow them to fester, sir."

What does Kershaw care about? Alan Kershaw. So let's see...

"We don't want any bad PR, Alan. If Blake came to Whitby. If time *didn't* do its work..."

Kershaw nodded. Swivelled in his chair. Looked across the harbour to the Abbey. Back at Brady. Narrowed his eyes.

I can see the wheels turning...

"You're right, Mike. We don't want to risk anything that would impact any of our careers. Or reputations. Or the reputation of the force. The force is paramount. Obviously. When does Blake come out?"

"I checked, sir. Friday. Four days from now."

"As soon as that?"

Brady nodded. Watched Kershaw's mind working.

'If the shit hits the fan it's going to reflect on me.' Yes, sir, it is. And you don't want Norman Blake telling his story. Or ending up in the harbour...

"You're right, Mike. Go and talk to them. Alice Simpson's family. See what progress you can make. Get them to see sense. Do whatever it takes. They're simple folk. Use your charm."

Use my charm? To tell them it's 'case closed' with Becky – and 'no bloody idea' with Alice?

Right...

Brady parked the Tiguan between two white vans. Glanced up at the bedroom window. Half-expected the curtains to twitch. Half-expected to hear a shout from inside. *'Piss off, Brady. Not until you've got something good to tell me.'*

Ruby opened the door. Nine-thirty and the black t-shirt, the just-got-out-of-bed look was long gone. Jeans, the denim shirt she'd been wearing when she'd turned up at the police station.

How long ago was that? I seem to have been knocking on her door for about a year...

She didn't speak. Gestured at the kitchen.

No cup of tea then...

Des and Brian were sitting at the table, both of them wearing clean overalls.

Not started work yet...

"Morning," Brady said. "Both vans?"

"Separate jobs. Late start though. Well, you can tell that. We're not covered in Autumn bloody Sunrise. Wanted to hear what you had to say first."

"Have you brought that for Ruby? Brady said. "It's lovely."

There was a framed picture propped up on the work-top. Whitby Pier at sunrise, taken from the beach. The sun halfway between red and orange, framed between the upper and lower levels of the pier. The sunlight reflected in a perfect heart as the waves ran back off the wet beach. A solitary seagull silhouetted as it flew across the sun.

"As good a picture of the pier as I've ever seen."

Brian nodded. "Aye. It's alright. Ten a penny are sunrises though. Every bugger with an iPhone's on the beach at sunrise. Stands to reason, you take ten or twenty, one of 'em's going to be alright. Good enough for Facebook anyway."

"You don't normally do landscapes in your spare time then? Seascapes, sorry."

He shook his head. "No. People mostly. Every face tells a story. An' Whitby's full of lined faces."

"I like them," Ruby said. "His sunrises. Takes a few from his back garden, don't you, Bri? They make me feel optimistic. But looking at your face, Mr Brady, I'm not. What've you got to tell us?"

Brady took a deep breath.

Ruby held her hand up. Shook her head. "No. You don't need to. Don't bother wi' your rehearsed speech if you've nowt to tell me."

"I have got something to tell you," Brady said.

"What's that then?"

Use my charm...

"Rebecca Kennedy. The case is closed."

Ruby reached across the table. Took his hand. Stared at him, hope burning in her eyes.

Please, Ruby, don't look at me like that...

"Does that mean you've arrested someone? Who? You have to tell me. Who is it? Tell me."

Brady gently took her hand off his. "I'm sorry, Ruby." He looked at the two men on either side of her. Felt their growing hostility. "All of you. All I can say is that the case is closed. We haven't arrested anyone. We *won't* be arresting anyone."

"What the fuck does that mean?" Des said.

Brian picked his mug up. Banged it down hard. Tea splashed out onto the kitchen table. "It means it's that bastard from Middlesbrough. It means they've found something else but they're not going to prosecute him. But they're certain now."

"No," Brady said. "There's a limit to what I can say, Mr Simpson. Both of you. But Norman Blake has *nothing* to do with this conversation. Or this investigation."

"Right, cock. You've told us the official line. Now tell us the truth."

"We're her family," Ruby said. "We've a right to know. Otherwise you're no better than all the others. And I helped your daughter. You owe me."

You didn't need to say it, Ruby...

Brady nodded. "You *are* her family. And you've a right to know. But only about Alice. I'm sorry to sound like I'm reading some sort of official statement, but that's all I can say, Ruby. Rebecca's death has nothing to do with Alice. Nothing at all."

"And you expect us to believe that?" Des said. "A month apart and you expect us to believe that bollocks?"

"I don't expect you to believe or disbelieve anything, Mr Simpson. I'm simply giving you the facts. Rebecca Kennedy's case is closed. Alice remains open – "

"And you're doing fuck all, the same as you've done for twenty years."

"No, we're not doing 'fuck all' as you put it."

That's why I drove to Cambridge. That's why I ignore my own daughter and spend Sunday afternoons on the Moors. That's why I went to talk to Morag. Because I'm doing 'fuck all...'

"Just because we haven't arrested someone – "

"That bastard did it," Brian said. "I know it. You know it. All of fucking Whitby knows it. And I tell you something, cock... If you won't get the truth out of him we will."

Ruby ignored her uncle. Looked at Brady. Spoke quietly. "I told you, Mr Brady. I told you I'd swing for him if he comes to Whitby. I meant it. My only daughter. If he comes to Whitby I'll make him pay."

The swagger and bluster of Des and Brian. The quiet threats from Ruby. Brady knew which one worried him more.

34

"I should resign," Frankie said. "Resign from the force and become a highly paid consultant. Then if you wanted to bounce ideas off me at lunchtime you'd have to take me to a posh restaurant. Not – "

"Do you want peas?" Brady said.

"Chips and peas. If I have fish I'll fall asleep in the afternoon. And I've got to take Mum to hospital. She needs a new pot on her arm."

"How is she?"

"She's alright. I put her in the shower, I tell her to make sure the pot doesn't get wet. Ten seconds later she's forgotten..."

"But the break's healing?"

Frankie sighed. "I guess so. No-one's said it isn't. But – "

"But this time next month – or next year – there'll be another break?"

She nodded. "Inevitably." Pulled the collar of her coat up. Turned and looked out over the harbour. "Scraps," she said over her shoulder. "Seeing as you're making me eat outside in the drizzle. Lots of scraps."

Brady laughed. Dodged the puddles as he walked through the alley to the fish and chip shop.

"Tell me about Cambridge," she said ten minutes later.

"I learned two simple facts."

"Which are?"

How much am I prepared to tell her? A lot more than I was prepared to tell Kershaw.

"I'm probably going to tell you more than I'm supposed to tell you – "

"We're surrounded by fish crates and lobster pots. You're safe. And everyone needs someone to confide in."

Yes. She's right. I do...

"One, Eric Kennedy killed his sister," Brady said. "And fact two. I learned that my power is limited. Very limited."

"So what happened?"

"You don't look surprised."

"Kennedy? You know me, Mike. I've never been a believer in the 'random stranger' theory. Occasionally? Yes. But put your money on the people they live with."

"I saw Kennedy," Brady said. "He's in his office, looking out over a perfect lawn in a college built by Queen Elizabeth's Chancellor. Two computer screens covered in incomprehensible lines of code. And 'yes,' he says, talking to someone three yards behind me. 'Yes,' he says. 'I killed her. I was home from university. The holidays. I was bored. We had a pharma party.'" Brady paused. "You don't need me to explain?"

Frankie shook her head. "No. There was one when I

was at uni. Several probably. But this one made the head-lines because someone died. That's what happened to Becky?"

Brady nodded. "He said she was inquisitive. Adven-turous. He probably wanted company. Aged twenty, prob-ably not very confident around women. A precocious younger sister? I doubt he could say 'no' to her. And when his parents came back from a night out he was unconscious and his sister was dead."

"And they never phoned anyone? Attempted to revive her?"

"No. I'm guessing she was clearly dead. Eric said his father took charge. Made the decision."

"Wasted police time. Perverted the course of justice."

"And a few others. Not to mention the impact on the town."

"But the town, the people in it. We didn't count."

Kennedy, Kershaw. The same contempt. Just showing it in different ways...

"No, not compared to his son. Who already had his brilliant career lined up. Kennedy made a logical deci-sion. What *he* saw as a logical decision. 'Rebecca can't be brought back: there's no point ruining my son's life.' Eric Kennedy said it was 'the greatest good of the greatest number.'"

"So reciting the works of John Stuart Mill he carries her onto the Moors and buries her?"

"Yes."

"In a backpack?"

Brady shrugged. "Eric didn't say anything about a coffin. So yes, presumably. Exactly like you said."

"Why did he choose that particular spot? Did he say?"

"No. Honestly, Frankie, if Kennedy's prepared to make a decision like that what does it matter where he buried her? Where he parked his car? By any normal standards he's mad. Maybe he just walked until he was worn out."

"Then took her clothes off and buried her."

"Or she was naked all the time."

"Where's her mother – Eilish – in all this? You think she went with him?"

Brady shook his head. "You know what? I didn't ask. It wouldn't surprise me. To say goodbye..."

"And then gradually – over the years, Kennedy's bullying – it all becomes too much for her?"

"Can you imagine it? Eric's graduation? Standing there afterwards? A glass of wine in one hand. A plate of sandwiches in the other. People must have heard about Becky. A few of them come up and sympathise. But Eilish knows the truth. Knows the price she's paid for Eric's glittering career."

"And the media. The press conferences she went through. 'Help us find Rebecca...' All the time knowing she's buried on the Moors. You know what amazes me, Mike?"

"What's that?"

"That it took her five years to crack. To make the final sacrifice for Eric. To protect him."

Brady stood up. Walked across to the side of the harbour. "It makes me bloody angry," he said. "Beyond bloody angry."

"There's nothing you can do?"

"Nothing, Frankie. Not a damn thing. I was warned off

in no uncertain terms. By... I don't know who by. Someone who looked like he'd climbed out of a tank in Afghanistan on Tuesday and strolled into Whitehall on Wednesday morning. He asked me if I wanted a reference. Passed me his phone. The Home Secretary's number. 'Go ahead' he says. 'Phone her.'"

"So what happened?"

"We sat in the College gardens. Emmanuel College. Admired the ducks. He gave me a flat white. How the hell does he know I drink a flat white?"

"Because Eric Kennedy told them you were coming."

"Right. Because they were waiting for me. You want his exact quote? 'Eric Kennedy could bugger the Queen at the state opening of parliament and we'd take no action.' Kershaw got the same message. Phrased more diplomatically, I assume."

"There must be something. He can't – "

"He can't what? Just get away with it? Both of them will. Kennedy and his father."

Brady shook his head. Looked at three small fishing boats moored in front of them. Two of them red and white, the third black and white.

And badly in need of a re-paint. WY333? There can't be that many fishing boats left in Whitby...

"You know what *really* makes me angry, Frankie?"

"No. Tell me."

"I can see both sides of it. I wish I couldn't. But I can. I'm driving back. I come off the A14 onto the A1. I'm at Peterborough and I'm a copper. Eric Kennedy has killed his sister. The law has to take its course. Yes, he's a Professor. And I understand what he's doing. But – "

"What *is* he doing?"

"Apparently he's all that stands between us and the Chinese turning the lights off. 'Whatever he did when he was twenty he's paid for it a thousand times over.' And bloody hell, Frankie, by the time I've reached Doncaster I can see it. Peterborough I'm thinking like a copper. Doncaster I'm thinking like a dad."

"How?"

"Look at Ash the other night. Ash thumps Shelley. Shelley stumbles backwards. Supposing she falls? Hits her head? Would I want the rest of Ash's life ruined? Of course I wouldn't. And that's what makes me so bloody angry. There aren't many people I actively dislike – "

Frankie smiled. "Jimmy Gorse?"

Brady laughed. "True enough. I wasn't so keen on him. There still aren't many people. But Edmund Kennedy's on the list. He's arrogant, he's a snob, he thinks other people don't matter. He deserves to pay for what he's done. But by the time I'd reached Doncaster I could understand his motives."

"Except you'd have called an ambulance."

"I would, of course I would. So maybe there's only part of me that can understand it. Anyway, it's irrelevant. Becky's been found. She can be buried. Orders have been handed down from on high. That chapter's closed. And Becky's death had nothing to do with Alice."

"You know that for certain?"

Brady nodded. "Kennedy was out of the country. The tank commander said did I want the proof?"

"And he gave it to you?"

"Yes. I didn't say 'yes' – didn't ask for it - but there it was when I got back. Copies of flight lists. Tickets."

"To show you they're serious."

Brady nodded. "Exactly that."

"So there's no connection?"

"Between the deaths? Or disappearances? No. Between the girls? Right now, Frankie we don't know. Maybe we'll never know. Mandy Jamieson said Alice had a friend at a posh school. Becky went to what Alice would call a 'posh school.' And she was adopted. Have I told you that?"

"So she wasn't like her parents. Or her brother. Becky could have had a wild streak."

"She *did* have a wild streak. So maybe they knew each other. And Mandy said Alice started acting strangely after Becky disappeared. Quieter, more withdrawn."

"What's Kershaw say to all this?"

"What do you think? I spoke to him yesterday morning. 'Let her rest in peace.' The same for Alice. 'Time will heal the wounds, Mike.'"

"That's bollocks."

"That's what I said. Not in those words. But no, I'm not having that – "

"No-one's having that, Mike. Not Ruby, not the town. Everyone knows the body's been found. Everyone knows you're investigating. What are you going to do? Issue a press release? 'We know who killed Becky Kennedy but we're not going to do anything about it? No, it wasn't the same person who killed Alice. Feel free to speculate, folks...'"

Brady nodded. "I've already seen Ruby."

"What did she say?"

"Not much. Her son and her uncle did most of the talking."

"You've re-opened the old wounds, Mike. Whether you wanted to or not. You can't leave them open. You have to close them. You owe it to Ruby."

"I owe it to Ash as well. My deal with Ruby's not going to last indefinitely. So there's only one solution."

Frankie nodded. Stared out across the harbour. "Find Alice's killer. Supposing the deaths *are* linked, Mike? It's still the most likely explanation. Supposing Alice went out to the house?"

"What are you saying now, Frankie? Eric Kennedy killed her? His mother killed her? That's the *real* reason she committed suicide?" Brady shook his head. "It's a nice theory, Frankie. But we've three days. We – "

"Three days?"

"The rest of today. Then three days. He comes out on Friday. So we haven't time for nice theories. We've time for basic police work. The work they should have done twenty years ago."

"Good," Frankie said. "I like 'basic.' Basic gets results."

Brady laughed. "I thought you were on sabbatical, DS Thomson?"

"I am. I fully intend to be." She shrugged. "But what woman can resist a twenty year old murder? Besides..."

"You're getting bored? I'll keep you in the loop."

Frankie glanced at her watch. "I need to go. Time to collect her. Remind her why we're going to hospital. But you'll do more than 'keep me in the loop,' DCI Brady. I'll expect a daily update. Even if it does only last three days."

She turned to go. Paused and looked back at Brady. "Seriously, Mike. What happens if Norman Blake comes for his fishing trip?"

"Seriously? I don't know. He's a free man. He's entitled to do what he wants. I've warned Ruby and her family. But what can I do? I can't arrest them for a few fevered mutterings over a cup of tea."

"They don't know when he's coming out of jail though. They can't know that."

"No," Brady said. "Thank goodness for small mercies. And Frankie..."

"What?"

"Thank you."

"What for?"

"This. This... talking it through."

Why is it so bloody difficult to say?

"Doing this. It's..."

She laughed. "I know. Me too. And thank *you*. It's not every day I eat chips and peas in the rain."

35

Back to basics. Back to basics with three days to go. Three days before Norman Blake gets off the bus with his lucky fishing rod.

Brady pulled Alice Simpson's file towards him.

Should I delegate this? Give it to Dan Keillor? I need to go and see Ruby. But if I don't know what I'm looking for how do I tell Dan what to look for?

He opened the file. Looked again at Alice's photo. The official school photo. The royal blue sweatshirt.

Deadpan. Looking straight past the camera. Almost like Eric Kennedy looked straight past me. Probably looking at one of her mates behind the photographer. Seeing how long it is before she has a fit of giggles...

Brady opened his phone. Looked at the photo he'd taken at Ruby's. Blonde hair, blue eyes, the knowing smile. Right on the edge of becoming a teenager.

He started reading the first statement.

Tamara Prince. One of Alice's friends. The girl Ruby mentioned...

Brady stood up, walked to the door of his office. "Dan? Spare me a minute?"

"What's up, boss?"

"There's a girl – well, woman now – who gave a state-ment when Alice disappeared. She was called Tamara Prince. See if you can track her down will you? I haven't any contact details but ring this number. Another friend of Alice's. Mandy Jamieson. Chances are she'll know if Tamara got married. What her new name is. Come back to me if you can't make any progress and I'll speak to Ruby."

Brady resisted the new coffee machine. Walked back to his office and picked up the witness statement.

Dictated by an 11 year old girl. And translated into witness-speak...

'We were down on the sea-front. Me, Alice, Mandy and three or four others. Jodie and Sarah left early. We weren't doing much. It started to rain so we went in one of the arcades. Then we had an ice cream. Alice said she had some money so she bought 99s for all of us. Then Alice said she had to go. She said she was meeting someone at three and couldn't be late.

She didn't say where she was going. She set off and walked back towards town. She left about quarter to three, I think. I looked at the clock to see how long it was before I had to go. My mum said I had to be in by half past four.

Alice was wearing her jeans and a grey hoodie. She walked off towards town. We didn't see her again.'

It was signed in a round, childish hand and dated.

Two weeks after Alice disappeared. Take your time, lads...

Brady looked at the picture on his phone again. Tried to read Alice's expression.

Where did you go, Alice? Where were you taking that knowing smile? If what Tamara says is correct you were walking for fifteen minutes. Did you cross the swing bridge or did you go the other way? Sandgate. Church Street. Up the steps to the Abbey...

He shook his head. Looked out of his office window. *Fifteen minutes. The best part of a mile. Whitby's a small town. She could have been anywhere.*

Ruby's statement didn't tell him anything he didn't know. Alice had gone into town. No, she didn't worry when Alice didn't come home. She'd done it before. 'I didn't report her missing until late the next morning. Maybe about twelve, something like that.'

The last sentence was ringed in red, two exclamation marks in the margin.

'We were second best, Mr Brady.' Maybe those exclamation marks were the start of it, Ruby...

It was a thin file. A third the size of Becky Kennedy's. No-one had seen Alice walking through town. From the moment she'd left her friends Alice had become invisible.

A young girl walking through town on a Saturday afternoon. Jeans and a grey hoodie. Of course she was invisible...

The last statement was from Brian.

He'd seen her two days before she disappeared. 'I called round to see Ruby at the house. One of her windows was sticking so I called round to fix it. Alice was just in from school. She seemed her normal self, didn't say much as she had a friend with her. She made a sandwich and went upstairs to her bedroom. That was the last time I saw her.'

Friend, silence, sandwich, bedroom. Sounds like Ash...

I need to speak to Ruby again. And Mandy. And I need to go down to the seafront. See how far Alice could walk in fifteen minutes...

Brady picked his phone up. Dialled the number. "Morning, Ruby. I just wanted to check you were in."

36

"So what is it today, Mr Brady? You've found her? You haven't found her? You've come to tell me you've lost interest?"

"It's not like you to be cynical, Ruby."

She shrugged. "Does it matter? Does anything I say matter? You want some tea? That's all I do these days. You, Des, Bri, Jason. Just a stream of men sitting at my kitchen table drinking tea. Drinking tea and talking bollocks." She walked over to the worktop. Turned the kettle on. Tore off a piece of kitchen roll. Dabbed her eyes.

"There. You've seen it again. Ruby Simpson crying. There's something to stick in your police file." She shook her head. "You tell me. What does any of it bloody matter?"

"This isn't like you, Ruby."

She's stopped fighting. For the first time the fight's gone out of her. Does this mean Norman Blake can go fishing?

"What isn't like me? Maybe I've just come to my

senses. Let Des and Bri deal with that prick from
Middlesbrough."

No, it doesn't.

"You're staying out of it then?"

"Me? I'm wasting my time. It's not going to bring her
back is it? Who knows? Maybe I'm getting sensible in my
old age." She laughed. Passed Brady a cup of tea. "Or
maybe it's hormones. I'm nearly fifty, Mr Brady. Maybe it's
the change. Maybe I'm turning into an old woman…"

"Ruby, I need to go right back to square one. Ask you
some questions about the day Alice disappeared. I know
that will be painful for you – "

Ruby shook her head. "Ask away. Drink your tea and
ask your questions. I can't give you any different answers
to the ones you've got in your file. But ask away."

*'Have you not read the file, Mr Brady? Do you imagine the
passage of time has changed the answers I gave your dull-
witted colleague twenty years ago?'*

At least she's not going to try and score cheap points off me.

"So it's a Saturday, twenty years ago," Brady said.
"What do you remember about the day, Ruby? Not
specifics. General stuff. How everyone was feeling. That
sort of thing."

"You want the truth? I was hung-over," Ruby said.
"We'd had a session the night before. The Black Horse.
Got in late. So that's the first thing I remember from the
day my daughter disappeared. My head splitting in two."

She looked across the table at him. "There you go, Mr
Brady. What everyone says is right. A bad mother. Ross
has taken himself off to play football, then he's off to a
mate's. Alice takes herself into town. And the bad mother

thinks, 'thank God they've gone' and goes back to bed to sleep it off."

"And you weren't in contact with Alice through the day?"

"No. How was I going to do that? This was twenty years ago. Not like today when kids have a phone before they've learned to walk."

"Did you notice what she was wearing when she went out?"

"What she always wore. Jeans. That grey hoodie. It was in and out of the wash like a bloody yo-yo."

"What about money?"

The question I always ask Ash. Have you got your keys? Have you got your phone? Have you got some money?

Ruby shrugged again. "I used to give her what I could. And she wasn't averse to helping herself to the odd fiver, the little tinker."

'Alice said she had some money so she bought 99s for all of us.' So that's where it came from. While Ruby's sleeping off her hangover Alice is helping herself from Ruby's purse...

"And then that night. You didn't worry when she hadn't come in?"

Ruby shook her head. "No. It sounds awful to say it now. Maybe I *was* a bad mother. There's a few people in town said I got what I deserved."

"No-one – "

"No-one deserves that. Course they don't. Doesn't stop 'em talking though. No, I didn't worry. She'd done it before. Stayed at a friend's. Forgotten to phone. And I'm still trying to get rid of my hangover." She paused. "Like I said to you. The first time you came. We were always second-best. Maybe it's my fault. 'Can't put that slapper in front of the cameras, can we? Bottle of Carlsberg in one hand. Fag in the other.'"

Don't reply to that. You don't need her any more depressed than she already is...

"What happened the next morning, Ruby?"

She sniffed. Reached for another piece of kitchen roll. "Ross comes in from his mate's. He'd rung me. He's a good lad is Ross."

"What about Alice?"

"I suppose it's about dinner time when I start worrying. She liked her Sunday roast did Alice. And by the time I'm doing the Yorkshire puddings I know there's something wrong. Mother's instinct."

She blew her nose. "Sorry. Like I said, I've had enough. That girl being found. Becky. I thought... for a weekend... It's the hope that kills you."

Two more questions...

"Where's Jason, Ruby? Ross is playing football, Alice has gone into town. Didn't you have Jason to look after?"

Ruby shook her head. "With his dad. Down in Scarborough. Used to go down there every other weekend." She shook her head a second time. "Maybe made a mistake there..."

"Why do you say that?"

"Maybe should have stuck with that one. Not the most exciting man in the world. But he was steady. His brain made the decisions, not his cock." She shrugged. "Right person maybe. Not the right time."

"But you're not with him. You're with your boyfriend. Where's Dennis McBride in all this, Ruby?"

"Dennis? I told you before didn't I? He's out. Told me he'd gone for a walk. But he's fucking some married woman. He sees me stagger back to bed with my hangover and he's off. Sees his chance. Like a dog with two dicks was Dennis."

"And when did he come back?"

She shrugged. "God knows. Some time Saturday night. Dennis wasn't a man you could set your watch by."

Brady nodded. Didn't say any more. Stood up. Told Ruby not to worry. To take care of herself. That he was going through the file. He'd be talking to Mandy again. Promised he'd keep her in touch.

Knew he was just making empty promises.

Closed the front door behind him and walked back to his car. Put his hand on the door handle.

Had the uneasy feeling that Ruby had said something important.

Whatever it was, I missed it.

HE CLIMBED INTO THE CAR. Dialled her number.

"Supposing Ruby's boyfriend did it?" Brady said.

"Good morning, Detective Chief Inspector. I'm well, thank you. Yes, we survived the new pot. She wet herself in my car on the way home, so not an entirely successful day. I'm sorry, was there something you wanted to ask me?"

Brady laughed. "OK. Sorry. Bollocking accepted. And I'm sorry about the car. I've just been with Ruby."

"They had the boyfriend in for questioning didn't they?"

"They had him in for questioning and let him go. No evidence. But..."

"But what?"

"But there's a hole in the story. Potentially a huge hole. The day Alice disappeared – Ruby says she had a hangover. She went back to bed. While she's back in bed Alice helps herself to a fiver from her mum's purse and goes off into town. Her son's playing football. The boyfriend disappears. Ruby says he's with another woman. 'Sees me stagger back to bed with my hangover and sees his chance' is her exact quote. The next day he refuses to answer any questions. He's got a record, Frankie. Theft, breaking and entering."

"Theft and breaking and entering aren't the same as murder. Besides – "

"I know," Brady said. "If the boyfriend did it..."

"Ruby *has* to know. She has to be involved in it. Or are we saying the boyfriend meets Alice in town and kills her? Then disappears back to Scotland? When did he go?"

"I don't know, Frankie. I'm clutching at straws. Not for one minute do I think Ruby's involved. If she is she's the best actress I've met in twenty years of doing this job. But Dennis McBride never said who he was with. 'Fucking some married woman,' according to Ruby. We've only got her word for that. But like I say, I'm clutching at straws."

"You are," she said. "I think you are."

"Ruby said something to me. Something significant. I can't for the life of me think what it was. There's some bloody connection I haven't made."

"What's next?"

"Mandy Jamieson. But not until tonight. I need some fresh air this afternoon. Space to do some thinking. What about you?"

"What's next?" Frankie said. "Thank you for asking. Give the car valeter eighty quid and hope for the best."

37

"You think you can be a copper without owning a dog, Archie?"

Brady walked across the road. Down the slipway. Unclipped Archie's lead and watched him sprint onto an almost deserted beach. "No, me neither," he said to himself.

Low tide but the waves were crashing onto the beach. Brady didn't have to look far for what he wanted. He bent down and picked up the piece of driftwood. Rested it on a rock. Stamped down with his right foot. Broke it in half. "There you go, Archie, two perfect sticks. Serious exercise time."

He threw one of the sticks towards the waves, watched Archie scamper after it.

Wind off the sea. Rain. Freezing cold. He doesn't care. 'Just throw me a stick and I'm happy.' If only life was that simple...

'We are to consider the case closed. No further action. As you can probably guess, I had a call from the Chief. Who in turn had received a call... Well, you know how it works, Mike.'

So Edmund Kennedy gets away with it. Buries his daughter. Lies for twenty years. Maybe drives his wife to suicide. What was it Grace used to say? 'Grant me the wisdom to accept the things I cannot change.' You weren't a copper, Grace...

Michael Brady pulled the collar of his coat up and walked after his dog. "Archie!"

The Springer looked up. Saw the second stick. Abandoned the first one. Yelped in excitement. Brady threw the stick, watched the wind catch it, hold it for a split second, drop it neatly into the centre of a rock pool. "Don't, Archie!" he yelled. "It'll be freezing." Archie took absolutely no notice...

Back to basics. When all else fails, walk your dog on the beach and go back to basics.

'I like 'basic.' Basic gets results.'

What have I learned from her being on sabbatical? I need her. That's what I've learned.

'Everyone needs someone to confide in.' Yes, Frankie, they do.

"Come on, Archie. Time to turn round."

Into the wind...

Brady threw the stick low and hard like a frisbee. Watched it bounce across the sand. Watched Archie skid to a stop as he caught up with it.

Three days. Supposing Norman Blake does come to Whitby. He's been inside for twenty years. Who's going to recognise him? Someone will. It's not a chance I can take. And Norman will say something. 'Hello, I've been looking forward to this for twenty years. They put me in prison for something I didn't do. My name? Yes, it's Norman Blake...'

He glanced up as he reached Sandsend. Realised he'd avoided it as he walked back to the car. Finally looked at the hill where he'd scattered his wife's ashes.

"I'm sorry, I've not been up for a while. Winter. This case..."

And something else. Someone else. I thought there'd never be anyone else.

Brady jumped over a stream the rain had made. Turned and watched it flow down to the sea, cutting a channel through the beach. Looked back up at the hill.

I thought there'd never be anyone else. And there isn't, Grace. There can't be. Because I'm her boss. And once you've crossed the line...

"Archie! Come on, mate. Time to go home."

Back to basics, Archie. Because I'm a copper. Because I've got a murder to solve...

38

"Come in," Mandy Jamieson said. "And you're alright, he's had his feed. He's asleep."

Brady laughed. "So I'm safe?"

"You are. Cup of tea? Coffee?"

"No, I'm good thanks. I'll try not to keep you too long."

Mandy led the way into the lounge. Sat on a cream settee and pushed a pale orange cushion behind her back. "Still painful?" Brady said.

She nodded. "Too old for it. Being pregnant is a young woman's game."

"My wife said seven months was about right."

I can still hear you saying it, Grace...

"She's right. After that you can't lie down. You're awake half the night. Your husband's sympathy has run out. Yep, seven months gets my vote."

"Can I take you back to that day?" Brady said. "You said no-one talked to you after Alice disappeared. There's a statement on file from Tamara – "

"Your guy rang me. Dan something? I told him she'd got married and moved away."

Brady nodded. "We spoke to her on the phone. She confirmed the statement. Said she couldn't really remember much."

Mandy raised her eyebrows. "No surprise there. She wasn't the sharpest knife in the box. Sorry, that's being unkind."

"No, you're fine. Give me someone's honest opinion any day. The last thing I need is you telling me what I want to hear. Tell me about that Saturday, Mandy. You're all down on the seafront..."

She nodded. "When weren't we down on the seafront? It's hard to tell one day from another. But there's a group of six or seven of us. Me, Alice, Tamara, two or three others that we usually went around with. It's bloody freezing but it's just before the clocks change. You know, it'll soon be winter. So we'd better make the most of it."

"The statement mentioned two others. Jodie and Sarah."

Mandy nodded. "They lived next door to each other. Sarah did well for herself. Trained to be a hairdresser. Won competitions. She's in London now."

"So you're all on the seafront. The witness statement said Alice bought you all ice-creams. Do you remember that?"

Mandy shook her head again. "She might have done. Like I said, twenty years and one afternoon on the seafront is like any other afternoon on the seafront. Did Alice buy ice-creams? She never seemed short of money, that's for sure. Given that Ruby didn't work." She shrugged. "But that was Alice…"

"Was she talking to anyone?"

"Honestly, Mr Brady, it's hard to remember. Alice was doing what Alice always did. Talking to everyone."

"But not to Posh Spice? You didn't see her with anyone specific?"

Mandy shook her head. "No. And I've been thinking about Posh Spice since you were last here. Half of me thinks Alice made it up. You know, like she wanted to impress us. But Alice was Alice. She definitely used to go up to the graveyard."

"How can you be so sure?"

"She used to tell stories. The full moon over the Abbey. The noise of the wind off the sea. We went on a school trip once. Marrick Priory – somewhere up in the Dales. The last term at junior school. There's ten of us in the dormitory. Alice is telling us stories about the grave-yard at night. I don't think any of us slept a wink."

"You said that after Becky disappeared she was quieter. Less confident. Not so sure of herself."

"Yes. Nothing I can put my finger on. But I do remember the feeling I had. I'm sorry, I'm not much use to you."

"You're fine. Don't worry"

No. I'm not making any progress. There has to be something…

"That Saturday," Brady said. "According to Tamara's statement Alice had to be somewhere at three. She left about quarter to…"

Mandy hesitated. "I think so. Now you say it. I don't

want to remember something – like you say, tell you what you want to hear. But... Alice was always the last one to leave. The rest of us had to be home. Alice seemed to suit herself. Didn't have any rules. So yes, she did go early. Whether it was quarter to or not I haven't got a clue. But yes, she definitely went early."

39

'Dot every I, cross every single T. Someone's been murdered, Mike. However late it is, however knackered you are, you owe it to them. Find the killer.'

He could hear Jim Fitzpatrick's voice. Brady rubbed his eyes, ran his fingers through his hair and pulled Sandra Donoghue's file towards him.

Back to the beginning. Right back to the beginning. Norman Blake didn't have anything to do with it. Definitely didn't. But let's be absolutely certain.

Brady looked up, half-expecting to see his old boss standing in the doorway, nodding approval. He started with the psychologist's report.

'Sandra Donoghue was murdered on Thursday August 22nd. Her partially-clothed body was found on waste ground behind Westmoreland Road Industrial Estate. There was no evidence of sexual assault. Cause of death was multiple stab wounds leading to loss of blood.'

What's it say later on? Can't be certain which was the fatal wound. Does it matter? No...

'The victim was reported missing at 21:05 on the night of August 22nd. Time of death was put at 9pm to 10pm. The body was not discovered until 10:30 the next morning, when two staff from Coyne Tyres and Exhausts went for a 'kickabout' in their break.'

So you lay there all night, Sandra. No distance from home...

'The stab wounds had been inflicted with some force. I would suggest that this was an attack from someone who had been rebuffed sexually, with the random nature of the blows and their severity suggesting anger.'

Rebuffed? Probably. Sexually? She's thirteen for God's sake. Let's not jump to conclusions...

'The killer is unlikely to be married or in a stable relationship and is unlikely to be 'successful' with the opposite sex. The victim was only partially clothed. Her blouse had been torn away: her jeans had been unzipped and tugged down in a sexually suggestive way. I am strongly of the opinion that the killer masturbated after the murder.'

Why? Because that was the fashionable theory twenty years ago. It's speculation. That's all it can be.

'The obvious conclusion to draw is that as the body was found near an industrial estate the likely killer is someone who knows the estate. In fact the waste ground is not easy to find from the industrial estate, but is used as a short cut between the nearby housing estate and the town.'

Why didn't they go with the obvious conclusion? Because they'd brought Norman Blake in for questioning. Because he ticked all the boxes...

'The pathologist has said that the stab wounds, were inflicted – in her opinion – by a chisel. In my view this does *not* mean that the killer is a tradesman. These are everyday objects that will be in most houses.'

Wounds inflicted by a chisel? Can he be certain about that? And 'everyday objects?' Have I even got a chisel? I don't think so...

'This was a disorganised, spur-of-the-moment attack. The killer does not, in my view, have the organisational skills necessary to work as, say, a joiner.'

Obviously written by someone who's never tried to get the joiner to come on the same day as the plumber and the electrician...

Brady pushed the file away. Ran his hands through his hair again. Picked his phone up and texted Ash.

You OK? I'm working late. Hope all's good with you and Bean.

We're fine. We've let Archie out. Given him too much pizza. Is it OK if Bean stays over?

Of course. Love you.

Stood up and looked out of the window at the back of the hospital.

It's no use. I need the view from Kershaw's office... Supposing the psychologist's conclusions are wrong? Supposing most of the report is right but he's drawn the wrong conclusions? 'Hard to find' does not mean impossible to find. Even if I do own a chisel I don't take it out with me. 'The killer is not a tradesman.' Why? If it looks like a duck and quacks like a duck...

Brady tapped *Westmoreland Road Industrial Estate* into Google. Clicked on the map. Dragged the little yellow man onto it. Clicked the compass arrows and looked around.

'Industrial Estate?' That's optimistic. Only four units this side. Tiny Tots Fun Zone. Hell's bells, I remember taking Ash to one of those. The noise. Like standing in the middle of the M25...

An employment agency. Coyne Tyres and Exhausts. Still going strong twenty years later. Congratulations Mr Coyne. What's that last one? Glazing and Joinery.

He spun street view through 180 degrees.

Tool hire. Accountants and business advisors. JJ Engineering. And 'to let.' Seven out of eight occupied.

He spun the view back across the parked cars and vans. Looked at the tyre and exhaust unit again. Realised he was wasting his time. Walked through into the main office. Stopped at Dan Keillor's desk and scribbled a note.

Dan – Westmoreland Road Industrial Estate in Middlesbrough. Google it. Look on street view. Phone the letting agents. Let's hope they haven't changed. I need a list of tenants from twenty years ago. Find out who was paying rent in 1996.

BRADY WALKED BACK to his office. Thought about ordering a takeaway. Didn't want to waste the time. Read through the file again. Had exactly the same feeling he'd had before.

They found Norman Blake and stopped looking. Should I go and see the OIC? See what Fraser Hogg has to tell me? Or should I go next door, admire the view and ask Kershaw about the confession he forced out of Norman Blake?

Brady scribbled 'Fraser Hogg' on his notepad. Put a ring round it.

First thing in the morning. He'll be retired now. He won't be far away.

He closed the file. Screwed his eyes shut.

Time to admit it. Reading glasses. Go and see an optician.

Heard Jim Fitzpatrick again. '*However late it is, however knackered you are...*'

Made himself open the file again. Looked at the copies of the newspaper clippings.

'Norman Blake was today found guilty of the murder of 13 year old Middlesbrough girl Sandra Donoghue. Sandra's family said in a statement: "We will never get over our sense of loss. A light has gone out in our lives and it can never be rekindled. Sandra had already represented her county in gymnastics competitions and was widely expected to represent Great Britain in the future. Now we will never know what might have been."'

Brady looked at the grainy, black and white photo of Sandra.

You've focused all your attention on Norman Blake. Because you've seen him. All your bloody attention...

Sandra. Smiling at the camera. A leotard with a zig zag pattern running across it. A trophy that's almost as big as she is. Hair pulled back into a pony tail. Like all gymnasts, looking impossibly young.

Brady closed the file. Wrote 'optician' on his morning list. Didn't put a ring round it. Switched the office light off. Wondered if his daughter, her best friend and his dog had left him any pizza. Wasn't optimistic.

40

Brady put his key in the lock and opened the front door. Couldn't decide whether the house smelled of wet dog or pepperoni pizza. Walked into the lounge to see Tom Hanks holding hands with Meg Ryan.

"*Sleepless in Seattle*? I remember watching it with your mum."

"Hi Dad. It's just finishing if you want football or anything, We're going upstairs. You're sure it's alright if Bean stays over?"

"Of course I am. If it's alright with your mum, Bean?"

"She's fine, Mr Brady."

"What've I said, Bean? Call me, Mike. You make me feel old."

"Alright... Mike." Bean disappeared upstairs, leaving Brady with his daughter.

"Did the three of you leave me any pizza then?"

Ash nodded. "There's plenty. I didn't eat much."

Brady looked at her. "You alright, sweetheart? You look a bit... Is something bothering you?"

"No, I'm fine."

"You sure? You look like something's hurting."

Ash didn't reply. Simply looked at him.

Her mother's even-you-can-work-that-out face...

"Oh," Brady said. "Is, er... Is everything alright?"

"Do you mean, 'are my periods regular,' Dad? 'Is everything happening as it should?' Yes, don't worry. But that doesn't mean... Well, it's crap if you want to know."

"Sorry, sweetheart. I'm useless. You know I'm here if you want anything. Sorry, that's an even more useless comment."

She surprised him. Walked over to him. Reached up and kissed him on the cheek. "It's alright, Dad. I know. I'm going to bed. I'll get a hot water bottle."

"Don't spend all night talking. Remember it's school tomorrow."

"As if we would..."

She walked upstairs. Came back two minutes later with a hot water bottle. Boiled the kettle and filled it. "I'll see you in the morning, Dad. Can I take Archie up to the bedroom to keep me company?"

"You've got Bean."

"Maybe we're having a party..."

Brady hugged her. Bent forward and kissed the top of her head. "Of course you can, sweetheart. And shout me if you need me."

"What for?"

He laughed. "I've no idea. Love you."

. . .

BRADY WANDERED through into the kitchen. Turned the kettle on. Changed his mind and turned it off again. Opened the fridge and reached for a beer. Decided he couldn't be bothered to warm the pizza. Ate it cold in front of the TV. Flipped through the channels.

Two hundred channels and there's still nothing worth watching.

Turned the TV off, finished the pizza and stared at the ceiling. Massaged his temples. Closed his eyes.

Woke up and looked at his watch.

Ten past midnight. What happened?

Got stiffly to his feet and nearly fell over Archie. Bent down and ruffled the top of his head. "Hey up, pal. You had enough of teenage gossip? Thought you'd come down here and listen to an old man snoring on the sofa? You want a biscuit? Silly question. Come on…"

Brady walked through to the kitchen. Put his plate in the dishwasher, the beer bottle in the recycling. Reached for the dog biscuits, still half-asleep. "Here you go, mate. Falling asleep on the sofa, Arch. That's not good. That's what old people do. Can't be doing that. You and me, Archie, we need to get fit. Starting next – "

Michael Brady stopped. Stood in his kitchen with a packet of dog biscuits in his left hand.

'That's what old people do.'

That's what I missed.

Not what happened on that Saturday. Nothing to do with her going back to bed. Nothing to do with Alice, with what she was wearing. Nothing to do with the fiver she pinched from her mother's purse. Nothing to do with the boyfriend.

A simple, throwaway comment.

He heard Ruby say it.

'Maybe I'm getting sensible in my old age. Or maybe it's hormones. I'm nearly fifty, Mr Brady. Maybe it's the change. Maybe I'm turning into an old woman...'

Heard Ash.

'Do you mean, 'are my periods regular,' Dad?'

Ash was thirteen. Developing normally. Alice had been eleven...

Brady reached for his phone. Scrolled through his pictures.

Alice with her mischievous smile. And Sandra Donoghue. Thirteen, posing with the trophy that was almost as big as she was. Hair pulled back into a pony tail. Impossibly young.

Looking the same age as Alice...

Two girls on the edge of puberty.

Two murders that are connected.

Not Becky and Alice.

Sandra and Alice.

A girl in Middlesbrough found on waste ground behind an industrial estate. A girl in Whitby who's never been found.

Not yet...

BRADY DIALLED HER NUMBER. Didn't think about the time. Didn't wonder whether she'd answer.

"You know this is stalking don't you?"

"I'm sorry, Frankie. I had to tell you."

"It's gone midnight."

"It's not Becky and Alice, Frankie. It's Sandra and Alice."

"Sandra? The girl in Middlesbrough? How?"

"I'll explain tomorrow. I'll come round. That's why I rang. To tell you. And to check when you're in."

"Lunchtime, I think. I don't know. I'm speaking to you. My diary's on my phone. Lunchtime."

"Thank you. I'll come round. I'll explain everything."

"Right. And you expect me to go back to sleep now?"

"I'm sorry. I... I just needed to tell you."

41

"Come on, Archie, enough's enough. The rain's getting heavier." Brady reached down and clipped Archie's lead on. Persuaded a very wet, very reluctant dog to finally leave the beach. "And you've not rolled in anything, pal. There's a first time for everything."

Two minutes later he opened the tailgate of the Tiguan. Archie jumped in, accepted the obligatory biscuit and sat down. Brady climbed in, pushed wet hair out of his eyes and wondered what excuse he could give Ash.

'Dad, the car stinks. You know the smell of wet dog sticks to my school clothes, don't you?'

Accepted that he didn't have an excuse.

He'd driven less than a hundred yards when the phone rang. He glanced at the car display. Mandy Jamieson.

"Mandy. What can I do for you at this ungodly hour?"

He could hear the baby crying. A man's voice. "Where's my shirt?"

"Where it always is. I'm sorry, Mr Brady, I hope it's not too early?"

"It's never too early, Mandy. I've just come off a very wet beach with an impossibly wet dog. What is it?"

She sounded nervous. "I hope I've done the right thing. I was in the supermarket last night. I bumped into Jodie. You remember, I told you."

"One of your friends? That was with you on the Saturday afternoon? The one that didn't go to London to be a hairdresser. Yes, I remember."

"I told her about the questions you asked me. I hope that was alright. She phoned me later. Said she thought she ought to talk to you."

Brady glanced in the rear view mirror. Indicated left. Slowed down and pulled over to the side. "Did she say what it was?"

"No. She said she shouldn't tell me. 'Just in case,' she said."

"Where does she live?"

"Mickleby Drive? Do you know it."

Brady laughed. "It's round the corner from where I grew up. Could you text me her number?"

"Sorry," Jodie Kemp said. "Getting the kids ready for school. It's a bit of a tip."

"Don't worry," Brady said. "How old are they?"

"Five and seven. Emma next door took them for me. I saw Mandy in Sainsbury's last night. She told me she'd been talking to you. She felt guilty. Said she didn't really have anything to tell you."

"But you might have?"

Jodie nodded. "Maybe. I think so." She looked at him nervously. "I'll be alright won't I? Telling you. Just, I've got the children."

Brady nodded. "Whatever you tell me it's fine. This is just you and me. I'm guessing no-one talked to you twenty years ago?"

She shook her head. "No. And then they arrested that man from Middlesbrough. And I sort of forgot about it. Except when I see the van in Whitby."

"Who's van?" Brady said.

"It's what Alice said to me. I went with her when she bought the ice creams. She opened her purse and there was twenty, maybe thirty pounds in there. She – "

"You're sure about that? The money?"

"Yes. She saw me looking. She winked at me. 'Plenty more where that came from,' she said. 'Starting this afternoon.' That's who she was going to see."

"The person with the van?"

Jodie looked up at Brady. "Simpson and Nephew, written on the side of the van. Des Simpson is someone's nephew, but he was Alice's uncle. That's what she said to me. 'Starting this afternoon. When I see my uncle.'"

"Boss?"

Brady glanced up. Dan Keillor was at his door, a piece of paper in his hand.

"Morning, Dan. Success? Hopefully you've done better than me."

Brady had barely slept. Walked Archie. Left the house at seven. Scribbled a note to Ash.

Sorry, sweetheart. Emergency at work. There's £10 in the kitchen if it's raining and you and Bean need a taxi to school. Hope you're feeling better this morning. Love you.

PS I fed Archie. Don't let him fool you.

He'd parked the car. Bought a bacon sandwich and a coffee. Given himself indigestion. Pored over the files again. Gone to see Jodie.

Come back. Two things on his list. Speak to Fraser Hogg. Speak to Ruby.

He hadn't done either.

"Why's that, boss?"

"I wanted to talk to the guy in charge of the Middlesbrough case. He's retired now so I told myself he wouldn't be far away. His wife phoned me back. Said he'd gone fishing. 'Is he back today?' I say. 'Probably not,' she says. Trip of a lifetime for his sixty-fifth. Pata – bloody – gonia. Standing on the edge of a lake in Argentina. No signal, obviously."

And Ruby. 'This is Ruby. I'm not here. Leave a message and I'll get back to you.'

"So tell me you've had some joy, DC Keillor."

Dan smiled. "I think so. The agents said they'd merged with another company. The ones who'd originally dealt with that estate."

"What did you say to them?"

"I said I wanted a list of tenants from twenty years ago. Nothing more, nothing less. And would they keep the request to themselves."

Brady nodded. "Good. What've we got?"

"They were really helpful. The girl I spoke to went off and found the old file. Read it all to me. So two of the ones that are there now were there twenty years ago."

"The tyre and exhaust place. We knew that. Who else?"

"The engineers. JJ Engineering. Two units were empty in the year we want. The landlords were doing repairs to the roof."

"So that leaves four."

Dan nodded. "A beer and wine wholesaler. She said they got burgled three times. Gave up in the end. Double glazing – but different to the one that's there now. Another wholesale place – "

"What type?"

"Trade, she said. Supplies for small tradesmen."

Brady raised his eyebrows. "No-one over five foot six then?"

Dan Keillor laughed. "Sorry, boss. You know, local tradesmen. Not the big building firms. And the last one was supplies for hairdressers. Hair and beauty," he said doubtfully.

"You're thinking how do you need a warehouse for a pair of scissors and a razor? Me too. But we're men. What do we know?" Brady held his hand out for the list. Looked at it briefly. "This one, Dan. Supplies for your small tradesmen. Jefferson's. Get in touch with them. Let's hope they're still in business."

"What do you want to know, boss?"

"I want to know if they sell paint, Dan."

.   .   .

HIS PHONE RANG. Brady glanced at the display.

One out of two...

"Ruby, thanks for coming back to me."

"No problem. What do you want?"

"Ruby, there's no delicate way to put this. But it's a question I need answering. Had Alice's periods started?"

There was a long silence. Then, "Twenty years after she died the police want to know if her periods had started? What's the point of that?"

"I can't say, Ruby. Just trust me will you? Had Alice's periods started?"

"You're different, I'll grant you that. No bloody joy with 'what was she wearing?' and 'who were her friends?' so you think you'll try summat new."

"Ruby..."

"Yes, if you want to know. Yes, she had the first one about two weeks before... Before that day. Will that do you?"

"Thank you," Brady said. "That's all I wanted."

"Good. Oh, and I've got a question for you."

"What's that?"

"Blake gets out on Friday. Did you know?"

"How – "

"How did I find out? A little bird told me, Mr Brady. So not long to wait, eh?"

The line went dead.

BRADY PUT his head in his hands. Raked his fingers through his hair. Sighed. Muttered, "fuck."

"Boss?"

Dan Keillor was back.

"Sorry, Dan. Some news. Not the news I wanted. Paint. Do they sell it or don't they?"

"They did, boss. They don't now."

"Did you ask them if they sold it at that branch in Middlesbrough?"

Dan Keillor nodded. "That's what I did. They said no."

Brady felt his heart sink.

One step forward, two bloody great strides back. Again...

"But they said people could order it there. Then they put it on the van from the main depot in Sunderland. And you could collect it."

Brady nodded. Watched the final piece drop gently into the jigsaw. "Thanks, Dan. Great work. Thanks very much indeed."

42

Brady reached for his phone. Opened *Photos* and passed it to Frankie. "Scroll through," he said. "Ignore the sunrises. Brian Simpson tells me any fool with an iPhone can take a good sunrise."

"Just when you thought you'd found a new career... What am I looking for?"

"Alice, looking mischievous. And Sandra Donoghue. The photo from the newspaper. They're next to each other."

He watched Frankie swipe through until she found the first one. Sandra holding her impossibly big trophy.

Looking younger every time I see the photo...

Frankie flicked her finger across the screen. Looked at Alice with her impish, knowing smile. Flicked back to Sandra. Back to Alice. Looked up at Brady.

"That's what links them?" she said. "The photos? What they look like?"

Brady nodded. "I think so. More than think so. Alice

on the edge of puberty. Sandra the same. Two years older but – "

"Gymnastics," Frankie said. "Delayed puberty. There was a girl in my year. Sometimes it happens naturally. The East Germans used to do it with drugs, didn't they?"

"Two murders *were* connected," Brady said. "But we got it wrong. Everyone got it wrong. It wasn't Alice and Becky. It was Alice and Sandra."

"So is it my random stranger? Is that who we're looking for? Or does someone connect them? I know you, Mike. You wouldn't be this excited if it was a random stranger."

"We both know it wasn't that. Like Ruby said. Why would he drive past Sandsend and Loftus? Why would he drive past all those other girls and pick on Alice? He didn't. And it's not a person that connects them, Frankie. Not to begin with. It's a place."

"A place?"

They didn't sell paint, boss. But they said people could order it. Then they put it on the van from the main depot in Sunderland. And you could collect it.

"A cash and carry warehouse. Jefferson's. Which sold paint."

"Paint... You're saying Des and Brian are responsible?"

Brady shook his head. "No. Not Des. Brian. Ruby's uncle."

"Christ, Mike. You know what that'll do to her?"

"I know, Frankie. I know. Let me go through it. Tell me where I go wrong."

She nodded. Didn't speak.

"I think – and right now this is only supposition – I

think Brian was obsessed with girls that age. Little girl one minute, teenager the next. He was there buying paint for the business. He saw Sandra. Meets her somehow. Open your laptop, Frankie. It's time to feel dirty."

FRANKIE REACHED FORWARD. Switched her laptop on.

"I hate this," Brady said. "I know it's what I get paid for. I know it goes with the territory. But every time I find a new way for people to inflict misery on each other a little part of me dies."

"But you knew this existed. That some men..."

"Of course. I spent six sordid months in Manchester's vice squad. I've just never had to give this particular kink a name. Tap it into Google."

"And you have a daughter," Frankie said.

"Yes, I have a daughter."

He hesitated. *Do I want to share this with her? Why not? She said it. 'Everyone needs someone to confide in...'*

"When I came to Whitby... It was all going to be so simple, Frankie. I was going to be a good dad. I was going to write a book. Walk my dog on the beach. And then one morning I'm sitting there with Patrick's laptop – "

Frankie raised her eyebrows. Smiled at him. "Which I let you take."

Yes. And you knew that, didn't you? Knew that once I had the laptop I'd have to do something with it...

"You did. And there I am with a bruised and battered laptop. But with all Patrick's secrets on it. And I've a simple choice. I can take it down to the police station. Tell whoever's on duty I took it by mistake. If I do that I give

ed3ed3ed3

up any chance of investigating Patrick's death. But I stay...
'Clean' is the only word to use."

"But you didn't..."

"No, I didn't. And the moment I pick up the phone to
speak to Scholesy. The moment I try to find someone to
unlock the laptop. That's the moment I cross the line.
And it's like... It's like that feeling when you go to the
wardrobe. You find something you haven't worn for a
while. You put it on..."

"And you think 'I've missed you. I've really missed
you.' I know." Frankie paused. Looked at him. "It's what I
feel now. I thought I needed the six months off. I wanted
a break: spend time with Mum while she still remembered who I was. And I *did* need the time. But there's an
itch..."

Brady nodded. "Yeah. I went to the wardrobe. I
found the clothes I hadn't worn for a year. I picked
my phone up. Made the call. Put the clothes back
on. And it felt... comfortable. Right. And dirty. And
part of me didn't want it and part of me did.
Because Patrick deserved justice. And it was up
to me."

*That's how it was. Exactly how it was. I never had this
conversation with Grace...*

"And now Alice deserves justice."

Brady nodded. "Alice. And Sandra Donoghue. And
Ruby."

"And it's up to you."

"No. It's up to us, Frankie. Because I need this. So do
you. Why was I at two thousand words in my book when
I should have been at twenty-two? Why have you got an

itch you need to scratch? Because this is who we are, Frankie."

"So bang it into Google?"

"Yes. Bang it into Google."

Frankie tapped the mouse pad. Brought the laptop back to life. Smiled at him. "You realise what this is going to do to my search history? God alone knows what ads will stalk me round the internet now..."

Brady shook his head. "I'm forty-three, Frankie. Any day now it'll be hair restorer. Little blue pills. Consider yourself lucky."

"What am I typing?"

"Hebephilia. H – E – B – E – philia. From the Greek goddess of youth. The daughter of Zeus and Hera."

He stood behind her. Watched her type.

"Click on Wiki," Brady said. "Let's have the basics, not the sensational."

"Right. And maybe Google will let me off. Decide I'm doing academic research."

Frankie opened Wiki. Read the entry out loud. "Persistent sexual interest by adults in pubescent children who are in early adolescence, typically ages 11 to 14 and showing Tanner stages two to three of physical development. Whatever Tanner stages two to three are."

"I didn't check," Brady said. "But we can guess, can't we?"

Frankie twisted round to look at him. "You were reading this last night?"

"What do you think? And sorry again for ringing you.

I just – well, it all fitted. I wanted to tell you. And yes, I spent last night sitting at the computer. Slept for about an hour."

FRANKIE TURNED BACK to the laptop. "There seem to be plenty of people saying it's an illness."

"They can say what they want. Murdering Sandra. Murdering Alice. That's not an illness."

"Halfway between paedophilia and – I can't even pronounce this one – ephebophilia."

Brady nodded. "Going up through the ages. And that's what links Sandra and Alice. They're right on the edge of puberty. Right on the edge of becoming teenagers. Young women."

"And all your roads lead to Brian Simpson?"

"You said it, Frankie. Put your money on the family. Words to that effect."

She stood up. Walked over to the sofa. "You're convinced? How convinced?"

"Enough to apply for a search warrant. Tomorrow morning."

"Why?"

"Because it fits. Maybe not all roads. Enough roads."

"Tell me."

"Brian takes photos. When I went to Ruby's he'd brought her one. It's there on the worktop. As good a sunrise as I've ever seen. That's when he said it to me. 'Sunrises are ten a penny. Any fool with an iPhone can take a good sunrise.' Then Ruby said, 'he takes a few from his back garden.' So I wonder where his back garden is.

He lives out near Hawsker. A house overlooking the sea. I drove out there. It's a bloody big house for a painter and decorator, Frankie."

"He doesn't have children. I thought that was the secret to being well-off? Two incomes, no children?"

"Except he's not married. 'Can't hold down a relationship,' Ruby said. But maybe he does have two incomes. And only one of them is painting and decorating."

"What are you saying?"

"I'm saying that's what he's doing. Taking photos and selling them. You're not telling me he's the only man in the world with an interest in girls that age?"

"And that's what happened with Sandra?"

"Right now I think it's as good a guess as any. I think he saw her one time. It's a numbers game with him. Ask enough girls, eventually one says 'yes.' Or 'maybe.' And he arranges to meet her…"

"Supposing one of the girls says something?"

"It's twenty years ago, Frankie. You know what it was like. Who's going to believe her?"

"What about the waste ground where she was found? I thought it was hard to find?"

"Hard doesn't mean impossible, Frankie. Maybe he met her somewhere else. Maybe she told him about the waste ground. It was near her house."

"And then it all went wrong?"

Brady nodded. "And he lost his temper. Reached in his pocket. Found a weapon."

"A chisel?"

"Suppose it wasn't a chisel? You've seen painters and decorators. Those knives they use for filling holes. A young girl... An inexperienced pathologist? It's an easy mistake to make."

Frankie looked at him. "You said she was naked from the waist up. You think he took photos?"

Brady shook his head. "No. Because it was dark. Getting dark. The psychologist's report was right. It's a disorganised, spur-of-the-moment attack. Plenty of the report was right. The police used it on the wrong person."

"There'd have been blood. DNA. All over his van."

"Yes, there would. But nobody looked."

"Because they'd got Norman Blake."

Brady nodded. "Because they'd got Norman Blake."

Frankie stood up. Walked over to the window. "It's wrong," she said.

"What? The case?"

"No. Sitting down is wrong. It's never seemed right to me. Someone's telling you about a murder and you're sitting down. The briefing room's bad enough. But this... Last night I'm sitting on the sofa watching some film I can't even remember. Now I'm sitting there and you're telling me about painters' knives."

"I'm sorry, I – "

"No, don't be. Like you said it's what we do. Who we are. Why did he kill Alice?"

Brady shook his head. "I don't know. The obvious answer is that she found out. Threatened to tell someone."

"You think she'd do that? At her age?"

"Given what people have said about Alice, yes, I do. He couldn't take the risk could he? And... I think he was taking photos of Alice as well. I saw one of

Alice's other friends. Jodie Kemp. She said Alice opened her purse and 'there was twenty, maybe thirty pounds in there.' Ruby thought she was nicking the odd fiver out of her purse. And that's what kids do if they want money. They nick the odd fiver. They don't steal thirty quid. That had to come from somewhere else."

"And one day she says the wrong thing?"

"Right. When I was talking to Mandy she said something. Alice was quieter, more withdrawn after Becky died. So I made the obvious connection. Alice knew Becky: the two deaths were linked. But supposing that was around the time she found out about Sandra?"

"Or he started to take the photos..."

"Or she found something. Started to have suspicions. Manages to keep quiet for a month. And then she lets something slip."

Frankie sighed. "What did you say about being dirty? It's like someone's turned a sprinkler on. Where's Des in all this, Mike? He's Alice's uncle. He works with Brian. He's a father-figure to him."

"I thought at first he was involved."

"Why?"

"Because of something Jodie said. She said Alice saw her looking at the money. Said she winked and told her 'there's plenty more where that came from. Starting this afternoon when I see my uncle.'"

"Des is Alice's uncle. Was Alice's uncle. Brian's her great-uncle."

"Technically, yes. But would Alice call him that? Jason said it when he was emptying Ruby's fridge. 'I'm going to see Uncle Bri.' My guess is everyone in the family calls him Uncle Bri.'"

Frankie was silent. Thinking. "OK. I'll go along with that."

'Bri's off to the cash and carry. Rather him than me. Drive across the Moors in the dark to collect paint. But if he wants to do it let him.'

"Brian was the one who bought the paint," Brady said. "Not Des."

"You're saying Des didn't know? You think that's possible?"

"Yes, I do. We see what we want to see. And how many times do people say it. 'He'd been having an affair for ten years. I had no idea.' 'She'd been fiddling the accounts for years. We only found out when...' We've both heard it a hundred times, Frankie."

FRANKIE STOOD UP. "Like I said, Mike. You know what it's going to do to Ruby if you're right?"

Brady nodded again. "The law has to take its course. I said it to Eric Kennedy. He more or less told me to piss off. But this time it does."

"And sometimes it leaves casualties. Ruby's going to be a bloody big casualty, Mike."

"Not just Ruby. Sandra Donoghue's family. But there's nothing we can do, Frankie. Two girls have been murdered. *One* girl has been murdered. One's almost certainly been murdered."

"It's a bloody mess, Mike. They live with something for twenty years. Finally find a way to deal with it. We come along and turn it upside down. Sandra's parents... They've probably come to terms with Norman Blake. Now they'll have to come to terms with someone else. A different monster."

Brady nodded. "But we swore an oath to uphold the law."

"Who will you go in with?"

"Just Dan Keillor. Jake Cartwright and whoever else is on duty as back-up."

"You think that's enough?"

Brady looked at her. "You don't need to say it, Frankie. I know you want to be there. I want you there, but – "

"But you can't process the paperwork in time?"

Brady laughed. "Something like that."

"What are you going to say to Ruby?"

Brady shook his head. "What can I say? The truth. I promised I'd tell her the truth."

"We've found out who killed Alice. It was your uncle. I'm very sorry, Ruby, the last twenty years have been a lie? Good luck with it, Mike."

"I know. I thought I'd touched bottom when I told Ian Foster his wife wasn't who he thought she was. This might be a new low. 'Sorry, Ruby, the man who brought you up? Your uncle? The guy you've just made a cup of tea? He's the one who murdered your daughter.'"

Frankie walked over to him. Put her hands on his shoulders. "You should take a holiday when this is over."

"I should. See my GP as well. Ask him to write me a prescription for an easy life. Six months of straightfor-ward, simple policing. Black hats and white hats. No shades of grey. But it'll have to wait."

"When do you get the warrant?"

"I'm seeing the magistrate at ten."

"When are you going in?"

"The afternoon. I want him at home. As soon as the light's not good enough for painting. I have to. They know when Blake's coming out."

"They can't. That's not public knowledge."

"I was on the phone to Ruby. 'A little bird told me, Mr Brady.'"

"Who?"

"I don't know. And right now it doesn't matter. What does matter is Norman Blake arriving in Whitby. Getting off the bus with his lucky fishing rod. And getting safely onto a boat."

"You don't know they'd do anything."

"No, I don't. But it's not a risk I can take."

43

Half an hour until sunset. The light fading.

Brady parked his car outside Brian Simpson's house.

"Two minutes, Dan. I want a word with Jake."

He climbed out. Walked back up the road a hundred yards. "You and Col stay here, Jake. I'll give you a call when – if – I want you to come in. But right now let's keep it low-key. He's gone sixty. We don't need to make it a crowd scene."

He turned and walked back along the road. Glanced to his right. Across a field and out to sea, a storm cloud on the horizon.

Twenty years. Twenty years of lying about Alice. Frankie's right. God only knows what this'll do to Ruby. When do I tell her? As soon as I'm finished here. Ten minutes to drive to her house...

"You've got the warrant, Dan?"

"Right here, boss."

"OK, let's do this."

. . .

Brian Simpson's white van was parked in front of the house, a black Audi TT next to it.

No, I wouldn't drive the van at the weekend either...

Brady rapped three times on the front door. Didn't have to wait long.

He was still wearing his overalls, a black t-shirt underneath them, a can of lager in his left hand.

"Brian Simpson, I am Detective Chief Inspector Michael Brady. This is Detective Constable Keillor. We have a warrant to search these premises. And I would like to talk to you about the disappearance of Alice Simpson and the murder of Sandra Donoghue."

The worn-out rock star in paint-spattered overalls stood belligerently in his doorway. "Number one I know who you are, so you don't need to get all official. Number two you can tell me what you're looking for. Or you're not coming in."

"Mr Simpson, this is a search warrant. Issued by a court. Authorising me to enter your house and conduct a search. Now I can do this in one of two ways. I can arrest you – "

"Arrest me? What the hell are you talking about? Arrest me? What for?"

Brady took a step back. Took his time replying. "I can arrest you in connection with the murder of Sandra Donoghue. And while you're being held in custody I can search your house, and take away whatever I think is relevant. Computers, clothes, cameras. Anything. Or you can co-operate. Let me in and answer some questions. And then we'll see if a search is justified."

And if you haven't worked it out by now the reason I'm

doing it this way is to protect Ruby. Because I don't want her to find out you've been arrested through the Whitby grapevine...

Brady looked him in the eye. "So the choice is yours, Mr Simpson. You can co-operate or you can't. Either way – "

"Bri? What are you doing out there? You're taking a bloody long time to tell Jehovah's Witnesses to piss off."

Ruby. What's she doing here?

The best laid plans... Every bloody time.

"What's going on? And... Mr Brady. Why are you here?"

Brady looked at Brian Simpson. Raised his eyebrows. "So are you going to let us in? Or do you want me to arrest you in front of Ruby?"

Simpson didn't speak. Turned his back. Stalked down the hall. Brady took it as a 'yes' and followed him. Saw him say something to Ruby. Turn left and walk into a lounge.

"Come on, Dan. And call Jake. Tell him to stand at the door. No-one else to come in. And tell Col to get some back-up. We're going to do a search. And we'll need some help."

The lounge was wood-panelled. Untidy. A single man's lounge. But the walls covered in black and white portraits. The lined faces of Whitby fishermen. Lives laid bare in a single photograph.

You've a talent, Brian. I'll grant you that...

A picture window ran the length of the far wall. A glass door in the middle of it. Decking outside, steps leading down to the garden. A low fence, the cliff top path. And then the sea.

'Takes a few sunrises from his back garden, don't you, Bri? They make me feel optimistic. But looking at your face, Mr Brady, I'm not.'

You've good reason today, Ruby...

There was a wooden table in front of the window. Two wooden chairs. Salt and pepper. A lonely coffee cup.

Simpson sat down on one of the chairs. Put his can of lager on the table. Gestured at the other chair. "Ask away, cock. All you're doing is telling us you haven't got a clue where Alice is. Like I said. Leave it to us."

"If 'leave it to us' is a reference to Norman Blake – "

"You know full well it's a 'reference to Norman Blake.' Never mind. We'll sort it..."

Brady glanced across the lounge. "You need to talk some sense into him, Ruby."

She shook her head. "I want to know where she is. That's all I care about. I've waited twenty years. It's long enough."

What are they planning to do? Camp at the bus station? Watch every bus from Middlesbrough? Maybe they are...

Brady turned back to Brian Simpson. "You used to drive up to Middlesbrough, Mr Simpson. You bought your paint from Jefferson's, which was on the industrial estate, close to where Sandra Donoghue's body was found."

He shrugged. "Still do, cock. Except they've moved across town. I'm a painter and decorator. It's the closest wholesaler. Or are you suggesting I get twenty litres of Sunburst Yellow off Amazon?"

"I'm suggesting that the waste ground where Sandra Donoghue was found is just behind that warehouse, Mr Simpson. That you knew about it. That maybe you arranged to meet her there?"

"You're talking bollocks."

"What's he on about, Bri?"

"I've no idea, Ruby. You said we were getting somewhere with this one. Strikes me he's even more stupid than the others."

Brady turned and faced Ruby.

It didn't have to be like this. She didn't have to find out this way. But he's giving me no option...

"Twenty years ago, Ruby – about two months before Alice disappeared – a girl was murdered in Middlesbrough. Her name was Sandra Donoghue. She was thirteen. Found on waste ground behind an industrial estate. Where Brian bought paint for the business."

Ruby shrugged. "So what? An industrial estate? What are you doing? Questioning every plumber, sparkie and brickie between here and Newcastle?

"No, Ruby, I'm questioning your uncle. *Just* your uncle. And I'm doing it because while Sandra Donoghue was thirteen she looked younger. Two or three years younger. Roughly the same age – "

'You know what it's going to do to Ruby if you're right?'

'The law has to take its course.'

And here's the first casualty...

"I'm sorry, Ruby," Brady said. Looked at her. Saw the realisation, what it might mean, creeping across her face.

"I'm sorry, Ruby," he said again. "She looked a lot like Alice. I think Sandra's death, Alice's disappearance, were linked. And there's only one person links the two girls. Can possibly link the two girls." Brady stood up, turned back to Brian Simpson. "You might be the link eh, Brian? Why don't you tell Ruby about your part-time job? About taking photographs of the girls?"

Brian Simpson rose to his feet. Defiant, the lines on his face suddenly deeper. Shook his head. "I've no fucking idea what you're talking about. No fucking idea – "

There was a noise in the doorway. Footsteps coming down the hall.

"Just fuck off. I'll decide if I can go in Brian's house or not."

"Sir, if I say you can't go in – "

Des was standing in the doorway. "What the fuck's going on? I'm supposed to be away tomorrow. Just came to check on a job for Monday. And bloody PC Plod here tells me I can't come in."

Brady turned to face him. "Calm down, Des. This has nothing to do with you. Do what PC Cartwright says. Go and sit in your van. Calm yourself down."

"Tell me what's going on."

"He's trying to arrest Bri," Ruby said. "Sits in my kitchen drinking my tea and then he comes here and tries to arrest Bri."

Brady saw Des glance at his uncle. Saw the expression flicker across his face.

A split-second. Enough.

He knows. He's known all the time...

"You know, don't you, Des? You know what happened."

"What's he talking about," Ruby said. "What's he talking about now? Someone tell me what's bloody happened?"

"Boss! Boss!"

Brady turned. Saw why Dan Keillor was yelling. Brian Simpson was through the door. Across the decking. Down the steps into the garden. Running across the lawn. Ten, fifteen yards. Only the fence between him and the cliff top path. Then the edge. Then the rocks and the North Sea.

"Brian!" Brady raced through the door after him. "Brian! Don't be bloody stupid."

Brady watched Brian Simpson put his left hand on the fence. Vault over it. Stumble slightly as he landed. Right himself. Stand on the footpath. Face him.

"Don't come any closer. One step back and I'm gone. Straight down to the rocks."

Brady was conscious of everyone rushing out of the house. Ruby, Dan Keillor, Des, Jake Cartwright. "Dan! Keep them back. Keep everybody back."

Saw something out of the corner of his eye. Two walkers coming towards Simpson. A young couple. Early twenties. Blue jackets, the girl with walking poles. He saw them stop. Stare.

"Turn round," Brady yelled at them. "Turn round and walk away. I'm a police officer. Turn round and walk away!"

Saw Brian Simpson glance at the walkers. Take a pace towards them.

"Don't you dare!"

Brady darted forward. Vaulted the fence. Felt his

ankle twist as he landed. Ignored the pain. Stood between Simpson and the young couple. "Do as I say," he said without turning round. "Turn round. Go back. And keep your phones in your pockets."

Brady glanced to his right. Saw that Brian Simpson hadn't been lying. Three, maybe four feet of the cliff top. Then the edge. Two hundred feet down. The waves breaking on the rocks.

"Keep them all back, Dan," Brady said, still without taking his eyes off Simpson. "Just keep them both back. 'Cuff them if you have to."

Brady felt his breathing slowly return to normal. Took a pace back.

Three options. He steps over the edge. He gives himself up. He attacks me. If it's the last one I want plenty of space. Make sure I'm nowhere near the edge.

"What's it going to be then, Brian? You going to take two steps to your left? Take Alice with you? Ruby's worth more than that. She's entitled to know. After all, Des knows what happened. That's what Ruby said to me. 'Des has always been there for me.' Guilt, eh? It's a powerful thing."

Simpson shook his head. "You're wrong. He didn't know."

"What are you talking about, Brian? Sandra? Or Alice? Or both. Because if it's both I don't believe you."

Simpson didn't reply. Glanced to his left. Down at the rocks.

"Don't," Brady said. "You've murdered one girl. Ruined God knows how many lives. But you're better than that. And you've got family. Ruby. Des. They don't deserve it."

"I'm not going to spend the rest of my life in prison. You think I want to go from this to some fucking exercise yard?"

I came to question him. Now I'm talking him out of suicide...

"No, I don't. But I don't think you want to jump either. Two hundred feet, Brian? What's that going to take? A second? Two seconds? Long enough to regret it. And supposing it doesn't kill you? Suppose you're lying there on the rocks? Broken. The tide comes in. Drowning. It's a bloody awful way to go. 'Like molten lava poured down your throat' someone told me. Friday afternoon, Brian. Might take us a while to get the rescue helicopter out."

Brian Simpson crossed his arms in front of him. Started to slowly sway from side to side. Stared at Brady. "Middlesbrough," he said. "He didn't know about Middlesbrough."

Brady nodded. "I think he did, Brian. I think Alice found out about Sandra. And Des found out about Alice. And he's known all along. God knows what that'll do to Ruby when I tell her."

I need to know where Alice is. Before he jumps. If he jumps. I need to know where she is...

"What did you do with her, Brian?"

Simpson carried on swaying. Looked down at the rocks. Didn't speak. Brady felt the wind getting stronger. Swirling towards the sea. Felt rain spatter against his forehead.

"Tell me what happened to Alice, Brian. Where is

she? Right now I don't care how she died. We can't bring her back. I do care about where she is. Ruby deserves that. Somewhere she can go on Christmas Day. On Alice's birthday. If you care about her..."

Brian Simpson didn't speak. Carried on swaying. Glancing to his left.

"Brian, there's something you need to know. I'm not a hero. I'm a copper. But more importantly I'm a father. And I intend to go on being a father. So I don't know what you're thinking right now. But if you're planning to take a step to the left – thinking that I'm going to heroically dive forward and save you... I'm sorry, the answer's no. I've done heroics. Some bastard called Jimmy Gorse on the end of the pier. And I thought afterwards – just between ourselves – I thought afterwards, when I was calm and rational, I thought about my daughter. And how much she meant to me. And you know what, Brian? If Jimmy Gorse killed me, my last thought as I lay dying would have been her. That I'd let her down. Hadn't put her first."

Simpson stopped swaying for a moment. Looked at Brady. "What are you saying?"

"I'm saying that's where you are now, Brian. You're on the end of the pier. And the choice is simple. Do you put yourself first? Take a couple of steps to the left. Escape? Get away with it? Or do you put your family first? Ruby. You brought her up, Brian. From the age of ten. You were more or less her dad, for God's sake. So what's it going to be? Two seconds of falling, knowing you did the wrong thing? Or come with me. And know you did the right thing?"

Brady felt the wind strengthen even further. Shivered as it cut through his jacket. Felt the rain get heavier.

Watched Brian Simpson start swaying again. Saw him lean forwards. Bend at the knees. Uncross his hands. Slide them down his legs. Rest them on his knees.

Like someone bowing. Accepting defeat. Waiting to be beheaded...

Brady took a pace forwards. Simpson said something. But it was lost in the wind. "Say that again, Brian."

Simpson looked up at Brady. His lips moved. For the second time the wind blew the words straight out to sea.

"Brian, the wind's too strong. Say it again."

Brian Simpson stared straight ahead. Past Brady. Slowly turned his head. Looked at the four people standing in the middle of the garden. Turned back to Brady. Finally found the strength to say it clearly.

"Under the fucking flowers."

Fell forward onto the cliff top path. Rolled onto his right hand side. Started to sob.

44

Brady felt the wind buffet him. The rain get even heavier. Saw Dan Keillor vault over the fence. Kneel by Simpson's side. Put the handcuffs on him. Place his left hand under Simpson's right arm. Pull him gently to his feet. Turn to Brady.

"What did you say, boss?"

Brady smiled. "Just what it says in the textbook, Dan. Told him I was too old to get wet and cold. Come on, let's get him inside. Over there. There's a gate. Take him back into the house that way."

Dan Keillor led Simpson towards the gate. Jake Cartwright and Des stood watching. "Jake," Brady called, nodding at Des at the same time. "In the car with that one, please. He's got a few questions to answer. More than a few."

Where's Ruby? Has she gone back inside? Can't worry about her now. These two to sort out...

"Through the gate, Dan. And keep hold of him. I don't want any stupidity."

Brady looked up. Saw Jake leading Des up the steps into the house. "You and Col take him down to the station, Jake. Book him in. I need to question him. And get some back-up will you? I need the house sealing off. And find someone to be with Ruby."

Wherever the hell she is...

Dan Keillor had steered Simpson through the gate and into the garden. "Up the steps and into the house, Dan. I'll be there in a minute."

He looked back at the garden in the fading light.

There, in the corner...

Brady walked over to the flower bed. One of the flowers, defying the wind, the cold, the salt air, still had a few deep red petals on it. Brady looked down, ignored the rain running down his neck.

"He gave you a view then, Alice. Becky on the Moors, you by the sea. Watching the sunrise. I'm sorry it took me so long to find you. I'll go and tell your mum. She's waited long enough..."

He walked back across the garden. Reached the steps leading to the house. Put his foot on the bottom step.

Heard the scream. One part anguish to three parts revenge.

"You! You fucking bastard! All these years and you fucking knew!"

Brady was up the steps in two strides. Stood in the doorway. Dan Keillor and Brian Simpson to his right, backed against the settee. Ruby two yards in front of them, a carving knife in her right hand.

A chef's carving knife. Short black handle. Long, sharp blade.

Ruby raised her left hand. Brought it across in front of her. Motioned for Brady to stop. Never took her eyes off Brian Simpson. "You don't come any closer, Michael Brady. This has nothing to do with you. This is family. My Alice."

"Don't be stupid, Ruby. Put the knife down. I know where Alice is."

Ruby nodded. Her eyes still staring straight ahead. "She'll wait. Five more minutes, she'll wait."

Brady took a step forward.

"Don't! I'm warning you. Either of you coppers move..."

She's right. A struggle. Four people. Anything could happen. Where the hell's Jake? In the car with Des. Where I sent him. Where's the back-up? Not here...

"Dan, don't do anything. That's an order. Ruby, put the bloody knife down. Leave him to me. You go and see Alice. Let me tell you where she is."

"I heard. We heard him. Under the flowers. Under the fucking flowers. I've stood in that garden on Christmas Day. He never told me. My little girl and he never told me..."

She lowered her gaze for a minute. Spoke softly, almost to herself. "My little girl. I stood next to her. And he never fucking told me."

Now. Gently, firmly, step forward. Take the knife...

Ruby suddenly straightened up. Stared at Simpson. Yelled at the top of her voice.

"YOU NEVER FUCKING TOLD ME!"

Lunged forward. Raised the knife.

Brady flung himself at her, left arm outstretched.

Felt Dan Keillor yank Simpson away.

Saw the knife flash down.

Felt something punch into his arm.

Felt the skin tear.

Felt the blood running warm.

Sank to his knees.

Saw Dan Keillor push Simpson onto the floor.

Saw him throw himself on top of Ruby.

Heard the knife clatter harmlessly away.

Wondered if they'd brought enough handcuffs with them...

45

Michael Brady adjusted the sling. Reached forward carefully. Opened the door of the interview room. Saw Dan Keillor on one side of the table, Des Simpson and a solicitor he knew slightly on the other.

"I got you a coffee, boss. There's a new machine."

"Is there? We live in hope, Dan. Thanks."

Brady sat down. Switched the recording on. Looked at Des Simpson and the solicitor. Smiled. "How do you want to play it, Des? You want to tell me the story? Or do you want me to ask a lot of questions? I'd prefer the former because my arm hurts like hell. But your sister missed everything important so I'm feeling magnanimous. And she's entitled to know. Like she said to me, she needs somewhere to go on Christmas Day. Somewhere to take Alice's teddy bear..."

Des Simpson opened his mouth to speak. The solicitor stopped him. "My client has committed no crime, Detective Chief Inspector. He would like it recording that you have held him overnight on the – wholly unwarranted I might say – suspicion of assisting an offender. And the condition of your arm, unfortunate as it may be, is of no relevance to Mr Simpson."

Oh piss off. Why do I dislike solicitors so much? Thank God Ash wants to be a vet...

"Do I take it then that I'm asking the questions? A young girl has disappeared, Mr Scott. Possibly murdered. It appears that Mr Simpson knew about it."

"I repeat, Detective Chief Inspector. He has committed no crime. As you well know."

Brady smiled again.

Why am I in such a good mood this morning? Possibly because I still have a left arm...

"When did you find out, Des?"

Des Simpson glanced at his solicitor. Scott nodded. An 'if you have to' nod. Des bent forward. Clasped his hands in front of him. Bowed his head. Spoke to the table.

"Eighteen months maybe?"

"Eighteen months after Alice disappeared? Or eighteen months ago?"

"First one. April time. I went round to Bri's. I thought he'd be there. I needed some paint for a job. Back then we were storing it at his place. Before we got the lock-up. There wasn't any in the garage. And..."

He shook his head. Stopped talking. Stared into space. Five seconds. Ten seconds...

"There's no paint in the garage," Brady prompted.

"No. Like I said, I thought Bri would be there. Found out later someone had run into the side of his van. That's why he wasn't there."

"So there's no paint in the garage... And you look somewhere else?"

Des nodded. "There's a door. Connects the garage to the house. Or I thought it did. So I think maybe he's put the paint through there. 'Cos he was getting a new car and I thought maybe he was going to keep it in the garage. And the door's locked. But I have a look around. And stick my hand up on the top shelf and have a feel for it. And there's the key."

"And what did you find when you opened the door?"

"Another room. And..."

"You don't have to answer," the solicitor said.

Des Simpson shook his head. "Yeah, I do. 'Cos he's right. Ruby's entitled to know."

"What did you find?"

"A photo. You know, a portrait. Lying on a desk."

"A photo of Alice?"

Des Simpson shook his head. "No. Just a girl."

'Just a girl.' Except she's someone's daughter...

"A girl I didn't know. But... Posed. You know..."

"About Alice's age?"

He nodded. "Yeah. About that age. And... I turn it over. And there's her name on the back of it. Kayleigh. And it stuck with me 'cos Bri's a bit dyslexic and he usually gets his spellings wrong. I and E, you know..."

"Then what?" Brady said.

Des Simpson shook his head. Bowed it lower. "I opened a drawer. To see what else there was. And that's when I found it."

"What did you find?"

"I found Alice's sweatshirt. The hoodie. The grey one she wore all the time."

"Des, I appreciate your co-operation. And I understand this is difficult for you. But I need to be sure of this." Brady reached for his phone. Showed him the picture.

Alice. Long blonde hair, blue eyes. Wearing a grey hoodie with 'Angel' on the front. Half smiling...

"Is that the hoodie?"

Des Simpson nodded.

"Could you confirm it please, Des? Just for the tape?"

"Yes, that's the hoodie I found. Alice's hoodie."

"I'm guessing Brian took the photo?"

"One afternoon when we were all round at Ruby's. He said Alice was a natural. 'Born for the camera.' I can hear him saying it."

"Do you want a break?" Brady said. "Are you alright to carry on?"

"No. Let's get this over and done with. Am I going to prison?"

No, you're not. But you've got to live with it. And one day you'll have to explain it all to Ruby...

"You haven't committed a crime," the solicitor said. "In this country not reporting a crime isn't a crime. So you don't have to say anything."

Des Simpson almost laughed. "Too late now. Besides..."

He's lived with this for nearly twenty years. He needs to tell me. Wants to tell me...

"How long was it before you said anything to your uncle?"

"Six months? I didn't know what to do." Des Simpson finally lifted his head. Spread his hands. Looked at Brady.

Like he wants my help. My advice...

"It was driving me mad. I thought, 'Ruby's coming to terms with it. What will it do to her?' Then – I was selfish. I'm sorry – I'd just got wed. Got a mortgage. Business was going well. We were busy. Maybe folks booked us out of sympathy. I just didn't know what to do."

"But in the end you said something?"

He nodded. "Couldn't keep it in any longer. The anniversary was coming up. Two years since she'd gone. And one day I just said it. We were in the van, driving out to a job. And I just said it. 'I know about Alice.'"

"And what happened?"

"Cool as you like. Bri pulls over. Phones the customer we're going to see. Tells her we need some more paint. 'We'll be half an hour late, Mrs Green.' Then he drives up on the Moors and talks to me."

"What did he say?"

"Says it was an accident. Said Alice was up there one day. She'd been on the seafront. Bri had collected her somewhere. He says she disappears and when she comes back she's wearing this blouse she's found..."

'Miss Donoghue's blouse was missing. The taking of clothing as a 'trophy' is well known.'

"And Alice says, 'can I keep it?' Bri says no. Told me he was frightened. Thought Alice would work it out."

She wouldn't have known about Sandra Donoghue. But Brian Simpson isn't thinking rationally...

"Alice says she wants to keep it. And it escalates. Brian

tries to grab her. She slips. He's having some building work done. There's a brick on the floor..."

"And so he decides to bury her in the garden?"

"He said he panicked. Didn't think. Said it was October. It had been raining. Said it didn't take any time at all. Then afterwards it was too late. And the police didn't seem very interested in Alice. And then they found that bloke – Norman Blake – in Middlesbrough."

Brady sat back in his chair. Slowly exhaled. Tried to imagine the scene.

Brian Simpson digging feverishly. Worried some walkers would come along the cliff top path at any minute. Worried someone would turn up.

Edmund Kennedy had sat calmly in his tent...

"How did he persuade you to keep quiet?"

"He just set it all out. We're sitting in the van. He unscrews the flask. Pours us both a cup of tea. 'Ruby's coming to terms with it.' 'You've just got married.' 'The business is doing well.' 'We can't bring Alice back, all we can do is take care of Ruby.' You don't understand. He was like a dad to me. I couldn't say no. And I'd kept quiet for six months. I thought I might go to jail."

"So you knew about Middlesbrough? Sandra, as well as Alice?"

Des Simpson didn't speak. Simply nodded.

"Des? Mr Simpson? For the tape?"

"Yes." He sucked his breath in. Shook his head. "Yes, I knew. He told me when we were in the van. Said he hadn't meant it. Like Alice it had all got out of hand. He said... He told me it was an illness. Young girls. He couldn't help it. Said he was going to get help."

And selling the photos was an illness was it? How many other girls were there after Alice?

"But he never did?"

"No. But... well, it was easier for both of us, wasn't it? A lie we could both believe."

Brady looked at him. "Like Norman Blake?"

Des Simpson nodded. "Yeah, like that. Maybe we did it to give Ruby some comfort. Maybe we half-believed it ourselves. You say something often enough and it becomes the truth doesn't it?"

"You told me I was useless because I couldn't find Alice. When I met you at Ruby's. 'Fucking useless' if I remember correctly."

"Yeah. Sorry." He shrugged. "Norman Blake... He became the truth. That was what Ruby believed. How could I change that? Say, 'Sorry, Ruby, got a bit of bad news...' I'm trapped, aren't I? Can't say anything. So I just tried to be there for her."

"And you've lived with it ever since?"

"Every day. My wife left me. She knew there was something wrong with me but I could never tell her what it was. Gradually it got too much for her. So I was on my own. Now I paint through the week an' run up hills at the weekend. Running away. Don't need to be a genius to work that out."

"Ruby said you're always there for her."

"Don't need to be a bloody genius to work that one out either, do you?"

Brady sighed. Picked his phone up and put it back in his pocket. "One last question, Des. Did you know Brian was still taking photographs? Still selling them?"

"No. Maybe. We didn't talk about it. I don't think he was doing so much now he's getting older. I did sometimes wonder though..."

"Wonder what?"

"Why no-one worked it out. The house, the holidays he took, the car. He did bloody well for a painter and decorator. Why no-one twigged."

Brady stood up. "Thank you, Des. I appreciate all you've told us. Obviously we've a post-mortem to do but... I'm guessing it'll confirm your story."

"So can I go?"

Brady nodded. "You're free to go, Des. We've no grounds to hold you."

I can't prove anything. Your solicitor knows I can't prove anything.

"I've no more questions. Not for today. DC Keillor will finish up all the formalities. I need to talk to Ruby."

And the best of luck when you finally speak to her...

46

The same interview room where I first spoke to her. A lifetime ago...

"I thought I'd have to come and see you in the hospital. If I got bail. A bunch of grapes and squirt that bloody gel all over my hands."

Brady laughed. "They wanted me to stay in overnight. Said I'd lost a lot of blood. I said no thanks. Taxi home at two in the morning."

"Just stitches then?"

"About twenty. But you missed everything important Ruby. Some damage to the muscle. But the specialist said it'll be OK. With time. And provided I do my exercises."

Ruby nodded. "That's good. I'm sorry. What will I get?"

"What will you get?"

"Wounding a police officer. That's the charge isn't it? Six months? I've never been inside. First time for everything."

Brady looked at her. A woman who'd lost her child.

'Find her for me, Mr Brady. I know she's dead. I know I'll never see her again. But find her. Give me a place to go on her birthday. Christmas Day. Somewhere I can take her teddy bear. Lay flowers. Find Alice for me, Mr Brady.'

"You only go inside if you're found guilty, Ruby. You're only found guilty if you're charged…"

"You're not going to?"

Brady shook his head. "No, Ruby, I'm not. Would it make my arm heal any quicker? Would it help *you* heal any quicker? I'd say a caution would be about right, wouldn't you?"

Ruby smiled. Nodded.

"Besides," Brady said. "I was in your debt."

"Shelley?" Ruby frowned. "She's a wrong 'un is that girl. You'll be seeing her again. But you and me… If you're sure. We'll call it quits shall we, Mr Brady?"

"More than quits, Ruby. If you answer me one question."

"What's that?"

"You knew when Norman Blake was coming out of prison. 'A little bird told me, Mr Brady.' Would I know that little bird, Ruby?"

"You've always been straight with me, Mr Brady. I'll be straight with you. Yes, you would."

Brady nodded. "I thought so. Thank you. So what are you going to do, Ruby?"

"Me? I'm going to walk up on the cliff top a lot. I know you'll have to move her. I know there's stuff you have to do. But that's where she was. So I'll get as close as your lads will let me. Twenty years. We've a lot of catching up to do."

"And you'll have somewhere to go on Christmas Day."

Ruby nodded. "Aye. That I will. And on her birthday. I'm guessing you can't tell me what happened?"

"You're guessing right, Ruby. I've spoken to Des but I need to interview Brian. Next job. So no, I can't. Not right now."

"But you will do? I'll have the kettle on." Ruby paused. "I did a bit of thinking overnight. And I'm too old for a night in the cells, I tell you that. But if Brian's the price I have to pay for it..." She sniffed. Reached in her pocket for a tissue. "And Des. If that's the price I pay for laying Alice to rest. Well, it's a heavy price. But it's a price worth paying. So thank you."

"You're welcome, Ruby. More than welcome. You let me know when Alice's funeral is won't you? Memorial service. Whatever you decide to have. I'll make sure I'm there."

The door opened. Dan Keillor walked in. "All sorted with Des, Dan?"

"Sorted, boss. You want me to..."

"Sit in on the interview? No need, Dan. I've told Ms Simpson we'll be issuing a caution. That seems about right. So she's free to go."

47

Michael Brady put the key in the lock. Pushed on his new front door. It resolutely refused to open.

"Frankie," he said. "You couldn't... With this arm..."

"You're not strong enough to open your own front door?" She looked him up and down. Nodded. "It comes to all men..."

Frankie put her shoulder unceremoniously to the door. "When's the builder start?"

"Monday morning."

"So he knows his first job..."

Brady stepped inside. Turned the hall light on. "Welcome to The Crow's Nest. You're the first visitor."

"I can't be."

"You are. The builder, the architect, Ash obviously. But you're the first visitor who's not family."

"You mean I'm the first visitor who's not going to cost you money..."

Brady laughed. "Unless you fall through the floor and sue me." He reached for the switch, turned the light on in the hall. "One of my better light switches," he said. "Only a fifty-fifty chance of being electrocuted. How the old lady didn't kill herself I will never know."

"So it's the light from our phones? Romantic..."

I need to say something to her. Have to say something...

"Yeah. And the lights from the harbour. Come on, I'll show you what's going to be the lounge."

Brady led the way upstairs. Carefully opened the door. "Remember what I said. Walk round the edge..."

She ignored him. Cut across the middle of the room. Stood by the window. Gazed out at the harbour, the lights reflecting off the water. "This is beautiful, Mike. You're definitely going to do it?"

"The balcony? Definitely. Chris has got a structural engineer coming next week. To work out how much steel we'll need. And then we extend the steel beams out of the window."

"I'm jealous," Frankie said. "Truly, madly, deeply jealous."

Brady gestured at a corner of the room. "Sit down," he said. "Enjoy the view."

Frankie looked behind her. "Those are the old plastic chairs from the police canteen?"

Brady nodded. "Yeah. I had one. Got another especially for you. I spent a couple of nights here when Ash was away. Just sitting and thinking. Trying to work it out."

"Alice?"

"Alice, Becky, Sandra Donoghue. The backpack. Deciding to go and see Norman Blake. I was in Ash's bedroom. There was a fishing boat going out. I thought about him wandering round Whitby. Going to see him seemed the obvious thing to do."

"You think he'll come here? Go on his fishing trip?"

"I'm sure he will. He told me it was the only thing that kept him going." Brady looked out at the harbour. "Twenty years for a crime he didn't commit, Frankie. He'll get so much compensation he'll be able to buy a boat. Go fishing every day."

Frankie ignored the battered chair. Stood next to him at the window. "Maybe he'll take you with him..."

"Don't say that. Dave will be back from Spain next month. I still owe *him* a fishing trip. And I've run out of excuses."

"You think Kershaw will get away with it?"

"Blake's confession? I'm bloody certain Kershaw will get away with it. Where's the evidence? There isn't any."

Do I tell her? Kershaw told Ruby when Blake was coming out? Yes. She might be reporting to him one day. She's entitled to know...

"Kershaw told Ruby," Brady said. "Or Brian. It doesn't matter which one."

Frankie nodded. "He was the only option wasn't he? You told Kershaw – "

"And Kershaw saw a chance of silencing Norman Blake. Removing any chance of him talking about the confession. Decided it was too good to miss."

"And like you say, he gets away with it."

"For now. It pisses me off, but..."

"You can't win them all?"

"I can't. But karma has tapped me on the shoulder. I've been compensated."

"How?"

"You haven't heard? What's happened to the police grapevine?"

"I'm on sabbatical, remember?"

"Even so... Kershaw's going."

"What? For good?"

"For six months. Maybe more. He called me in this morning. Revealed the answer to the mystery. Why he's been away so much. Why he invested so heavily in a new suit. 'Smug' is not an adequate word, Frankie."

"What's happened?"

"He's been appointed to some special commission. Six months considering the future of the police service. 'Outreach and inclusivity.' 'Community engagement.' Every bloody management cliché you can think of. So he's in London for six months. Maybe more."

"Does that mean..."

"Yes it does. When you come back Michael Brady will be the boss of bosses. *Capo dei capi*. Providing the Chief Constable stays on the golf course..."

"So Whitby will be a crime free zone?"

"An earthly paradise, Frankie. Not so much as an underweight lobster smuggled ashore under cover of darkness."

"What could possibly go wrong..." she murmured.

"He said I could use his office."

"And will you?"

"Sit there with Kershaw's ego wall behind me? Have him looking over my shoulder for six months? No thanks, I'll carry on staring at the hospital's back door."

"What about your other bête noire?"

"Edmund Kennedy? I'm ashamed of myself, Frankie. I went out to see him. I wanted him to know... It was an act of petty revenge. Let him know that I knew about the chess pieces."

"The chess pieces?"

"Yeah. He's got a chess board set up. The pieces hadn't moved for thirty years – "

"Miss Havisham plays chess?"

"Something like that. He told me it was a snapshot of the first time Eric beat him. Eric told me it wasn't. 'I'd taken his bishop as well.' I wanted Kennedy to know that a 'dull-witted copper' knew his little secret."

"Your way of getting even?"

"I suppose so. Like I said, I can understand what he did. But it pisses me off that he'll get away with it. Anyway, I get Jake Cartwright to drive me out there. Have my small act of vengeance all lined up. And someone's beaten me to it."

"Who?"

"Morag. The housekeeper. I go through the door and almost fall over the packing cases. I told you she had a boyfriend down in the village? He's seen one episode of *A Place in the Sun* too many. Bought a house in France. She's going with him."

"So Edmund Kennedy's left to cope on his own?"

"Or not cope. He sure as hell won't know how to make Dundee Cake."

She looked at him in the fading light. "You need to let it go, Mike."

He knew what she meant. Asked her anyway. "Let what go?"

"Kershaw. Kennedy. Not every case is perfect. Some of the bad guys get away with it. Not every loose end gets tied up."

Brady turned towards her. "Becky and Alice," he said.

"What about them?"

"I still can't decide if they knew each other. My gut feeling is yes."

"But you could be wrong?"

"I've been wrong about most things in this case. Twenty years later? We're never going to know for sure. I'd just like to think of them climbing the steps to St Mary's together. Standing in the churchyard, looking out over the town."

"Hiding behind the gravestones? Frightening the tourists?"

Brady laughed. "Obviously. What else do you come to Whitby for?"

"There's one other thing," Frankie said. "Kennedy, Kershaw, Norman Blake, Becky and Alice. You've forgotten one thing."

"What's that?"

"The Lilla Cross."

"What about it?"

Frankie smiled at him.

She knows something I don't. The same expression as Alice. The grown-up version...

"What about the Lilla Cross?"

"Why did Edmund Kennedy bury Becky's body there?"

"Because he couldn't be seen. Because it was as far as

he could carry her. Because he finally found a bare patch of ground. Somewhere he could pitch a tent."

"You're sure of that?"

"Sherlock Holmes, Frankie. When you've ruled everything else out what's left is the truth. And we've done that. Edmund Kennedy carried her until he was sure he couldn't be seen. Until he couldn't carry her any more."

Frankie shook her head. Smiled again.

That expression. That smile. Why do I find it so annoying? And so bloody attractive at the same time...

"Like I said, it comes to all men... Would you like a clue, Detective Chief Inspector?"

"As you seem to think you've solved one of the great mysteries of our time, yes."

"History," Frankie said simply.

"History?"

"History. And *Edmund* Kennedy."

"Edmund?"

"Come on, Mike. You've *met* him. I had to Google him. Go online and find a picture. And look up his father. *And* his grandfather..."

Brady stared out of the window. "I'm not going to be beaten by this, Frankie..."

"But you might be some time." Frankie walked away from him, pretending to search the room. "Where's the bookcase? I've been meaning to read *War and Peace*."

Edmund Kennedy. His father was called Oswald. History...

"What was his grandfather called?" Brady said.

"Edwin. And that should do it for you."

Edwin... And the chess piece. The king. It was him. The braided beard...

"A line of kings?"

"At last. Edwin, Oswald, Edmund. The ancient kings of Northumberland. Him, his father, his grandfather. They must have thought they were descended from those kings. A family folk tale. That's why he called his son Eric. King of Norway and King of Northumberland. Eric Bloodaxe."

"And you think he was convinced of that?"

"Yes. You just said it. When you've ruled everything else out what's left is the truth."

"And that's why he chose the Lilla Cross?"

"Because of the inscription. 'Erected about 620AD over the reputed grave of Lilla, an officer of the court of Edwin, King of Northumbria, who died saving the life of the King.' He must have thought Lilla would watch over Rebecca. Guard her. Keep him and his son – his heir – safe."

Brady turned and looked at her. "So having made a cold, logical decision, he did that? Relied on a Christian burial site?"

"Yes, he did. Maybe there's some superstition in all of us, Mike. Even Edmund Kennedy."

That smile again. I have to say something...

"Frankie..."

She walked across the lounge to him. Reached up and put her finger on his lips. "I know. You don't need to say anything. You've already said it. 'Because I need this. So do you. This is who we are, Frankie.' That was what you said at my flat. And if you're my boss one of us has to give it up."

"And we can't."

"No, we can't."

Brady took her finger in his left hand. Brought it back to his lips and kissed it. "Ruby said something to me. 'It's not just the right person. It's the right time.'"

Frankie nodded. "The wisdom of Ruby. She's right."

And we both know it...

Brady looked at her, the lights from the harbour leaving half her face in shadow. He reached forward. Put his middle finger under her chin. Tilted her face gently up.

"There's one other thing I need to say to you."

"Which is..."

"You're wrong. I'm sorry to say this, DS Thomson, but there's a fatal flaw in your theory. You may not be as clever as you think you are."

Frankie's eyes narrowed. She took a step back. "What's that?"

"Eric Kennedy's son. He's not called Edwin or Edmund. Or Olaf or Ragnall, or... any other Norse name I can think of. What I know and what you *don't* know, Frankie, is that his son's called Isaac. And while I'm only a simple copper, I do know there wasn't a King of Northumberland called Isaac."

Frankie shook her head and sighed. Walked out of the room and down the stairs. "Come on," she said over her shoulder. "You're paying for the fish and chips. Assuming you can eat them with one arm."

"Why me?"

"Because you didn't pay attention in History. And you very clearly didn't pay attention in RE either. Or you'd know who Isaac was."

Brady closed the door of The Crow's Nest behind him and followed her out into a clear, starlit January night. Down a flight of steps to the side of the harbour.

"Who was he then?"

"In the Bible. Isaac was the husband of Rebecca. Calling his son Isaac... I'd say it was Eric Kennedy's way of acknowledging his guilt. His way of apologising to his sister."

Michael Brady knew when he was beaten.

"I admit defeat," he said. "Do you want peas?"

Frankie put her arm through his. "Of course..."

48

"Hello, sweetheart. I didn't know if you'd still be up."

"I was giving you ten more minutes. You smell of fish and chips, Dad. How did you eat fish and chips with one arm?"

Brady laughed. "Carefully, Ash."

"Have you been sitting by the harbour with Frankie again?"

"Sitting by the harbour and shivering. I was bringing her up to date."

"Telling her how you got stabbed?"

"No. Her sister's a paramedic. She was the one who came up to the house. Patched me up and took me to hospital. So I'm guessing she told Frankie."

"Your boyfriend's been stabbed."

"Ash, I am not Frankie's boyfriend. I won't *ever* be Frankie's boyfriend. I'm her boss."

Ash nodded. Surprised him by not pursuing it. "A woman came round to see you."

"Yeah? Who was that?"

"She said her name was Ruby. She seemed to know who I was. Anyway, she said she needed to say thank you. And she brought you a present."

"She's related to Shelley Clarke. Her mother's cousin. And she didn't need to do that. What is it? A bottle of whisky?"

"It isn't a bottle of anything. I put it on the worktop."

Brady walked into the kitchen. Knew immediately what it was. The oblong parcel wrapped in brown paper, two ends taped down, fraying string round the middle of it.

There was a message written in red felt tip on the wrapping paper.

Looks like they were right. You were a sharp bugger. Thank you. Hope you find a place for it.

Brady laughed. Managed to unwrap it.

She'd had it framed.

A frame that looks like driftwood. Perfect, Ruby. Thank you.

"What is it, Dad?"

"A picture. For the new house."

Ash glanced at it. "Sunrise. That's nice. I like sunrises."

"Me too," Brady said. "Especially when I'm on the beach with Archie."

"I'm going to bed," Ash said. "Wake me up early will you? I didn't finish my essay."

Brady nodded. "Will do. And Ash..."

His daughter turned. "What, Dad?"

"Nothing. I'm proud of you. I love you."

She walked over to him. Hugged him. Remembered

his arm. Hugged him more gently. Brady kissed the top of her head.

"I love you too, Dad. But make sure you don't stay up too late. And don't stay up all night texting Frankie. Not that old people can text with one hand..."

"I told you – "

But she was already halfway up the stairs.

MICHAEL BRADY REACHED for the picture. Put it on the mantelpiece. Sat in his chair and looked at it.

Whitby Pier at sunrise. The sunlight reflected as the waves ran back off the wet beach. A solitary seagull silhouetted against the sun...

Why do I like it so much?

A picture of the pier taken by the man who murdered Sandra Donoghue. That will remind me of the man who murdered my best friend.

Because it's a bloody good picture.

Because I caught them both.

Because maybe I'm a half-decent copper after all.

Because you can't run away from your memories.

He bent down and ruffled the top of Archie's head.

"And I like sunrises, Archie. Ruby was right. They make me feel optimistic..."

REVIEWS & FUTURE WRITING PLANS

Thank you for reading *The Echo of Bones*. I really hope you enjoyed it.

If you did, could I ask a favour? Would you please review the book on Amazon? The link to do that is here.

Reviews are important to me for three reasons. First of all, good reviews help to sell the book. Secondly, there are some review and book promotion sites that will only look at a book if it has a certain number of reviews and/or a certain ratio of 5* reviews. And lastly, reviews are feedback. Some writers ignore their reviews: I don't.

So I'd appreciate you taking five minutes to leave a review and thank you in advance to anyone who does so.

What next?

This is the third book in the *Michael Brady* series. The fourth book will be published early in 2022.

There are also two Michael Brady short reads/novellas, telling his back story in Greater Manchester Police from the time he first became a detective.

The Scars Don't Show tells the story of his first murder case. *Crossing the White Line* takes place roughly two years later.

If you'd like to receive regular updates on my writing – and previews of future books – you can join my mailing list by clicking this link: https://www. subscribepage.com/markrichards

SALT IN THE WOUNDS

His best friend has been murdered, his daughter's in danger.
There's only one answer. Going back to his old life.
The one that cost him his wife...

'Salt in the Wounds' is the first book in the Michael Brady series. It's available on Amazon and in paperback.

"Fabulous! Had me gripped from the start. Reminds me of Mark Billingham's detective, Tom Thorne."

"Loved the book from the first page. Straight into the story, very well-written. Roll on Brady 2."

"Loved everything about this book. A gripping plot with unexpected twists and turns. Believable characters that you feel you really know by the last page. I could smell the sea air in Whitby..."

THE RIVER RUNS DEEP

Good people do bad things
   Bad people do good things
   Sometimes it's hard to tell the difference...
   Gina Foster's body has floated down the River Esk.
   It looks like an accident. But Michael Brady has his doubts.
   It's a year since his wife died. He's back in the police force, trying to prove himself to a new boss. And be a good dad to his teenage daughter.
   Is it murder? Or does Brady need it to be murder?
   Brady's convinced the answer lies in Gina's past. But his boss is doing everything he can to stop Brady finding out what that past was.

'The River Runs Deep' is the second book in the Michael Brady series. Again, it's available on Amazon and in paperback.

"Really love this crime series. Believable characters and good pace to the storylines."

"Another fabulous book. The characters are really

developing, the story is well told and there are enough twists and turns and dead ends to keep you on your toes. Great new series to follow."

"The depth of the characters is so good I couldn't stop thinking about the story for weeks after I'd finished it."

ABOUT ME

I spent the bulk of my working life in the financial services industry – but always with a small voice inside me: 'Let me out,' it said. 'I'm a writer.'

In 2009 my brother died of cancer – and it was one of those pivotal moments in life. A time when you realise you either pursue your dream – do what you've always wanted to do – or you forget about it for good.

So I sold my business, sent my stripy ties to the charity shop and started writing. I've worked full-time as a writer since then. Starting from scratch I built a business as a freelance copywriter and content writer – something I still do for a small number of clients.

Then, in the spring of 2016, I had the latest in a long line of mid-life crises and invited Alex – my youngest son – to come for a walk with me. I wanted to do a physical challenge before I was too old for a physical challenge and – despite never having done any serious walking in my life – asked Alex if he wanted to walk 90 miles on the Pennine Way, one of the UK's toughest national trails.

The walk took us five days, and the result was *Father, Son and the Pennine Way* – a book that now has more than 400 reviews on Amazon, the overwhelming majority of them at 5*. 'Brilliantly written, insightful, brutally honest and laugh out loud funny.' And my personal favourite among the reviews: 'I was laughing so hard at this book my husband went off to sleep in the spare room.'

The book is available on your Kindle and in paperback. Here's the link to the Kindle version.

Father, Son and the Pennine Way was followed by *Father Son and Return to the Pennine Way* – picking up where the first book left off – in 2018 and *Father, Son and the Kerry Way* – 125 miles around South West Ireland – in 2019.

We had intended to do another walk in 2020, but the pandemic put paid to that. Covid also meant that I lost two clients in the 'day job,' meaning I finally ran out of excuses for not writing a novel. That was the start of *Salt in the Wounds*.

You can find all my books on my website, or on my Amazon author page.

JOIN THE TEAM

If you enjoy my writing, and you would like to be more actively involved, I have a readers' group on Facebook. The people in this group act as my advance readers, giving me feedback and constructive criticism. Sometimes you need someone to say, 'that part of the story just doesn't work' or 'you need to develop that character more.'

In return for helping, the members of the group receive previews, updates and exclusive content and the chance to take part in the occasional competitions I run for them. If you'd like to help in that way, then look for 'Mark Richards: Writer' on Facebook and ask to join.

ACKNOWLEDGMENTS

This book was written to the sound of crashing walls. While I was writing it, we were having a new kitchen fitted. Some writers work to the sound of waves gently lapping on a tropical beach: *The Echo of Bones* was written to the sound of a drill going through industrial bricks...

...And if you don't believe in the long arm of coincidence, you should. Our builders were BMC Builders: the boss was Brady Michael Carey. And my thanks to Brady – and his team – for the many conversations about my Michael Brady's new house.

Builders aside, I'd once again like to thank the serving and retired police officers who gave me advice and corrected points of detail. In particular I'd like to thank Graham Bartlett – someone I hope to have a working relationship with for many years to come.

As always my reader group on Facebook was helpful and supportive in equal measure. Two, in particular, went the extra mile for me. Thank you all – and especially Carolyn Towse and Philip Wood.

My biggest thanks, of course, go to Beverley, my wife. Professionally, for her advice on autism and Asperger's: personally for reading what were sometimes very rough drafts. Far more importantly for understanding my constant need to disappear upstairs – only to re-emerge and say, "I need to do some more research. Do you want to come to Whitby? Again..."

Mark Richards

September 2021

Printed in Great Britain
by Amazon

24055425R00219